PRIVATE
PRIVILEGE

PRIVATE PRIVILEGE

Simon Astaire

QUARTET

First published in 2008 by
Quartet Books Limited
A member of the Namara Group
27 Goodge Street, London W1T 2LD

A catalogue record for this book
is available from the British Library

ISBN   978 0 7043 7143 9

Typeset by Antony Gray
Printed and bound in Great Britain by
T J International Ltd, Padstow, Cornwall

FOR MILO

Happy is England! I could be content
To see no other verdure than its own;
To feel no other breezes than are blown
Through its tall woods with high romances blent;

John Keats

His left hand was tightly clasped around my neck, squeezing it with callous force. The cue in his right hand was poised, ready to strike me across the head. Sean, a sinister criminal, took aim and started to swing. I closed my eyes, preparing for the blow.

Then a miracle happened: a big black hand belonging to a stranger grabbed the cue and threw it across the pub floor; the astonished crowd of locals fell back in paralyzed silence.

'Do you know who this is?' demanded Jimmy, a former middleweight champion from Doncaster.

'No, who is it?' snarled Sean, his face livid with outrage.

'Yes, who am I?' I heard myself asking out loud.

*   *   *

'So this is Colditz,' shrieked a boy as I hesitantly took my first steps to my new school, Montgomery House, the alma mater to many Prime Ministers whose names, with other greats, glared out at me from my house walls. I'd never felt so lonely, not even when I was sent away to my prep school when I was just nine.

Although it was early September and should still have been relatively warm on the outskirts of London, a cold chill blew through the streets.

My father was keen to show me the graveyard at St Luke's Church situated past the dense orchard on the northern edge of the summit of the knoll where the young Lord Colherne famously used to lounge by a gravestone, look towards London, and pen his wistful romantic poetry.

'It is important to seek the many hidden places on this beautiful school estate,' he advised, his tall domineering figure leading the way, his vetiver cologne drifting through the air.

We found the tomb in question and my father gave a special fanfare as he directed his hand to introduce the stone where Colherne wrote and lazed his days away.

'Look. Find the plaque that commemorates the hours he spent here . . . read it out to me, my son.' My father half-closed his eyes, lost in reverie.

'BOLLOCKS,' I read.

'What?'

'BOLLOCKS,' I repeated.

'Don't be so insolent, Samuel.'

'No, father, that's what it says.'

Some wag had graffitied on the sacred stone.

'Must have been some nasty ignorant yobbo from the local town.'

'Oh yes,' I doubted; and I was right. The school was not quite how it was when my father had attended it some thirty years before, and I was about to join the change.

My father left soon after his hastily cut short tour, and I made my way to the big noticeboard at the bottom of the sweeping stairs besides the main door to the house to find out where my trunk should be carried and with whom I would be sharing my first year at public school.

I was going to share with someone called Langley, in a room apparently at the top of the Headmaster's House. As I assembled my thoughts, I caught sight of a boy with brown curly hair just ahead of me rounding the corner. As I thought he'd be able to point me in the direction of my study, I called out, 'Hey, hello,' but by the time I'd struggled with my trunk around the bend I'd missed him and I was left standing alone in the inhospitable and desolate corridor.

Langley was a complicated work; he was tall, willowy, with little personality and had an obnoxious smell that I had never encountered before. He didn't say much but I later found out he was the son of a General in the British Army. Langley left the room after a few minutes, and I unpacked my things and stuck up a poster of Raquel Welch in a ravishing bikini pose above my bed to keep me company during the wintry nights.

* * *

The new boys gathered in the Main Hall like a flock of worried sheep. Mr Webster, our housemaster, resembled an over-fed Labrador, with butterscotch-yellow hair sprouting from every orifice. He had a deep-voiced Scottish accent and a thin mouth. Individually we were called and had to answer 'Yes, sir,' loud and clear, and then return as soon as our names were delivered. The whole process lasted quite a few minutes, as there were ninety boys in our house. In all there were ten houses in the school grounds. Mr Webster gave a welcoming speech to all the boys and then spoke of his hopes for the coming term. I connected with no one that evening and deliberately kept my head down, apart from the ritual embarrassment and humiliation of having to climb up on a table, like all the new boys had to, of course, and nervously sing the opening verse of a curious choice, 'Men of Harlech'.

Leaving the hall, a podgy blond-haired senior boy with a cane in his hand poked my back and bawled at me in the most unpleasant terms to get my 'damned hair cut; you look like a bloody girl'. Charming, I thought, and how welcoming; but I knew I was in no position to answer back.

Up the creaking staircase and back in my room again later, I discovered that Langley had clearly found my Raquel to be offensive, for he had torn the poster to shreds with a scrawled word on top of the pile, written in red marker pen: 'DISGUSTING'. I started to feel like the stranger and could not understand how anyone could take umbrage with such a magnificent creature.

How I needed my pillow that first night. I hugged it close like a long-lost lover and smothered my face deep within it, hoping that my nightmare was in fact just that, and I would wake up in the morning in my warm bed at home in Oxfordshire, far from the cruel and unwelcoming world I had just joined.

*   *   *

Mr Harris, our form master, looked about a hundred years old. He shuffled into the classroom wheezing away, and barely made it to his desk. This was perched on a platform looking down on the entire class of twenty boys all immaculately turned out in new blue blazers, grey trousers, smart white shirts and our black ties to commemorate the death of Albert, the Prince Consort of Queen Victoria. As Albert had been dead for over a century, I reckoned it might have been time to get over it, but I kept this irreverent thought to myself.

'Bomber' – as he was known by all the boys, after the RAF's Air Chief Marshal Sir Arthur 'Bomber' Harris from the war, decided that as a timetable had not yet been set we would entertain ourselves by discussing who in the classroom had a relation that was a war hero.

'So would anyone like to open up this theme?' enquired Bomber, surveying the class with his rheumy blue eyes.

There was not a word, not a movement. The class remained dormant.

'Come on boys, one of you for God's sake?' his dandruff flying off his shoulders.

I found my hand reaching for the sky with one other, a

small fair-haired thirteen-year-old sitting next to me. I desperately wanted to keep a low profile for my first weeks but I seemed to have my hand up before I had properly considered what I was even doing. He chose the boy beside to go first.

'My name is von Nadelheim, sir, and my family proudly remember my grandfather who was a war hero. He was *Oberbefehlsleiter* Reinhard von Nadelheim and he killed many communists outside Stalingrad. He was executed after the war but the number of so-called innocent children also killed in the church that afternoon has been greatly exaggerated since by the Soviets.'

'Um, interesting. Thank you, von Nadelheim. Next.' He seemed perplexed, as if he had misheard what had been said and then in quick action pointed directly at me.

'My name is Samuel Alexander and my grandfather was a war hero, sir . . . '

'Ah, was he the late Field Marshal Harold Alexander, one of our great military commanders and, inter alia, an old boy of this school?'

'Er no, sir. He was a member of the Dam Busters raid.'

Bomber seemed mightily disappointed. The Dam Busters were the RAF squadron famous for annihilating strategic dams during World War II with their bouncing bombs.

'What did he do? Did he clean the planes out?' piped up an unamusing twit sitting two rows in front.

'No, he fucking didn't, you prick,' I muttered, too loudly.

'Hey, out,' spluttered Bomber. Within ten minutes of my first class in my new school I had been removed. Was this the start of a trend?

Bomber was understanding, though; he let me off with a severe warning but without further punishment, and told me to be on my way.

'You stay out of trouble, young man,' he wisely advised.

'It is far too early to get into that sort of malarkey.'

I found out a couple of months later that my grandfather did not in fact fly with the 617 Squadron but made the costumes for the 1955 film, *The Dam Busters*. The comic was not so far off the mark after all.

I made my first good friend that morning. Andrew Grafton, long fringed blond hair hanging heavily over his eyes and far taller than a thirteen-year-old should be. He put his hand on my shoulder and cautioned me not to over-react. His newly acquired broken voice told me that if I opposed every caustic remark, I wouldn't get past the first week. Grafton, although he had a considerate side, had a kind of gloom that hovered over him like an unwanted companion and how he himself lasted even a week in the school was a miracle.

*   *   *

'Boy! Boy! Boy!' howled Summerfield.

And so we ran like a wretched bunch of mice to answer his ill-tempered call. This was our introduction to fagging, an institution first introduced to the school in the sixteenth century and four hundred years later, still in full swing. Older boys were responsible for the young and the resultant abuse of many thirteen-year-olds, if recorded, would fill a library.

The rule was simple. Whoever reached the yelling senior last, paid the penalty. The call could and would happen at any time of the day and generally at the most in-convenient moment. I was inevitably at the rear of the group of out-of-breath pubescent boys and so I was ordered to run Summerfield's 'tosh', neither too hot nor too cold. Public school had its own language and certain words were substituted with upper-class slang: like 'tosh' for 'bath', for instance. Summerfield, a senior boy, who had greeted me with his cane on my first night, turned out to be my curse and from our first blink of a meeting, we loathed each other.

The bath was deep, and the whole process could take up to ten minutes with both taps on. There were six baths in this chilled wind-swept room with icy stone floors. One of the worst punishments that a new boy could endure was 'a cold tosh'. While he sat naked in the empty tosh the sadistic prefect would run only the cold tap to the brim. Your body would go into shock as the freezing water built up and by the time the whole process was completed the promise of revenge to the perpetrator was sealed.

Summerfield threw his unappealing damp dressing-gown at me. 'It better be warm.'

'It will be,' I replied.

'I didn't ask for your opinion, you piece of shit.' He was short, slightly podgy, and had a chunk of blond hair that gave the impression of a bad wig. The son of some Scottish landowner, he was an angry tyrant who liked to vent his spleen against anyone junior. For now I remained necessarily courteous and servile.

He lay in his bath, his lardy stomach hovering over the water, satisfied that my job was well done.

'Go away now and revise for your new boy test, you little creep. Failure is not worth contemplating. Chop chop.'

Nice, I thought. He was right about one thing though; failing the new boy test wasn't worth contemplating. You were tested on all school rules as well as other insights, such as all the special school words and the various nicknames for the masters – Bogie Earle (snot hanging from his nose), Ducky Morrison (highly camp appearance), Bomber Harris, Gripper Yates (long sideburns), Noddy Lawson (who looked remarkably like the lead singer of the glam rock group Slade) were some we had to remember – along with which shops were out of bounds, old boys' accomplishments, and a lot besides. A boy in the year above you was instructed to take you through the test and if you failed then he was punished. He was known as your 'Shepherd', his task to guide the new sheep through the maze of school rules.

Hood was fifteen going on forty. He had been through a terrible time; his mother had committed suicide when he was nine and his enormously wealthy father paid him little attention. He, like me, and many of our contemporaries, was crying out for help. The trouble was that we didn't exactly know what we were asking for and our screams were lost in the fog of authority and hierarchy.

Hood took his duty as my Shepherd seriously, but not before he introduced me to the best place in the grounds to have a smoke. The cigarette represented both a reason to hide and a reason to meet in Dunsmore Wood just to the side of the main school. It provided a quiet place to revise for the new boy's test and also to demolish a packet of Player's No. 6.

Hood simply forced me into knowing every detail of the school. Failure would mean that he would have to stay confined within the school grounds until I had passed the test; and as that could take weeks, he was not willing to take any chances.

'You've been smoking for a while, haven't you? You don't "Humphrey Bogart" them like some new boys.'

'Humphrey Bogart?'

'Oh, he was an American film star that had a cigarette glued to his mouth, he was mummy's favourite,' and his words loitered in the hesitant warm wind. I broke the silence.

'Yes, I was once caught smoking at my first school back when I was eight. I hardly knew how to tie up my shoes, but there I was dragging away trying to act sophisticated.

14

Miss Andrews, the headmistress there, found a few of us puffing in the loo and told us to immediately hand over our cigarettes. We didn't know what we were doing but we all had these fancy brands we'd taken from our fathers: Dunhill, Rothmans. We crammed into her small office and emptied our pockets. One of our gang, Tony Waldergrave, looked at her all innocently and through chubby cheeks said, "Miss Andrews, do cigars count?" At which point Tony pulled out of his pocket his father's cigar, which was nearly as tall as he was.'

By the time I was called into the prefects' study, I was word perfect and on leaving their sanctum with full marks and a pass, I smiled at Hood with gratitude and relief.

He slapped my back. 'Let's go into town and celebrate.'

'But don't we need the housemaster's permission?' I asked.

Hood smiled, 'Permission? We don't need permission, we need unshrinking audacity,' and we laughed and hit the local town.

I wasn't to see much more of Hood, as only a week later he had vanished from school life. His father had decided to emigrate to Australia and like many from this time he receded from my life.

*　　*　　*

I was asked to report to a Mr Herbert's office early in the morning before breakfast. A small hunched man emerged from the shadows early each school year to ask new boys just one question, their full name. With this information he carved each surname with full initials on to the house wall. Here you would join previous greats and not-so-acclaimed old boys. I have never been sure why he did not just look up our names on our entrance papers, but as he asked for your name he looked searchingly into the eyes. He copied your answer in thick black ink on to a scrap of paper.

'Name?' he spat, his phlegm reaching my blue blazer.

'Samuel Henry Ignatius Thamen Alexander.'

'Very exotic,' he replied uninterestedly, writing down my name in his beautiful handwriting. His hands were well worn and his fingers heavily lined and curved like claws.

In fact my full name is Samuel Jack Alexander but as I walked into this gloomy cubbyhole of an office, I was on a quest to lighten my day and to pursue something with a twist of the different.

Although he had been engraving them for over forty years he took no further notice of my name written on his sheet, and I left the room to wait in anticipation to see his work etched on to the house wall.

My father's name was there from the war years and he had taken great pride in showing my brother Tom and me his full name when he first took us both to visit the school. I was only five at the time but I distinctly remember standing in that same hall as he pointed out his name and saying whilst doing so, 'One day your names will join mine and countless others.' From that moment there was no doubt in my heart, I would be going to Montgomery and no other public school would be contemplated.

When my name finally appeared on the dark wooden board between J. E. Abbott and T. W. Bellemy, I shuddered. At the time I had thought it to be such a good joke almost amusing but on seeing it clearly now – S.H.I.T. Alexander – I squirmed and prayed that my father would not visit, let alone want to see my name.

But luck was not to be on my side and only seven days on, my father was in the area and put in a surprise appearance. I was up in my study when a boy knocked purposefully to announce that my father was waiting in the hall.

'My father,' I screamed, and scrambled off my bed to run down and meet a less-than-happy patriarch.

No words were uttered, there was just my father pointing at my name and then purposely pointing at my brother's and then at his own.

'But father, I don't understand how it happened.' I started my defence in high voice but I knew that I had none He did not wish to listen but walked out of my sight and returned to his waiting car. When my father was angry no words were said. I sulked back to my study and felt miserable and very alone. I sat on my bed and stared at the ceiling, angry that he did not even want to hear my hasty excuse. It emphasised our pitiful lack of communication. With his attacks running through my mind, I felt homesick; I felt impotent and unable to reach for anyone and in truth, I needed my mother; she would understand and have the patience and love to sympathize.

Without any fanfare the board carrying my name was removed and replaced with my correct initials, S. J. Alexander. I heard from my mother during my first school holiday that my father had to pay for a new board and Mr Herbert's extra time. The poor man had to chip away with dozens of names that covered that slice of wood. With my name listed firmly in the middle, he had no choice. It cost my father £500 and cost me a real scolding from my mother.

'Don't be senseless, Sam. Stupidity, especially from you, is inexcusable. You have really disappointed us.'

For my mother to even raise her voice was unfamiliar and her piercing words made me swear that I would try to behave for at least the next twelve weeks.

*   *   *

The housemaster, Mr Webster, announced that in the next few days there would be a fire practice. We were to proceed in an orderly manner fully dressed into the housemaster's garden to the rear of the house. Although it would only be a practice, we should take it very seriously and anyone seen behaving badly would be severely punished. What a drag to have our short sleep interrupted by the sound of a bell. I also didn't see why we should have to dress. If it were a real fire, surely the minutes wasted putting on your trousers, shirt, shoes, and tie could cost a life, but no one would listen to common sense.

Days drifted by, each absorbing the other until many of us had forgotten the warning of the impending practice. And then at about three o'clock one morning, while most were in the deepest of their dreams, the bell sounded. I slept on and on until Prefect Warwick literally kicked me out of my bed, 'Get up you fool, there's a fire drill.'

My eyes still closed, I pulled my trousers over my pyjamas and my shirt over my head with my tie already attached.

I ran out of the door and was speeding down one landing on to the next when I heard a blood-curdling scream. It was James Gregory, a tall camp seventeen-year-old who had the reputation of having the biggest penis in the house. Unfortunately, I witnessed his reputation with my own eyes. The poor soul, in the hurry to make it out of the building and into the garden, had pulled up his flies and caught his foreskin firmly in the zip. He was rolling on the floor in agony. What to do? I certainly didn't want to physically help.

I chased Warwick, but he ignored my pleas and told me to stop talking and move on. I ran into the garden where I was the last to arrive bar one. The roll call had already started. My surname beginning with A always meant that I was one of the first to be called. Mr Webster bellowed out my name, 'Alexander.'

'Sir, we have . . . '

'Here just "sir" will suffice.'

'No, sir,' I yelled.

'What do you mean "no, sir"? See me later, boy.'

Why is it that masters become stupid and don't listen when things don't go according to their plan? A generalization perhaps, but true nonetheless. I walked up to him and put my face directly in front of his.

'Gregory is dying, sir. He has caught his penis in his zip.'

'Why didn't you tell me, boy?' was his reply. He dropped his board carrying our names and dashed with terror etched on his face to poor Gregory's room. He hurried in a way that suggested this had probably once happened to him too.

Poor Gregory was rolling on the floor, agony carved on his face. The fire practice was immediately postponed and we were ordered back to our rooms. As we were leaving, Gregory appeared looking red-faced and traumatised. A huge cheer went up amongst the boys and an embarrassed Gregory sheepishly returned to his room once he saw that the whole drill had now been cancelled.

He thanked me for calling the alert.

'What happened next?' I asked.

'Webster told me to think of something else, and then he pulled the zip down without warning. He just did it.'

As we walked back, Shearer, a boy who had arrived the same term as me, fell to the ground and started to shake. He was having a seizure and shook with his tongue hanging out of his mouth.

'Do something, for heaven's sake,' someone shouted at me.

I froze for a moment, then to my shame ran away to my room, unable to cope. I thought about that night many times afterwards and it haunted me. I realised that I was a coward and I did not like myself for it. Shearer was epileptic and I realised that he could have a fit at any time. He simply needed to have support when he found himself in

19

danger. I swore that night that cowardice would not mark my life.

*   *   *

'There seems to be some confusion here, boy. Are you or are you not a Jew?'

'My father is but my mother is not, Mr Harcourt,' was my hesitant reply.

The Reverend Brian Harcourt was a very grey man. Grey hair, grey skin and a grey attitude; an old-fashioned bore.

We were asked to report to the Reverend's office to be tested out for the choir and also for his lurid eyes to give us the once over. His reputation was widespread; he had his favourites and it was no surprise that they usually were the better-looking boys.

I felt challenged by his question, possibly because of earlier experiences suffered at prep school involving my religion, but maybe because my reply had to be fleeting and well-thought-out. This wasn't the moment when you decided if Jesus was the Son of God; it was a time to calculate how your hours would be spent in the coming years. The choir would certainly not do. Compulsory attendance at six services during the week and then choir practices on top were going to be very limiting for out-of-school activities. Even if you had a voice like Nat King Cole, which I didn't, it was still best to sing tone deaf so as not to leave any doubt for the reverend and music head, John Oxlade, who resembled how I imagined God to look like with long white hair, white beard and outstanding bright blue eyes; it was curious as Mr Oxlade was only in his late twenties.

Jews did not have to attend the school chapel; their only religious 'order' was instead to meet up with the other

Jewish folk on Sunday morning to have a discussion with Rabbi Isaac Landau.

'I am a Jew.'

'Hmm, are you now?' Reverend Harcourt did not seem convinced.

He then turned to Oxlade and spoke phlegmatically into his ear.

'Well you might as well go away, which seems a pity as I saw a part of you that might want to serve. And if I remember rightly your brother Thomas attended school chapel most regularly.'

'In our family it is a matter of choice, sir.'

'Very well, then.' The Reverend was yawning now. 'As I say, a pity. I thought you had talent.'

I had no idea what he meant, but I thanked him and shook Mr Oxlade's weak hand, which took him by surprise.

'I heard you had a voice; it seems a shame that your faith should get in the way.'

I told Mr Oxlade not to be that disappointed.

*   *   *

I had never really taken into account that I was Jewish until I was sent away at the age of only nine to a prep school on the coast of north-east Suffolk. The 'milk' trains that left Liverpool Street bound for Southwold were terribly daunting for someone so young. Life at my prep school was a huge chasm for someone so vulnerable to overcome.

I changed radically from the experience and believe that the stoic wave I gave to my parents from that train, without being allowed to show any emotion, altered the whole fabric of my life. So I learnt from an early age that to reveal your feelings was a sign of weakness and as the train slowly rattled out of the station away from my home, security and my parents, I would sit quietly with tears welling up in my eyes and turning my face to the window so that no one else could see me.

It was three weeks later when I got the first threatening note placed on my desk. A piece of paper crudely ripped from scrap with the words 'JEW GO HOME' scrawled on it. 'How bizarre,' I thought and did not know what it meant. It was my first encounter of anti-Semitism and until that moment I had no idea that in the eyes of some others I was different. My father kept a kosher home and when he sent me away to a place that had had very few Jews in its history, he merely insisted to the school that I didn't eat pork. And so every Sunday when the whole school was served pork sausage and beans, I had to take the slow lonely walk to the kitchen, past the long table of other whispering boys, to pick up my beef sausages. I was seen as the outsider and because of it, not trusted. Most thought that the sausages represented my religion. Being seen as a stranger doesn't help when you are locked up full-time with a bunch of pre-pubescent boys in search of their own identity.

I'd reported the note immediately; it was my prep school headmaster who explained with wisdom and care what it meant and what I had encountered. An hour later I left his office with a head full of information, and horror, on the persecution of the Jews through the ages.

The notes continued; left either in my desk or in my locker. And finally to my acute embarrassment at the morning assembly, the headmaster warned that if this campaign of hate continued, the police would be brought in and the culprit would be instantly expelled. The notes soon dried up and after that, other than the occasional remark, my time there was relaxed and at times comfortable. I do remember, though, once being cornered by the prep school English master accusing me of writing the notes myself.

'Why would I do that, sir?'

'To leave the school and return to your cosmopolitan way of life,' he hissed.

Most odd, but false accusations and theories about my behaviour would follow throughout my school career.

*   *   *

Rabbi Landau had a heavy East European accent. At ten o'clock every Sunday this tiny man would make his way to the school grounds carrying an assortment of religious books, to the science rooms to meet his congregation. Just twenty Jewish boys were at Montgomery during my time and most of them were the sons of highly respected and successful businessmen. I was welcomed by the rabbi but by no one else. It was not the warmest reception and yet again I felt an outsider. The rabbi asked that I addressed the class about what I thought or knew about Judaism.

'I know a good Jewish joke.' The class fell silent; and the rabbi nodded for the act to begin.

'OK, this man had been kosher for seventy-five years and so not once had he tasted pig. Not once had he drifted from his kosher upbringing. So he decided that for his seventy-fifth birthday he would go to the best restaurant in town and order pig. He just wanted to know what it tasted like.

' "Pig please?" he asked the waiter in this posh restaurant.

' "We will bring the finest roast we have, sir with all the trimmings," the waiter replied.

'As he waited for the dinner, he happened to see his rabbi walk into the restaurant with four senior members of his own congregation. They sat at the table next to him.

' "Good evening, rabbi." The rabbi gave him a warm smile.

'At that moment, the swing doors to the kitchen burst wide open and in marched the proud chef holding a silver plate with the head of a roasted pig sizzling, pointed ears, a huge schnozzer and a bright green apple stuck in its open mouth. The beast was placed directly in front of the man.

'He smiled weakly at the rabbi. The rabbi was speechless, the members of the congregation stunned.

' "What sort of restaurant is this, rabbi? You ask for a green apple and look what you get?" '

The boys turned away embarrassed. There wasn't even a hint of laughter. It was a tough room

'Thank you,' said Dr Landau. 'Now let's move on.'

*   *   *

Chief Kwame Mensah Ngonlomah was the scariest boy during my time at school. Physically daunting as he walked down the street, boys would flee to the other side of road as the pavement cracked beneath the big Ghanaian's feet. He was deeply unpleasant, insecure and had a huge chip lying on his broad shoulders. I would usually run into him during break where he ate his sandwiches like a lion devouring his kill. He would sit at the next table divulging his latest slaughters as his sycophants nodded their heads: 'Yes Kwame, brilliant Kwame, how amusing Kwame.'

Occasionally one of his acolytes would shout, 'That is not a very nice thing to say about Kwame, Alexander,' and he would turn round and scowl, but that was about all the menace he slung in my direction. He regularly turned his hate to others, though, and should he decide that he didn't like you, whatever it may have been, your face, your hair, or even your laugh, then God help you: Kwame would be out to serve incredible pain.

The yearly school boxing tournament was announced and the hot favourite was inevitably Kwame Ngonlomah. It took place on one sultry afternoon in the rather worn gym close to the 1st XV Rugby pitch. To win the large Jack Dempsey Trophy you would need to win two preliminary rounds followed by the final. Three one-minute rounds may sound short, but it certainly is not when you're being walloped at full pelt by an over-eager sixteen-year-old. Then the plea for mercy is never far from your lips.

For his first fight, Ngonlomah battered Slewka, an over-brave Canadian, into a crunching submission late in the first round, meaning in precisely fifty seconds. Slewka was certainly game, with arms flailing around like an out-of-control windmill before walking straight into a devastating left hook. Crunch. The Toronto-born Slewka fell as if a bullet had been lodged in his head.

As usual, parents had been invited to watch the massacre of their own children and poor Mrs Slewka, terrified that her A-grade student had suffered brain damage, jumped through the ropes, and tripped over the lower rope, in a desperate attempt to comfort her semi-conscious son.

'I am all right, Mom; I just wanted to be brave for you and Dad,' his voice weak, his eyes half-dead.

His mother helped support his frail body out of the hall and we got ready for the next onslaught.

Charles Batty, twin brother to Paul, was next to be served up on a plate for the ferocious Ghanaian. Charles had the unfortunate reputation of not possessing a brain in his head; in fact many could not understand how he'd even passed the entrance examination. Brother Paul fared little better.

Charles entered the ring with an inane smile stuck to his face. In the corner stood Paul, there to support the unavoidable. Hands up to protect his face he stormed towards his opponent like a car out of control. Ngonlomah, with one punch so beautiful in its action, silenced his enthusiastic opponent. Charles Batty fell to the floor with a thump and the count was discarded to save time. His twin continued his smile even when a doctor was called; poor Charles had been knocked out cold. Five minutes later he had recovered to full health but probably with less functioning grey matter than before, and there wasn't much to begin with.

I sat ringside chewing my Juicy Fruit gum, enjoying the gladiatorial encounters and relieved that I had ducked out of the humiliation that many were suffering. For one insane moment a few weeks earlier, I had thought it would be a good idea to test my resolve in the ring, but I woke up to reality and decided to be a spectator. 'You are no fool,' remarked my uncle, a connoisseur of the game. 'Only fools fight.'

The hall was beginning to suffocate with hysterical parents, eager students baying for blood and fighters covered with sweat. I needed air and went to the line of trees directly opposite to have a much-needed pee. Standing there looking up to the sky stood a thoughtful Ngonlomah.

'Beautiful punch, Kwame.'

He did not answer. 'You showed him.' Again he did not answer.

I was about to crawl a little further up his arse when he asked, 'Do you want to be in my corner?'

'When do I begin?' I replied, not daring to even contemplate turning him down.

Ngonlomah was dressed in his white silk shorts with black stripe, not unlike Muhammad Ali. He was shadow boxing around my head and developing a mighty sweat. It was time to lead my talented fighter into the ring. The hall crackled with a mixture of anticipation and boos. Grafton, surprised to see me leading out the number-one bully in the school, shouted 'What are you doing, Alexander?'

I put my index finger to my mouth and shushed him but it was too late; by then the entire hall joined in with boos that echoed round the gymnasium, and cries of 'wanker' were spat in my direction.

I even saw parents hurling insults. 'You creepy crawly,' hissed one lady, prodding at me with a stick.

I was getting so used to being despised that I thought people liked me. I lifted the rope and Ngonlomah stepped into the ring ready for battle. The spectators were baying for blood and not just from the fighters.

Our opponent was Javed Khazandar, a deadly Omani who had no fear whatsoever. Known in the trade as a brawler, he lacked grace and skill but made up for this with sheer intensity of punching power. A fighter with a stable stance, he threw hard slow punches to devastating effect. It was a perfect match which would be remembered by all who had the privilege to witness the extraordinary contest. Khazandar and Ngonlomah would fight to the death and enjoy doing so.

Blood spurted out from each corner of the ring, teeth were lost and eyes were closed. In a three-round fight, it should have been stopped after the first but it continued as these two brave and foolish souls fought to the very end. The third round will go down as probably the most violent anyone has ever seen at Montgomery, as they traded blow after blow. Ngonlomah, a boxer-puncher whose normal tactics were to punch hard, move away, jab and go in again to wear his opponent down, threw any idea of this to the wolves. He simply stood tall, loaded his punches and didn't let up. The final bell sounded and a decision went to the judges. The PE teacher Mr Riggs, the rugby coach Gripper Yates, and, unexpectedly, the music master Mr Oxlade, unanimously gave the decision to Ngonlomah.

Ngonlomah was awarded the trophy and I danced around the ring holding his prize aloft. The boos were deafening and my popularity sunk to an all-time low. Even Ngonlomah didn't appreciate my efforts. A few days later as I walked by him on the street, the big Ghanaian elbowed me and I had to go the sanatorium to have a suspected broken jaw examined.

In the following weeks, I saw Khazandar walking in town swatting flies that didn't exist. When I said 'Hello,' there was no recognition, just a punch drunk look.

*   *   *

For the second year we were going to be able to choose with whom we would like to share, but only subject to it being agreed by next year's head of house, and making a good choice could make life easier. Langley and I both agreed that we would never be friends, had nothing in common and were from two different worlds. He planned to share from September with an acne-ridden genius, Richard Poole, known to us as 'Brains'. Far more his pace, I thought. I would visit Brains a number of times a term myself, as for fifty pence a go he would do my maths homework for me. What would have taken me a hefty hour of hard intense work, Brains would complete in fifteen minutes and get it virtually all correct.

'Thank you, Brains, you're a pal,' I would say as I picked up my work. He never answered and would simply put his fee in his pocket and start on his next commission.

In my first school year in the house, most of the friends I had made, and I am talking about three, were in the year above me, and so my sharing options from September weren't going to be that good. One boy I hadn't noticed much, as he kept to himself, was Justin Deane. Justin was the brother of the popular Christopher Deane, who was due to take up the position of head of house at the start of the next school year. The brothers were quite different from anyone else. They had been brought up in Haiti on the island of La Gonâve and had that island sense about them: a certain freedom in mind and movement.

28

They were very close and tactile which was incongruous to many at the school, who dealt with touch as a kind of leprosy. I thought it would be a bright idea to approach Justin on two counts. First he was the brother of the libertarian Christopher, which would allow a certain amount of free rein next year, and second he seemed calm and would potentially understand my idiosyncrasies.

'Hey Justin, do you want to share with me next year?' I asked nervously, as my alternatives were limited and I knew this would be a very good idea.

'Yeah, no problem,' he replied, but fairly dispassionately, I have to say. And there we had it. I put our names forward, Justin's brother as head of house elect signed it off, and for our second year we were given a very good room above the eccentric and Frampton-obsessed Dixon.

Dixon played 'Show Me the Way' continuously through the day and into the night, and each time I hear that track it fills me with dread. Certain songs consumed the public school boy's head during that period and if you didn't like Deep Purple, Genesis or Yes then you were considered an outsider. I was considered an outsider.

Dixon had decorated his room with strips of silk bought during a recent trip to India and the resonance of music kept us distracted most of the term. He sat most of his days cross-legged turning the pages of *Slaughterhouse Five* with a smile on his face. The smell of grass was continuously wafting up to our room as well, and how he escaped punishment for that misdemeanour was amazing.

He was the palest seventeen-year-old you were ever likely to encounter. Unbearably thin, regularly stoned on his supply of dope. He was seen only at roll call and floating to and from his lessons doused in patchouli. He had an admirer in Charles Moore, who broadcast to anyone who cared to listen that he was in love with Dixon and would do anything for him, and anything meant anything. Dixon would use this intense, dangerous passion as far as he could. This was not just teenage love, first crush, but more like a deranged infatuation. Studious and scholarly, Moore would easily be seen from the outside as a diligent student who would fit well into the public school system before heading to honours at Oxford, but even at my tender age of fourteen I could see it differently. The air of neediness that followed him told a far more complicated story.

*   *   *

Come September, and back at school, Justin, and I met up in our new study. Justin's brother was now head of house, and apart from the unwelcome news that, as expected, my nemesis Summerfield had become a prefect, the new year seemed to offer grounds for optimism. For a start, we were no longer the new boys any more; the fresh intake would now have to respond to the demands of fagging instead of us.

Justin and I had no problems with either our taste in posters, our music, or our smell, and the first couple of months ran smoothly without incident and with pace. By now the personality starts to assert itself and friends are made who stick with you until you leave and if lucky beyond.

The rat pack was being shaped. Andrew Grafton, monosyllabic, academically very bright and a side that would reveal itself only occasionally; that side being an unhinged lunatic. Tim Winter, a year older and with the kudos of having a distant cousin who was a bass player in a heavy metal band. Winter was a kind and considerate person, who on the face of it didn't want trouble but learnt differently, and in no time his nickname was indeed 'Troubles' Winter. Lord David Burford was probably the best looking one of us, a refined English aristocrat. Sex-obsessed and luckier than everyone, he would make his way down town to seek out the local crumpet and promise them love, respect and a room on his estate, none of which he was able to deliver.

'But David, I thought you loved me,' was a plaintive cry I once heard from a townie girl directed at Burford's room, which faced the main street.

'Oh, go away, will you? I never said anything of the kind,' he was heard to yell back.

He had a wicked laugh, curly brown hair and a beautiful heartfelt smile, which many people joked at the time would have let him 'get away with murder'.

I met up with these usual suspects for the first smoke of term in Dunsmore Woods. All of a sudden I noticed a new face had joined us.

'What are you doing here?' I asked.

'I felt like a cigarette so I just followed you in here.'

It belonged to Nimmo Smith, soon to be known as 'Spit' because he could gob with the accuracy of Robin Hood. It was his very first day at a new school and the sheer audacity to just join in without being asked immediately made him a friend and one of us. Born in Bristol the only son of a lawyer, Nimmo Smith loved football and Bristol City, and gave the impression of being older than his years. He also had a great laugh that made him sound like Muttley from the cartoon *Wacky Races*.

'I just want to have fun and am not going to let anyone stop me,' were virtually the very first words I heard my new friend utter.

As the autumn progressed, we spent more and more of our free time in a dank and derelict house off Wales Street on the north side of the school grounds. As soon as lessons drew to a close we would meet in this unkempt construction with torn and stained mattresses flung across the filthy floor. The intense smoking of cigarettes and talk of girls occupied our long hours and even back then we supported each other with the knowledge that we were all alien to the majority. We should, however, have concentrated on how we were going to survive the Establishment and avoid the trouble that was gathering like an ominous storm.

*   *   *

My new room had more than size going for it; Justin and I had a fire escape hanging from one of our windows. You could clamber out of the window on to the platform and descend a ladder down to the garden. The garden led, of course, to the back road and then on to the local underground station. The tube was our salvation and within twenty-five minutes the sanctuary of central London could welcome you.

Oh, how I remember those escapes with that nagging fear that an observant master would catch sight of you and within minutes of being captured your school career would hang in the balance. Whenever I went on that journey, I always imagined that I was a prisoner of war escaping the Nazis but being helped by the local resistance, one of whom would be a beautiful, sultry, courageous French girl, smoking a Gauloise cigarette, who thought I was handsome but didn't particularly like or trust me. I got so distracted in my fantasy that one time I was nearly caught before I'd even reached the bottom of the fire escape.

A disguise was needed, and having seen an interview with Laurence Olivier only a few weeks before where he had said that fake teeth were his best concealment from adoring fans, I purchased some from a local magic shop. I found a discarded pair of my father's glasses, a heavy coat, and that was that. I looked like a young George Harrison with big teeth. In fact I probably looked like me with big teeth.

*   *   *

It was a straight choice. You could either choose community service or do as the majority of the school did and join the Corps. I, of course, went for the least popular, mainly because community service involved frequent visits to the town, going to the movies and enjoying the delicacies in the local Wimpy bar. The Corps, on the other hand, had to spend a disproportionate amount of time in another uniform doing a great deal of exercise under the supervision of a commanding officer who would usually be a power-crazy prefect. No choice really.

Wednesday afternoon, I reported to Mr Rose, the dull, taciturn master of community service and he looked up from his glasses rather suspiciously; he raised one eyebrow and asked, 'Why do you want to help those less fortunate?'

'Because of exactly that, sir. They are less fortunate than me.'

'Hmm,' he pondered. He clearly didn't believe me for a moment and in reality I didn't even believe myself, but it gave an excuse to leave the grounds and that was too important a gift to muck up.

'What do I have to do, sir?' I asked willingly.

'Well, let's see now.' He looked through a pile of papers. 'On the whole you will be visiting the elderly and will be asked to do their shopping, make sure that their house is tidy, which I should think will be quite a leap for you, and generally be an overall help. I suggest that you find a friend to go with for the first few weeks. Anyone in your house will do.'

I was in luck; Andrew Grafton also wanted to steer clear of the Corps, mainly to avoid getting his hair cut.

The same Wednesday the two of us set off cheerfully to meet an elderly woman called Mrs Wheeler. We walked into town past the cinema, through the High Street and found Gilson Road where a group of terrace houses greeted us. We knocked on the yellow door of number 24 and then saw the bell and pressed it instead. There was no answer, so we knocked on the door but there was still not a murmur. We looked at each other, thinking that we were in luck. We could now leave and enjoy a visit to the town. Just as we were walking back on to the street, the yellow door creaked opened and there greeting us was an elderly woman, grey hair, huge earrings and a little too much make-up. Her face encouraged conversation and was the type that put people at ease.

'Don't be in such a hurry. Come in boys, come in now,' she called. We followed her into her warm, rather cramped house full of her possessions, which covered the ages; I noticed a bookshelf filled with Agatha Christie novels, pristine in condition and seemingly unread. She walked slowly into her living room and then slumped into a large deep chair, dust spreading from the cushions, and looked straight into my eyes. Her stare was potent; she had piercing green eyes, alive and vibrant. She handed us a long piece of paper which listed her shopping and we headed for the local Co-op and on to the nearby fishmongers to buy her kippers.

We whizzed round the Co-op, taking less than half an hour, so we reckoned we had time to stop for a quick milk-shake and some egg and chips drowned by HP Sauce. Ebullient with stomachs full, we returned to Mrs Wheeler's. We unpacked the shopping, put it carefully away, and when finished asked if there was anything else to do.

'Make a pot of Earl Grey tea, please dear, and pour yourselves a cup.'

We put the kettle on, found the teapot and a strainer,

and located which tea caddy had the Earl Grey in it. We made up a tray with chocolate digestives and sat with her as she told us her story.

She spoke fast as if she hadn't had much conversation recently. She spoke of a lost romance. It was during the First World War.

Her mind still sharp, she described her first true love who'd lost his life in the mud of the trenches in 1918. She mused that he wore the same school uniform as we did, and remained surprised that we still wore that black tie. They had met in town and their clandestine relationship continued for three years until he left school and joined the army.

'We used to meet at a tea-room just off the High Street and hold hands as if we would never let go. We had no chance, really; we were from two different worlds. But I have thought of him every day since he left us.'

She found out that he had been reported missing, presumed killed, when her letters were returned, and she went to the school to ask the bursar what had become of him. His body was never found.

'I mourned alone and still mourn today.' Her pain was tangible.

I changed the subject and asked what she had done as work. To my surprise, she asked Grafton to fetch something out of a drawer in the sideboard near the fireplace. Grafton found a pack of cards.

'Bring them over to me,' she said, 'I used to read these.'

They were old, overused tarot cards that had worked their power and advice on the many who needed an answer.

'I am actually psychic, you know,' she continued. 'I communicate with spirits, but I haven't used my gift, oh, for such a long time. I find it very tiring these days; very difficult to concentrate in the way that I used to. I made a good living once and clients were always pleased with the accuracy of the reading.'

'Can you read my cards?' I asked, perhaps too keenly.

'Not now, but I will one day.' We finished our tea and just as we were leaving she said, 'In future, boys, come straight back with my shopping. You can always have your milkshake on your way back to school.' I looked at Grafton, and Grafton looked at me. And so it begins, I thought.

*   *   *

The housemaster called me to his room. I was convinced that he was going to bring up some misdemeanour of mine, like my unauthorised use of the fire escape, but there was no mention; instead he had something else on his mind.

'Alexander, you have that showbiz type of feel about you, don't you?' I both shook and nodded my head, not sure what the right answer to this was supposed to be.

The housemaster continued. 'We have Mr Preston who is the President of Root Soda, you know, the big American fizzy pop outfit, visiting the school tomorrow morning and he has asked for a boy to show him around. I believe you are the man for the job. You can miss tomorrow's lessons and show Mr Preston the school you have grown to love . . . Now don't interrupt. You will be representing the school, so I would expect you to be on your best behaviour and to be a good ambassador.'

I was amazed by the recognition. I thought Mr Webster hated me, but this small sign of belief might be painting a different picture. Perhaps they did see a talent or maybe they just thought I had some showbiz charm and this was something to which an American would relate. Whatever the reason, I was instructed to go to the headmaster's office the following morning at ten o'clock sharp.

I had only actually met the headmaster once and that

was before I had even started at the school. One June afternoon after I had passed my Common Entrance, my mother and father and I shared tea with him. They spent most of the time talking about my brother, Thomas, and only rarely looked in my direction. It did not matter, though; the tea was delicious with hot scones and melting butter and thick slices of carrot cake which I stuffed down in a gulp. The headmaster gave us a tour of the house, which was part of his building. In point of fact, it was my father who gave the tour; the headmaster joined me and my mother as bystanders as my father waffled on about this and that. As we passed his study, the headmaster managed to get a word in and joked that the only time boys visited that side of the building was when they were either being expelled or if they were going to become head of school.

As I turned up at the headmaster's office, those words resonated in my mind. I rang his bell and the door was answered by his assistant, looking like the Wicked Queen from *Snow White*. Rumour had it that she was having a relationship with God but it turned out to be just Mr Oxlade. Supposedly they were once caught in the act in one of the music rooms, but the only eyewitness to this was Burford and he was well known for his exaggeration. I tried to wait patiently but started to tap my fingers on the armrest of the throne-like chair I was sitting in.

'Can I have a glass of water, please, Miss Phillips?'

'It is Mrs Phillips and the answer is no,' and she crossed her legs and pursed her very cherry lips.

So she was married; and I was still in the process of working out her marital arrangements and finding her acutely desirable when the headmaster suddenly appeared from a small side door.

'Alexander, could I introduce you to Mr Raymond Preston, the President of Root Soda. Please show him around the

37

school. Mr Preston has an interest in anything dated before the turn of the twentieth century, so I would suggest you show him the Maths Schools that were built in 1893; but, of course, you know that.'

'Turn of the century?' I thought. He had to be kidding, but I kept my smile fixed and said, 'It would be my pleasure, sir. Hello, Mr President.'

Mr Preston had a wide welcoming face, big generous eyes, not a strand of hair and a walking stick. He looked in pain as he took steps and he quickly explained that he had recently stumbled down some stairs and was lucky to still be walking at all.

'Where shall we go first?' he asked, voice resonating as if he smoked heavily.

'Well, I think we should go and see the Maths School as the headmaster suggested.'

The Maths School was built in the year the headmaster gave and was known now as the Old School. The big oak door welcomed us and in we walked to the classroom from another age. Carved into the walls were 'signatures' from bygone times.

'My father told me that he had once signed his name here. Now let me think where.' I walked to the back of the class and searched and there carved deeply in the wood was 'Alexander 1942'; his name had found me.

'He says that he got six of the best for that deed.'

Mr Preston spent time looking at the markings and was clearly captivated by my tales of public school life and the little history I knew of Montgomery. He chuckled and had the eccentric habit of talking to himself after I had finished a sentence. He was a delightful man; I liked him immediately. After we'd finished in the school he asked where we were going to go next. I suggested the churchyard on the knoll where Lord Colherne wrote his poems and mused over his early loves. After my VIP nearly died of exhaustion from the moderate climb, we sat on the grave where I had spent my first evening with my father and we looked into the distance where London stood. The day was bright and sunny and I felt happy. I didn't make a feature of showing him the plaque itself, as I had noticed the word 'Bollocks' had now been replaced with 'What a load of crap'.

'Listen, young man, I don't need to see the school that you're expected to show. Show me your school. Show me what you do and how you really live.'

I was suspicious, but he assured me that he could be trusted and so with my heart open I started to reveal to him where I would take the clandestine cigarette, my routes to escape into town, and Dunsmore Wood. In fact two boys ran in the opposite direction when they spotted me and the elderly gentleman with a cane, walking by the dense trees and close branches. We stopped off for lunch at Mr Baresi's Italian restaurant, an establishment set on the outskirts of the estate where parents were seen taking their children for an up-market meal. It was expensive but faced little local competition as the only alternatives were places in the town like a Golden Egg restaurant, the Wimpy bar – my particular haunt – or various greasy cafés.

Mr Preston regaled me with his long career and I listened intently as he spoke to me as an equal rather than a teen-age delinquent. He had been raised in New York and had travelled from the slums of the Lower East Side to the top of the corporate ladder.

'I hope to visit New York soon. My older brother Tom is living there now, working in a bar,' I responded excitedly.

As his success had grown, he explained openly, life became more difficult and he was unable to grab the moment for the pleasure it was giving.

'You must learn to enjoy the present. Don't think of

tomorrow or yesterday, live for now and life will work in a more flowing and peaceful way.'

Wise words from my new older friend and although at the time the words resonated, they have become more profound as the years have fled by. The food and company was a joy and the bill was heavy, but his shiny American Express card gobbled it up and we both left with full stomachs and treated by each other's company. After lunch I escorted him to his waiting Daimler as he needed to get back to London.

'I will tell your headmaster what a charming young man you are and that you are an asset to the school. Also, if your brother in New York needs a job tell him to call me and I'll direct him to our personnel department.'

He handed me the perfect business card engraved with name and rank and gave me a firm shake of the hand.

'Always shake as if you mean it. It gives the right impression. I shook President Nixon's hand a few years back, and he shook like a wet fish. I knew from that moment he was no good.'

'I won't forget,' I promised.

For a boy who remained devoid of compliments this was a big day. The headmaster did receive a flattering letter weeks later and he called me back to his office for a second time. He congratulated me on representing the school so well, but a bit like when a doctor gives you clean bill of health, you feel untouchable and ready to take risks. As I closed his door behind me, I chuckled to myself at the prospect of being far naughtier.

*   *   *

'What's wrong with you?' I asked Justin, as my roommate walked into our study looking as if his nearest and dearest had died. I wasn't far wrong.

'It's my brother. He's been expelled.'

40

This simply could not be true. Even with my small knowledge of the workings of a public school, a head of house is virtually untouchable and especially someone as popular as Christopher Deane. But no, it was an expulsion. When it comes to drugs, there is not much argument with the authorities. A huge plastic bag of dope was found in his study; some said it was enough to cater for half the house, but like all rumours or gossip sure to be exaggerated. Many thought he had been set up although he was an infamous habitual smoker. When a search was made of his room it was clear that someone had betrayed him. He had hidden his treasure in a box placed below a loose floorboard, and the floorboard was only accessible by moving a heavy cupboard. Three masters had visited his study whilst he was at lessons and found the incriminating evidence within minutes of entering the room. Nothing else was moved. They knew exactly where to look and what they were looking for.

Justin fell heavily on to his bed with a thud and stared at the ceiling. The silence was painful and I pretended to finish off an essay, something far distant from my nature. Then there was a knock on the door and in came his brother, now out of uniform and giving the air of someone just released from prison.

'I am sorry; I didn't mean to let you down.'

The brothers embraced and their hug was long and firm. I left the room without a word and walked around the house looking for solace. I ran into David Burford. We were amazed about what was happening and curious where this jolt to the monotony of the school system would take us.

Burford whispered the news. 'Things are bound to change round here. I've heard that Christopher Deane was stitched up by Summerfield. And Summerfield is now going to be made head of house. You know what that means.'

Deane was the first head of house in over two hundred years to be expelled, which was quite a stretch, so these were isolated times. Burford was right; things were about to change and not for the better. Christopher left that very night, which is the rule for expulsions; once out, you do not hang around. His brother Justin slept quietly and still that night, although the muffled sounds of despair were faintly audible.

The following morning Mr Webster, the housemaster, gathered the boys together. We stood to attention as he marched into the hall. Photographs of former house groups with dates wafting back to the turn of the century stared down at us from the oak-panelled walls. The tension was heightened and resembled that moment when there is a sudden break in television for a 'newsflash'. The news was not going to be particularly pleasant.

The housemaster theatrically cleared his throat, sounding like he was dealing with something that had been lingering there for a good few hours. He didn't hold back with his announcement: Summerfield would be taking over as head of house and long before he should have.

'These are most unusual circumstances, but I have engaged the advice of my other prefects and Summerfield is the man to lead us through this unfortunate set of circumstances.'

'Engaged the advice?' I thought. What a load of codswallop, but the decision was set.

Summerfield then took centre stage and virtually barged the housemaster out of the way. You could hear the proverbial pin drop and we looked on as Summerfield took up a Churchillian stance.

'The behaviour in the house has reached an all-time low and in fact has become an embarrassment. Things are about to be very different. I will make sure that respect and discipline is installed in every one of you. I know there's not long now until the Christmas holidays, but there will be no slacking in this house. Our last head of house allowed slovenly behaviour to manifest itself, and this is not acceptable. We shall root it out.'

I saw Justin tighten his fists and his knuckles whiten. I then noticed that his brother's name had already been expunged from the wall. Within hours the process of re-moving any memory had begun. Once expelled there is no forgiveness from the school and a boy is banned from returning to the grounds for fifty years. There will never be an invitation from the school's association to join, which means that you will not be invited to an old boys' reunion. Your son will not be invited to take part in the school's entrance examination. And finally and probably the hardest institutional slap, you may never wear the old school tie; an absolute disgrace in the eyes of the public school system. We were released and made our way to our studies filled with a certain amount of dread.

Although generally very quiet, Justin now seemed to disappear further within himself. He did not seem at all present and spent his days with headphones clasped to his ears listening to Bob Marley or sauntering around the house in a daze. Although I asked regularly how he was, he didn't want to discuss his innermost feelings and I respected his solitude. We shared a room but in truth I was very much alone. The postcard would arrive and he would carefully place it in his book and I would occasionally catch his furtive eyes reading the words written by his ostracised brother. Since that first night, I heard no tears; he was quiet and uttered little except when he switched off his sidelight, and before falling asleep would always wish me a good night.

*   *   *

43

'Perseverance, perseverance. Effort, and more effort,' bellowed Summerfield in his hectoring way. He was lecturing us about the upcoming January school cross-country run. He believed that this was the opportunity to show the rest of Montgomery that our house was no longer the laughing stock and to hold aloft the Annasmore Cross-Country Cup, recently renamed after Giles Annasmore who died whilst trying to complete the last mile of the race.

I was told that Annasmore had had a heart attack from a blood clot. For someone so young this was highly unusual. Although it had happened ten years before, I was haunted by the story and started to have palpitations about the forthcoming race. Each boy was expected to take part and finish the race. Time would eventually be added up from the first forty finishers from each house and the house with the best time would be named as the champions.

I was sick with worry at the prospect of running the race when I met Burford and Grafton. It was just not my sport and with the added complication of hypochondria drifting into my brain, I was becoming a little neurotic.

'It's going to be a disaster,' I said. 'I just seem to lose breath at an early stage and panic if strange boys overtake me.' My paranoia was hitting new heights. 'What are we to do?' I was looking to my friends for guidance.

'Cheat,' said Burford, leading me into trouble with that one word 'It would be quite easy, actually.' He explained that the run started on the main race track, and yet the majority of the chase was run through Balfour, five acres of woodland on the border of the school grounds. It was named after James Balfour who had been headmaster for over forty years the previous century; he reportedly died on the job whilst calling out a name during roll call.

'Listen,' he suggested, 'during the first ten minutes we can lose the crowd, hide in the woods and then rejoin when the race is coming to a close.'

'How will we know it's near the end?' I asked. There was no answer.

I slept badly that week, tossing and turning as the fat little face of Annasmore haunted me. He had been in our house so I had searched out his name on a school photograph. There he sat cross-legged like many of us, face open and smiling, very much alive and embracing his time. Before a geography lesson I was piling my books on to a desk and caught a glimpse of a name carved around the ink well; it was Annasmore and I screamed in horror just as Gripper Yates was marching in.

'Pull yourself together, Alexander,' he ordered.

I spent the rest of the lesson jittery and when Gripper finally directed a question, I was unable to make a sound. Losing patience, he tossed me out of class. Afterwards I told him I'd seen a ghost but, in response, he put me in detention where I had to write out a thousand times, 'During the week, ghosts do not exist in classrooms'. I did not complain, I just wrote.

Community Service gave the perfect opportunity to talk to someone in the know.

'Mrs Wheeler, I am being haunted.'

'Who by?' she asked.

'A thirteen-year-old boy who went to my school.'

'Do you mean a dark-haired boy called Annasmore?'

I fell off my chair. The old lady, whom I was meant to be looking after, dashed to the kitchen to fetch me a glass of water. I pulled myself together and looked at my resident psychic. In a few days I had turned into a neurotic with an acute form of spectrophobia.

'Don't worry,' she laughed 'I read about it in the papers

at the time. But be careful how you run the race. That I can advise.'

'My health?"

She tutted and smiled which I took to be a good sign; she surely wouldn't sound so joyful if I was going to die.

* * *

We met on the running track dressed in our house games kit, pink rugby shirt, white shorts and pink socks. Our house colour was pink, not the most distinguished but the most fashionable. The three of us huddled together as Mr Riggs, the PE master, got out his starter's gun. The professionals amongst us looked straight ahead, the amateurs looked at the gun; I looked at the gun.

Riggs shouted, 'Get ready, set,' and a shot was sounded. A throng of boys ran across the track, up the hill and towards the woods. On reaching the trees, we vied away from the crowd and headed towards the more dense part and hid behind an overgrown holly bush. We were joined by Spit.

'But I thought you were a good long-distance runner?' said Burford.

'Yeah, but I wanted a fag.' His answer was short and emphatic. He took cover and lit up.

It started to rain and we were beginning to be drenched and extremely uncomfortable.

'How long do we have to be here?' I asked Burford, our ringleader.

'Well,' he was looking rather hesitant; 'I saw the record for the race was one hour, set in 1961, so we should wait for an hour and twenty, and then rejoin the race.'

'And what time did we set off?'

He did not have a watch. 'Great,' I thought and looked to my other musketeers to come up with another plan. Spit said that we needn't worry as he had a watch and we had set off at about two o'clock.

The rain became stronger and we were now completely drenched. I kept asking for the time and it seemed as if Spit's watch was moving very slowly.

From our hideout we could see the rest of the school taking their laps round the course. The groups were dispersing and soon fewer and fewer boys were passing our vantage point.

'Do you think we should join in?' I asked.

For someone who didn't want to run, I was now eager to make a sprint to the finishing line. It was becoming very clear to all of us that there had been a miscalculation and we were way back in the field, and already the sun was setting in the evening sky.

We decided to rejoin after seeing Varney, the most over-weight and slowest boy in the school, gasping for air. We hurried out of our hiding place, saturated by the unforgiving rain and miserable. As we ran along, things became very clear, that we were at the back of the once-crowded field. Other than Varney there wasn't a boy in sight. We ran out of the woods across the fields towards the finish; and yet there was no finish, as boys were clearing up and there was little evidence that there had even been a race in the first place. We had bungled and we were coming in last but one. I yelled at someone who was making his way back to the house.

'The race finished about an hour ago,' he replied.

How could that be? But we knew we were going to be in real trouble now. And sure enough Summerfield, with his face as red as a baboon's arse, was heading directly towards us.

'Where the fuck have you lot been? You're a fucking disgrace!'

47

Thinking on my feet, I said that Burford had twisted his ankle in the woods and we had come to his rescue. 'Brilliant,' I thought but he didn't buy it.

'Don't lie to me, you little toe-rag.'

'But it's true, take a look at his ankle,' I continued our defence.

He looked at the ankle in question and Burford rather pathetically made it act limp.

Summerfield's disgust was overwhelming. 'Go and change and report to my study . . . immediately.'

Once back in the house we scurried along the gloomy corridor to his warm room and he greeted us with two of his prefects, Warwick and Shaw, standing either side of him. Although physically smaller, Summerfield looked down on all of us.

'You are vermin. A disgrace to our house and to the name of this school. I will do my utmost to straighten you out but if that fails I will make sure you don't see the year out in this establishment.'

I wanted to answer but I didn't have the energy; we had been caught and knew that punishment awaited us.

'Go now, undress and come down to the tosh room with your towel. Five minutes, no longer.'

The cold tosh had arrived. This was a miserable, angry day and the bathroom itself was as cold as stone. Summerfield and Warwick made us line up behind the baths and ordered us to put the plug in, sit in the empty bath and switch on the icy water. I will never forget how bone-chilling the water was, nor how raw the pain. It took forever and the prefects chuckled sadistically as the water level built. I wanted to complain, I wanted to plead for mercy but I knew that it would be useless. I saw Spit in the neighbouring bath, lips turning blue, skin shrivelling. Poor Spit, he had only been at the school for a few weeks. Burford was groaning; Grafton almost seemed to be somewhere else, probably already plotting some dark revenge.

The whole process lasted fifteen inhumane minutes. The torture was complete; our frozen bodies clambered out and ran rheumatically with shrivelled penises to our thin, unwelcoming towels. I hobbled to my room and dived into my bed, clinging on to my covers and trying to warm my shivering body. The chattering of my teeth, the stiffness of my hands and the redness of my nose were my companions that night. I reflected that I had tried to cheat in the school cross-country race, was caught and had to face the consequences of experiencing medieval torture. I had made a choice and allowed myself to be consumed by delusion. I lay in my bed disconsolate, but twenty-four hours later I had placed the sadistic retribution firmly in a closed box and I was ready to challenge authority once again.

*   *   *

Valentine's Day always conjured up fear amongst the boys in the school. Reputations were brushed aside with a heavy swipe in a morning when no cards arrived at the breakfast table. Others grew overnight as a stack of mail waited proudly with scent drowning the envelopes. There was no hiding place that day. A date in the calendar that grew in importance thanks to the growth of mass-produced greeting cards.

I had completely forgotten it was February 14th as I'd not long had my birthday. Suddenly it was the evening before and Burford was boasting that in the morning he expected a record delivery of fifteen cards.

'I have made my regular calls and will not be surprised if I beat the all-time record.' He talked smugly and like a pollster assessing the votes in an election.

Oh God, I thought, I'm not going to receive any and I had spent the previous months full of stories that countless girls had fallen for my charms. My tales were developing into catastrophic hysteria and yet I couldn't resist this fantasy figure I'd created.

Troubles chirped up, 'Well I wouldn't get too cocky; Sam here will give you a very good run for your money.'

I smiled weakly and if I had been standing at that moment, I probably would have collapsed. It was too late now to get to town, buy up the cards and forge the writing on the envelope. I dragged hard on my cigarette and kept quiet for the rest of the evening. How could I have been so foolish and so unaware of the upcoming celebration? I tossed with every turn throughout the night and dreaded hearing the morning bell. Perhaps I could be sick, pretend to be so violently ill that the boys would forget the date, and focus on my health. No, that wasn't going to help, so I decided that I would sneak into town and send some off and just explain that they must have been lost in the post. But this was not going to work either, as they'd arrive too late, no one would believe them, and so by breakfast time the bell sounded as if it was marking the day of doom. I had not found one decent solution which was going to save my Lothario stature in the eyes of my friends. I dressed as if going to a funeral, and the funeral was mine. I would just have to hope that I could keep my head down and things might pass by unnoticed. I tip-toed gently down the stairs, already acting with quiet low profile.

The table of carefully placed letters was as predicted: envelopes drenched with exotic and brothel-like fragrance and block capitals written mockingly to hide each sender's identity. Yes, Burford had a pile waiting in assorted colours, but whether it was instinct or the fact that I had thought of doing it myself, it was clear to me that they all came from the same individual, namely Lord Burford himself. Brains even had one and picked his up quickly and hid the evidence in one movement into the inside pocket of his blue blazer.

'Didn't see any for you?' my so-called friend, Troubles, asked me.

I smiled nonchalantly but it was too late. When boys sniff a trapped animal they pounce and don't let go until the victim is either dead or very wounded.

'And we thought you were a big ladies' man,' smirked a faceless swine.

The whole house seemed to be laughing as I walked into the Main Hall.

I picked up my cereal, poured my milk and walked slowly to my seat. Perhaps I had generated this whole episode with my internal fear, but somehow my fellow housemates turned the spotlight of the morning firmly on to my head.

Then the homosexual jibes started to cascade in my direction. Camp voices sounding like Larry Grayson asked me to pass the sugar or hand over the butter, 'Oh no, of course you need that.' I never understood the connection between the public schoolboy's aversion to homosexuality and someone truly not receiving a Valentine card.

I munched on my cornflakes and concentrated on examining the cereal dissolving into the milk when a silence drowned the scornful room. Looking up I saw the housemaster of all people carrying the largest bunch of red roses ever, almost big enough to swamp his portly figure. He was walking in my direction and on reaching my shoulder plonked the bouquet of flowers with its overwhelming redolence right in front of my food.

'For *moi*?' I asked.

'Yes, but not from me,' the housemaster replied.

'Ah, that is a pity, sir.'

'They were delivered to our door by mistake, Alexander; it seems someone loves you.'

Amongst the sheaf of roses was a small card tucked into a typical pale florist's envelope.

'Who is it from? Is it signed?' asked an obnoxious nasally sounding prat sitting to my right who only moments before was accusing me of doing terrible things with animals.

I opened the envelope and took the card to my chest and then glanced at what was written. 'Have a lovely day, love you, MUM X'.

'No, it's not signed,' I said, as I crumpled the card into my pocket.

I gathered up the roses and hurried to my room; I leant against my door and looked up to the heavens with my hands clasped and thanked God and Mum for coming to my rescue in my hour of need.

*   *   *

It was Monday, 8.30 a.m. and morning assembly was about to begin. On the first day of the week, the entire school gathered in Speech Room to hear the engagements for the coming seven days and to listen to a rather dull lecture from the headmaster, usually about how responsible we had to be as he advised us that we were 'the future heart-beat of the nation'. A big yawn and certainly an incorrect hypothesis. Mr Henderson, the headmaster, was like a quasi-mythical figure that hovered around the school but was rarely encountered from a boy's view. He had pre-viously been head of English at a public school in the north of England, famous mainly for producing good rugger players. He had the appearance of a lock forward and although in his mid-fifties looked fitter than virtually anyone else at Montgomery. He was handsome and had the air of a sober Burt Reynolds, but anyone who had the pleasure to meet him always reported that he was fantastically boring and virtually any word uttered would create a wide yawn. This Monday, however, was different. The head announced that late on Sunday night after the little school museum had closed to the public, its Turner painting had been stolen.

J. M. W. Turner had once painted a local scene and a Montgomery old boy, who'd later owned it, had bequeathed it to the Montgomery Foundation. The value of the painting was colossal whilst the blow to the school's morale could be more. The headmaster warned with caution in his voice that there might be journalists swarming around the grounds and we were under strict instructions not to converse with these members of Fleet Street. The police, on the other hand, would also be asking questions, and we were told to be helpful with our answers to them. The head went on to advise that the police believed that the crime was carried out by a member of the public between ten o'clock and midnight and that the thief would be apprehended and soon. 'Well, well, well,' I thought, 'never a dull moment in this place.'

It was that afternoon that I met my first newspaper hack. 'What's your name? Know anything about the robbery, son?', a man with a husky voice and yellow teeth asked.

Instead of not talking to this suspicious individual, I sang like a canary.

'Yes we've heard it was one of the visitors to the museum and that it was not one of the boys and anyway no one from this school would have the guts, and a mysterious man was seen at the entrance late last night after ten o'clock holding a multi-coloured umbrella, and . . . and . . . and . . . '

I ended my statement with the wish that I didn't want my name mentioned, but a contribution to my dwindling funds would be much appreciated. He smiled, gave me a five-pound note and told me not to worry about names.

'Perhaps we could do business in the future. There must be countless good stories around this place. Got any royals here?'

He handed me his card, after scribbling his home number on the back with a leaking blue biro. He then walked away looking for his next victim. The following day my first headline appeared in the *Mail* reprising my words: 'Turner Theft Latest: Umbrella Man Sought'.

The police were around too, asking their own questions.

'Excuse me, young man, did you see anything suspicious going on last Sunday?', an over-eager man in a raincoat enquired.

'Are you a copper or a hack?' I immediately responded. My tone was arrogant and certainly misjudged. His cheerful countenance changed to a stern one and he pulled out his police warrant card.

'I'm a Detective Sergeant, sunshine, and I would like you to answer my question,' he said indignantly.

I told him I had seen nothing, but my whole attitude was foolish; I could see that he made extra notes about my conduct and my demeanour.

'What's your name? We may want to talk to you again.'

I was now a suspect, well so I thought, but it worried me little as I was innocent. When he'd finished with me, I ran to our derelict house and told Burford and Grafton about my encounter with the cops. How impressed they were, as only young teenagers can be, and we laughed and joked about the possibility of being called for a 'line up' or whether we should take on the role of detectives and track down the robbers ourselves; surely there would be a reward?

I think it was two days later, far into the night, when my deep sleep was shattered.

'I need to tell you something.' I moved slightly, my eyes barely open. Justin was standing looking down at me. He was shaking my shoulder, trying to wake my comatose body. With my eyes now slightly open, he then spoke his first words to me in days.

'I stole the painting.'

Somehow the news put my body into shock and my brain was unable to process what was going on.

'What did you say?' I asked, wiping my eyes.

He repeated those words: 'I stole the painting.'

I didn't believe him. 'You stole the lighting?'

I had misheard him again and I gasped for air. Now wide awake, I took in what he said and began to listen properly to his bizarre story. He explained that he was angry and after his brother had been expelled, he decided that he would get some money and join Christopher who was now working in a surf shop in California.

'How are you going to sell the picture?' I asked.

'We have a friend, who has a friend, who is a fence and he'll be able to sell the painting on.' This was becoming more ridiculous and I sipped a glass of water whilst taking it all in. I had noticed he was going on about 'we' and asked who else was involved.

'It was really Dixon's idea,' he explained and he was doing it for the money so he could get out of the school and travel the world. Charles Moore was involved as well, because he was so stuck on Dixon, and he wanted enough money to be able to follow him. They planned to set up shop somewhere in Peru, he added.

'Peru?' I said, 'Why in fucking Peru? Do they think they're Butch Cassidy and the Sundance Kid?'

This was the most Justin had ever conversed with me since we met and still I found it hard to take it all in. His confession was precise, measured and unemotional, cold in fact. I, on the other hand, trembled either with trepidation or excitement.

'Where did you hide the painting?'

'Well that's the reason I told you. It's under your bed.'

I sprang from my sheets as if they had been set on fire and hurriedly looked under the bed with my torch. And there, poking out from the bed-sheet it was wrapped in, was the unmistakable gleam of a gilded frame. I smiled with disbelief, looked again and then lost it.

'Get it out of here and I fucking mean now, you idiot. I've, been shooting my mouth off round the school like I was involved, but only because I knew I wasn't. Now I am.'

I was furious, petrified the Sweeney would be kicking our door in at any moment.

Within minutes all three culprits were in our room dealing with the problem. Dixon was paler than ever before, Moore fussing and Justin explaining to the others why he'd felt compelled to tell me.

'Just hold on a little longer, we should be able to shift it before the week is out.' Dixon was trying in vain to placate my anger. I was having none of it. They soon gave up after I'd rejected an offer of a ten per cent agent's cut by grabbing hold of Dixon's skinny body and shoving his groin hard against the corner of my desk.

They took the painting from under my bed, and went off to hide it in the roof space of the art school, which was easy to reach from our room by clambering on to the fire escape and going down through the garden. The evidence had all been removed by four o'clock and the air of innocence returned to our study.

I had so many emotions running through me. The disbelief that the painting had been hidden under my bed, that my roommate was involved and that they had had the audacity to drag me into their mess. If anyone had found the painting, no one would have believed that I was innocent after all my bragging. It would have been the end of not only my school career, but probably everything else.

I decided not to tell my other friends. How I wanted to, not only because I was upset, but because I wanted to gossip. Each time the robbery was brought up in conversation, I kept quiet or tried to change the subject. I was surprised that no one saw that I was hiding something but it seemed they didn't.

The following days passed without incident. The police did not re-question me, which was a relief as I am sure I would have found that difficult, and the school returned to near normality. The relationship with my roommate was strained but as we never had a particularly communicative connection before the incident, it was relatively unchanged.

*　　*　　*

I had drifted to the Wales Street house after lessons one day, and there were Dixon, Moore and Justin talking to a man in a donkey jacket that I'd never seen before. He was a dodgy-looking character too. He had hair like the housemaster sprouting from everywhere: his nose, his chest, his ears, his eyebrows.

He was just leaving when I arrived in the doorway, and he called out to the others, 'Before the end of the week, lads, OK?'

The three boys smiled at him and rubbed their hands with satisfaction, while I moved to let him get past.

He looked at me. 'What can I do for you, laddie?' he asked with bad breath.

'You could have a shower,' I replied and he swore at me and moved out of my sight.

Dixon wore a self-satisfied, smug look. 'I told you things would be all right,' he boasted.

'I knew you would fix everything for us. Lima here we come!' said a rather pathetic Moore, gazing forlornly with doe-like eyes at Dixon, his imprudent hero.

'You must be mad,' I remonstrated. 'How can you even entertain trusting a man like that?' But my words were useless and fell to the dirty fag-butt-littered floor. The boys were never going to listen and although the obvious stared them in the face they chose to disregard it. I realized that afternoon that if someone wants to believe in something because it makes them feel better, even if their choice is way off the mark, they will. And reality will return and then bite and wound you.

The boys left the building, but I remained looking out of a broken window, glad I was not involved.

The next few days moved in slow motion and nothing was mentioned. If I passed any of the 'villains' in the passage we nodded and moved on: not a word was said.

After an afternoon of games I returned to my room to find Justin hunched over his trunk, packing furiously.

'How are you?' I was asking the obvious. He had just been sent to the headmaster and had been expelled from the school. The fence had gone to the police that morning and turned the boys in. The likelihood was that he had made a deal with the police to keep himself or one of his mates out of prison. I have no idea whether that was true but the result was the three boys were expelled that day and were banished before six o'clock. The headmaster apparently saw them all individually and expressed his surprise and disappointment that it had been boys from the school.

'I just can't believe you would let Montgomery down in this way,' he kept on repeating. Dixon, like Deane, had shown little emotion and made no comment.

Moore on the other hand had blubbed for mercy: 'It was Dixon, he seduced me and forced me into it.'

But his pleas were ignored and after he was sent from the headmaster's office he was blanked by Dixon who had heard the loud cries of innocence spilling from under the headmaster's door. No charges were being brought as the school wanted the episode to vanish, especially as the bad publicity would hang over the school like the smell of dead fish. It all happened so quickly and was done.

Justin put his hand on my shoulder and looked me straight in the eyes. 'I never wanted to involve you and not for one second did I want to hurt my friend.' He spoke as if he were really older than he was. 'The headmaster and housemaster both asked whether you were involved or if you knew anything about it. I told them you didn't. I'm sorry for everything.' And with that he turned his back, bag on shoulder and disappeared from my life forever. I barely knew Justin but was impressed with his dignity and wisdom at the end; and then, like a handful of sand slipping through your fingers, he was there and, within seconds, had vanished.

I walked out of my study to find Grafton, Burford and Winter all eager to hear the inside scoop; and so we made our way to our Wales Street house to gnaw on the well-eaten bone. My heart wasn't in the story that night; I felt the school was on a crusade to rid itself of the 'characters' and I suppose I felt threatened. Yes, I knew they had stolen and stolen big, but I felt that a side of them was innocent, perhaps with the exception of Dixon.

'I am going to miss Justin,' I heard myself saying.

'Not if they don't replace him in that large room of yours,' Winter instantly replied, looking for a positive take on the situation.

'I suppose you're right,' I said, but I wasn't convinced.

We crept away from Wales Street; it was dark and the air was crisp. Roll call was minutes away and once again names would be missing. As I was approaching the house from the other side of the street, I saw an orange Austin Allegro draw up with a woman in her fifties wearing a tweed coat, heavy-rimmed glasses and carrying the burden of the world on her shoulders. A dog was barking from the back seat. She was meeting her son. Her son was Dixon. Dixon slung his possessions into the back of the car. There was no embrace, just a feeling of resignation from both sides. Oh, the ordinariness of it all. The car drove away from the house with not a word shared between them. Probably the poignant silence continued throughout their journey home. The words and recrimination would surely come later.

The housemaster surprisingly didn't explain why the three boys had been expelled to the gathered house, but just that they had and it was time to move on. He read out our names slowly and the response from the boys was, on that night, very different. It was sombre and monosyllabic. We were told to go our rooms and finish our work and lights out would be early tonight, in fact directly after our nightly prep.

Mr Webster knocked on my door and asked if I had a minute. It was the most cordial he had ever been to me. He said that it was a sorry affair and that he was shamed that it had happened on his watch, in his house. The gruff Scots accent became more intense when he promised that this sort of behaviour would not be repeated. As there would be no changes for the boys and their studies until after the summer term, I was told that the room would remain mine for the rest of this school year. Ah, what luck, a room to myself in my second year. The 'private privilege' of having your own study began at the start of your third year so I was ahead of time. There was light through the darkness and I decided there and then for the coming weeks, I would

60

keep to myself and avoid trouble. Easy to write and entertain, but mighty difficult to put into practice.

'Deane told me you had nothing to do with it and knew nothing about it; this must have come as quite a shock?'

I did not answer. A day later, Brains ran to my room and told me that someone was calling and it was important. I picked up the house phone and heard a voice I vaguely recognised.

'Want to tell me who did it?' asked the voice.

'Did what?' I replied.

'Stole the painting?' It was the hack with the bad teeth that I had earned a fiver from.

'I don't know what you are talking about and anyway I have no comment.'

I put down the receiver and returned to my study, satisfied that at least I had done something right for the first time in months.

*   *   *

There had always been fierce rivalry between Montgomery and Selwyn College. They had an unyielding distaste for each other. By reputation, and probably by fact, Selwyn was the more aristocratic whilst Montgomery smelled of new money. Montgomery was regarded as a second choice to many who failed to get into Selwyn. But my family had Montgomery school in their veins and Selwyn was regarded at home with disdain.

There is a classic story that well describes Montgomery's relationship with Selwyn. It portrays the Monty, a term given to boys who have attended the school, as an arrogant yobbo and an oik, and it was regularly told around the public school circles, giving the air that a Monty was a lesser mortal in manners and etiquette.

A Monty and a Selwynite walk into the gents to have a

pee. After the Monty finishes he does up his flies and walks out. The boy from Selwyn meanwhile goes to wash his hands and dries them thoroughly. Outside, the Selwynite approaches the Monty.

'At Selwyn, we are taught to wash our hands after we have been to the loo.'

'At Montgomery,' replies the Monty, 'we're taught not to piss on our hands.'

*   *   *

The rivalry was running stronger than ever, reaching its zenith at the Selwyn versus Montgomery match at the Oval Cricket Ground in Kennington on the south side of the River Thames. The match had first been played in 1805 and was one of the oldest fixtures in the sporting calendar. Now, with football hooliganism in England all the rage, trouble was about to surface in the midst of an upper-class cricket match. It was like Liverpool versus Manchester United, but posh. A group from my school arrived at the Oval on the Saturday morning with weapons hidden down their trousers and taped to the inside of their jackets, ready for a good melée.

The match took place on the last Saturday of term. School was over at eleven o'clock after the final roll call, and then we were picked up by our parents and taken directly to the Oval.

My father had hired a box for the day and it gave a fine view not only of the game but the skirmishes springing up in the stand directly to its right. There were about fifty boys singing their hearts out to the football chants of the day. Why the masters did not stop the banter I have no idea, but it was presumed that they were sung with good nature. How a song with the words, 'You are going to end up in an ambulance,' can be perceived as good nature, I will never know. Soon after lunch the atmosphere turned. A group of ten boys from Selwyn approached Dave 'Coatsy' Coates, a giant of a boy with a Grimsby Town scarf tied to his wrist, and demanded that he and the rest of his gang should shut up, stop being yobs and behave like the gentlemen they weren't. Well, that was that and a counter-charge was mounted and the frustrations and aggression that had built up over the term spilt on to Oval Cricket Ground. The Earl of Blythe had one poor Selwynite on the ground and was systematically punching him in the face.

'Do him, Chris,' yelled Nick Keswick.

'No fucking names, Nicko,' retorted the Earl as he continued his onslaught.

'But you just called me Nicko.'

I watched from the safety of my father's box and felt contented that I wasn't the only obstreperous boy at the school.

Grafton caught my eye as I was leaning over the balcony to get a better view. He beckoned me with his index finger. The headmaster of Montgomery was in the box sharing some thoughts with my father at the time. The box was full of alcohol, and was being consumed by my father's contemporaries at a most alarming rate; I made a discreet exit. The head was still unaware that his school was involved in a full-scale riot.

Grafton opened his jacket and revealed a contraption not unlike a home-made bomb.

'What's that?' I asked.

'A home-made bomb,' he answered.

'And what the hell are you going to do with that?'

I followed quietly as Grafton led me to the gents, near to the Pavilion.

I kept watch whilst Grafton stuck the mechanism to the innocent white porcelain cistern. He turned the small switch with some difficulty, as his hair was nearly touching the tip of his nose, and seeing anything was becoming increasingly difficult. He ran to the door waiting for it to detonate. Nothing happened, absolutely nothing.

'Well, that was exciting,' I laughed.

He didn't understand what had gone wrong and the two of us went back into the loo again to discover what had happened. Starsky and Hutch we weren't: Laurel and Hardy more like. The container exploded without warning, more with a whimper than a bang, but with enough juice to crack the porcelain and allow gallons of water to escape.

A steward, hearing the noise, ran towards our direction. He immediately caught us and held us both by our collars. The water continued to flow and was now flooding the whole area.

'What have you done?'

'Nothing,' was our instant response.

He let go of us for a second and asked for our names. I gave mine, also my school and house. He asked Grafton the same question.

'Henderson, Eton and King's Scholars.'

He jotted them down and told us that we would be reported to our respective schools. 'You're just bloody hooligans – what is this country coming to?' Oh, what a fool I had been. I had honestly given my full name and address whilst my more astute ally had acted quickly and pretended he was someone else. I was now in real trouble and dreaded that my expulsion was just around the corner. I returned to my father's box downcast and angry that I was going to be in trouble for such a stupid ill-conceived prank. The headmaster was still there drinking yet another large gin and tonic. I moped in the corner, now that the confident witty soul I had been only a few minutes before had evaporated.

Go to the headmaster, I thought, and twist the story

into a hard-luck tale. From the sound of it, the fighting was still in full flow below us.

'Excuse me, headmaster. Sorry to bother you, but . . . '

The head gave me a gin-induced smile and then heard my story on how, when I was passing the gents I'd heard a disturbing noise, and had gone in to investigate. The headmaster listened, seemed to believe me, swayed and told me not to worry.

Then he was pulled to one side by an anxious-looking Mr Oxlade.

'Sorry, I have to go,' he announced to the gathering. 'It looks like the school is in a state of revolution.'

*   *   *

It was always the same; my school report would arrive a week after the end of term with a heavy thud on the doormat. It was delivered by the local postman, George Chambers, a man who always had a smile on his face and had been delivering post in the area for the last thirty years. George was an ardent Sunderland supporter who although now in Oxfordshire, would take the train every week to follow his first love, a team that played more than 250 miles away from his front door. He would walk up our long drive whistling a football tune that would shatter the silence and make the birds fly away in terror.

'It's here, it's here, it's here,' he would yell whilst posting my report through the letterbox, making sure the whole household was prepared for the bad news. In the times that I was awake he would grab my ear and bore on about the history of Sunderland Association Football Club.

A few years earlier, in 1973, Sunderland celebrated their finest moment when, thanks to a single goal from Ian Porterfield on a rain-swept Saturday afternoon at Wembley, they won the FA Cup by beating the favourites, the indestructible Leeds United. So happy was George, that he was drunk not only with happiness but with whisky for weeks that followed. Post went astray and complaints from a minority of the locals mounted to the point that George was dragged in front of his superiors and sacked. This created such dismay amongst the majority, who liked George, that a petition was quickly organized, by none other than my father, to reinstate him. My father even led a march in George's support, which set off from the White Bear pub to the milestone just outside the village. Banners were held aloft with 'Reinstate our Postman' and 'Is it a sin to be happy?' on them. Although only a distance of two miles it made the point and my father led the villagers with confidence, like a pair of trousers that really fit.

Within days, dear George miraculously got his job back and everybody celebrated in the pub where the march had started with loud toasts and hearty cheers. Even at my tender age I was allowed to join the celebration and got to drink a bit of someone's Guinness. That afternoon I had looked at my father with my heart full of pride.

My mother knocked on the door and told me to get up. I groaned, knowing that, to follow, I'd have the boring formality of my father sitting stonily behind his desk, while slowly reading out bits of my report and making remarks about my behaviour in class.

I ate my breakfast steadily and played for time by asking for kippers, which I then drowned with vinegar.

'Hurry up, Samuel; he's waiting.'

'Mum, do we always have to go through this? It's so dreary.'

'Yes we do.'

I shrugged my shoulders and made my way to my father's office, which was more like a library with a desk placed in the centre of the room. My father had a passion for books and had collected and preserved them from a young age. He kept them in strict alphabetical order by author and his proud collection included some first editions of Charles Dickens which he seemed to cherish more than his own family.

He asked me to sit down and then, thumbed through the sheets, making obtuse sounds each time he turned a page. After he had finished waiting, I sat staring at the multitude of books waiting to hear my father's summary.

'French – Good, History – Very Good, Geography – Good, Latin – Very Good. Well, well; they think you might be an asset to the school. The housemaster believes that you have a good, honest attitude. He believes that you can reach the very top.'

I was so amazed that I wanted to check this was my report and that George the postman hadn't reverted to his old ways and delivered it to the wrong address. I asked if I could see it with my own eyes but father denied the request. 'No, this is addressed to me,' and he pointed to the envelope, 'but I am very pleased with you.'

It was time for a celebration. I had received a good report, and as I left the library my mother hugged me warmly as if a doctor had given me the all-clear.

*   *   *

The hangover from the cricket match was evident on our return the next term. David Coates was expelled during the summer holidays for his part in the fighting. No charges for grievous bodily harm were brought to court but his school career was over. Two other boys from different houses were expelled and a fourteen-year-old from Selwyn was dismissed for carrying a flick knife and threatening a master with it, who had told him to quieten down. The headmaster gave a stern lecture about the disgrace that many had brought on the school's name. He talked about the state of the nation, the social unrest and how the country was disintegrating in front of his eyes. He concluded that over his dead body would he allow the school to follow. 'You are leaders, do not forget that,' he shrieked; I shook my head.

The cricket match would never again be held at the end of term thus spoiling a long tradition and would instead be played just before the eighth week. Many who were guilty of participating in a near-riot had avoided the wrath of the school as the summer holidays that followed the match had softened any idea of a full-scale enquiry. The bombing of the bathroom was never again mentioned; I kept my eye on Grafton, though. The prank had left a wintry chill running down my spine; I wondered where my friend was heading.

The first day of term, I was given my own room outside the bathroom on the old side. I became used to the free-flowing flush occasionally reverberating around my head at night. Within hours, my room was covered with my footballing heroes and my favourite girls. Long sexy legs covered the ancient cream wallpaper. I knew that once the housemaster had carried out his routine inspection of what was hung on the walls some of my finer portraits were going to be removed.

Mr Webster usually emerged within the first few days during our evening prep hour and with a keen eye for the unwanted, would mark the unacceptable items with a heavy black pen, reminiscent in a way of Langley on my first day at the school.

'Please don't ruin the picture, sir, I could take her home,' I would plead but his cruel streak would not listen and he smirked as his pen scribbled over anything that he considered too risqué.

The window overlooked the High Street and the area

below the school library. Our new smoking sanctuary was on the same floor, a small landing under the stairs of yet another fire escape but thankfully inside. As soon as I had finished my interior decorating I made my way for the first fag of the term. This small space would become our home for the majority of our free time. The usual suspects were there; we spoke excitedly about the holiday. Sex was of course the main subject but there were many Billy Liars amongst us, boasting about conquests that were very distant from the truth.

*   *   *

My visits into London became more and more frequent over the following terms. Leaving the school at nine o'clock on Saturday night, taking the exact route each time. Down the fire escape from my old room, behind the library, past the art school, and down a steep road shadowed by the dense woods, and on to the tube station. This remained the most dangerous part of the escape, but rarely did we see a master and if we did the platform was so large we were able to avoid him. Then it was on to the Metropolitan line into central London, and freedom. When I reached the streets of London, the joy was overwhelming. This particular night the fire escape hanging from my room, which we regularly used, was being fixed and so it proved to be impossible to return via our usual route. The group of us discussed the quandary. We decided that the only remaining option was to sneak through the housemaster's study which would lead to the relative safety of our rooms. The study was at garden level so a climb was not needed. The housemaster spent most Saturday nights playing cards with his wife and fellow housemasters, Mr Bagley and Mr Briggs; it had become a ritual, a tradition for them and Mr Webster could be heard most days on the fun they shared over the card table. If a distraction was needed whilst dealing with Mr Webster, you brought up playing poker and he would forget what he was dealing with and bang on about the fun of a good game.

Troubles Winter offered to leave the window ajar for us, and we were set.

'You make sure you do that, Troubles, or else we'll be in real trouble,' I warned. He promised and we trusted him.

We set off to London confident that our return would be without incident. By the time we reached the party in Earls Court, any thought that trouble might lie ahead disappeared and we spent the night chatting to a group of girls from St Paul's. The clock was heading for midnight so we said our goodbyes and headed for the tube before it all shut down. Our train was empty except for a drunk singing John Miles's 'Music' at the top of his voice.

'I hope Winter remembered to open the window.'

'He promised me. He's a good guy, don't worry; it'll be fine,' I replied.

There was not a soul on the street and our walk back to the house was littered with just the sound of clunky footsteps. The window had been left off its latch as arranged and Grafton pushed it open easily and very quietly. He climbed up and with a push he lowered himself over the ledge and into the office. Once there he turned around, smiled and beckoned Burford to follow. Up went Burford, slightly more drunk than his friends. He pushed open the window wider this time. He looked at me, waved, and walked through the housemaster's study.

Just me to go, it was all clear, the plan was working perfectly. I climbed up the short wall, grabbed the bottom of the window and with one giant step lowered myself into the study. I pulled the window down and replaced the latch. I then began to tiptoe across the study floor and just as I was doing so, I heard footsteps making their way to the door. I froze for an instant, what was I to do? I speedily retraced my steps and hid behind the dark red drawn curtains directly behind Mr Webster's desk. I could see through a crack in the curtains that it was the housemaster himself walking directly to his desk. I stood upright holding my breath, knowing that the slightest murmur would be catastrophe. I firmly believed that the future of my life at public school was hanging by a thread. He sat down only a few inches from where I was standing. I could see he had taken some papers out of his side drawer and had begun reading them. What had happened to the card game? Again I held myself straight, breathing as quietly as possible. I could see and count the specks of dandruff on his shoulder. I was unsure how long I could last there. I was wilting, I was going dizzy. I looked at the clock ticking away on his cluttered desk. I had been standing there for nearly an hour and was beginning to fall asleep.

Mr Webster's muttering and comments as he was marking kept me awake, jolting my head upright as it was in the process of falling. I was so close to his shoulder that I could actually read the names written on the papers in front of him. The clock's ticks became louder and I could see that another hour had passed. It was the longest two hours of my life and I was about to hand myself in, ignoring the consequences, when the housemaster gently put the lid on his pen, straightened up the papers and walked towards the door.

He paused, switched off the main light to the office and opened his door, but as he was walking out he turned round, stared at the curtain, the very curtain I had been standing behind motionless for two hours, and said, 'I don't know about you laddie, but I am going to bed,' and with that he was gone.

I never found out whether he knew who it was but the

punishment had been served and whatever else he had thrown at me, nothing would have been worse than the hours I had just experienced.

*　　*　　*

Although we'd shared a room for our first year at the school and therefore spent many weeks of school life together, I honestly knew very little about James Langley. Yes, I knew he was the son of a high-ranking officer in the British Army and he didn't particularly like my taste or approve my lust for the different, but other than that, I really had little concept of his mood or whether he was happy or sad to be part of this privileged life.

He would come into our study, put his books down on his desk and scribble into his diary his innermost thoughts. He would never say hello and rarely looked in my direction. His nose was always blocked so that the sound of snorting was consistent and at first extremely irritating, but after a while it just became part of the furniture and I hardly noticed it. Other boys, however, would snort as they passed him and mutter 'pig' under their breath. He was strange, different and for most boys that is disconcerting and hard to handle. When he attended roll call, boys would shift away from him as if he carried a contagious disease but he never reacted, he just stared into space and did not utter a sound.

Langley was in my class and would stroll in and quietly sit at his desk, straighten out his pens, place his rubber in the same position every day by the disused ink well. Within seconds someone would flick it to the ground and start to play soccer with this small object. He would fleetingly dive to its rescue and more often than not the master would walk in, scold him for not sitting at his desk and a relentless jeer would be sounded until the master told us to shut up and silence would surface. I was sometimes part of this mean streak but it seemed at the time to be nothing more than prankish behaviour.

It was Field Day for the Corps. Field Day, when all the Corps went on field excursions in the autumn, usually pretending to kill each other and act as if they were in an actual war. Being in the minority and serving my local community instead, I missed all the shenanigans of khaki and orders. I spent a leisurely afternoon with Mrs Wheeler watching the afternoon film on television. It was *The Yellow Rolls Royce*, starring Rex Harrison and Shirley MacLaine amongst others. A cup of tea and a warm fire was the perfect tonic from the draught and woes of the school.

'You'd better not be late today, young Sam. There isn't a good feeling coming from Montgomery tonight.'

I looked at her and could see the face of concern staring back. I hurried away and was not surprised when a silent hall welcomed my return to roll call.

Most of the boys were still dressed in khaki and I was the last one to walk into the assembly room. I gave David a nod and in return he gave me a look to keep quiet. In marched Mr Webster, sternly looking at the ground; he joined the top table of prefects and addressed the house.

'Today an incident took place during Field Day on the school grounds. Langley, a member of our house, was set upon by four unidentified members of the school and suffered concussion and broken ribs. He remains in hospital this evening and his condition is stable. There is no suggestion that members of his house were involved but if it turns out to be so, the boys in question will be expelled immediately. Bullying will not ever be tolerated.'

The housemaster walked straight out and we were all sent to our rooms.

There was no question that Langley had become a victim.

He had little social grace and no charm. He was unclean and never washed his hair. His white shirt was grey and his trousers were ripped around the pockets and remained so.

In short, he had no respect for himself. We knew that was hard to tolerate but he was easy prey and that night I chastised myself for my role in joining the laughter when he walked into our classroom. I had suffered the intimidation of the bully and his thirsty pack when at prep school, but it wasn't until that night the scar resurfaced.

Although questioned many times by the school staff and by the local police when his father took the matter to them as a criminal case, he refused to point the finger at anyone and merely said that he was challenged from behind by four boys but was unable to recognise the faces. Rumours were abundant about those who had committed this cowardly act, but nothing could ever be proved.

Langley was in hospital for five days and although given the chance to leave the school, he chose to return to the house. As he walked through the corridors, boys would avoid him. One day I literally bumped into him walking past the kitchens.

'How are you feeling?' I asked. He mumbled that he was alright and seemed to want to talk on but before I could follow it up with another question, he walked away and a chill of loneliness followed him through the corridor.

I called out after him. 'Hey, Langley, if you need to talk, just come up to my study.'

However, despite my offer, he didn't come to see me.

*   *   *

Grafton and I spent time together in the holidays in each other's company and on one particular afternoon before Christmas we headed into London, Kensington Market to be precise, a flea-bitten second-hand clothing bazaar off

Kensington Church Street. There we saw a sign advertising ear-piercing for just fifty pence in a narrow store drenched with the smell of patchouli and selling bits of hippy jewellery and paraphernalia.

'Let's do it,' he suggested.

I had to think fast, knowing that if my father ever saw it then life would not be worth living; but a decision was made and it was done quickly and with some pain. To quote Grafton, 'You squealed like a little girl'.

I stood up, proud of the loop spinning round my ear, knowing that it was in a small way a grasp for independence.

'Your turn,' I said to Grafton and pointed at the happy-looking hippy that had just performed the operation. Grafton stared at me as if I were mad.

'I wouldn't do something so stupid,' and he walked out into Kensington High Street. And in a small way that encapsulated Grafton, measured in everything he did with no instinctive nature, and happy to let others get into trouble whilst watching it happen without a share of guilt.

As for me, having chosen to take up the challenge, I sauntered down Kensington High Street with a newly found confidence. I approached a pretty young girl.

'Like my earring?' I asked, shoving my ear into her face.

'No, you look like a wanker.' And I did.

*   *   *

My father found out pretty soon about our excursion to the erstwhile jewellers. He banged on my bedroom door.

'Let me have a look at your ear,' he yelled. 'Are you out of your mind? Take it out.' I removed it in front of him and as he stormed out of my room he turned and said, 'Don't play around with your body until you are eighteen,' and slammed the door behind him. That could be mighty tough, I thought.

*   *   *

75

On the first day back after the Christmas holidays we gathered as usual for the opening roll call. The housemaster addressed the gathered. 'We will be one short this term. During the holidays James Langley took his own life. He was found hanging from a rope by his father in his bedroom. I tell you this detail because I want you to know that his loneliness and sadness was caused by many different aspects but one of which we have to take responsibility for. I am as much to blame for not recognising the seriousness of what was happening and all you boys must question yourselves for any role that you may have taken in making him unhappy. We are all responsible.'

He dismissed the house and as I walking out of the hall the housemaster beckoned me over.

'Come to my study immediately,' he said, 'I need to talk to you.' I took that long walk and in those moments tried to recognise if I were a bully and partly guilty of this tragedy. I certainly wasn't the one that harmed him on that cadet exercise, but yes I had been wrong for simply being a spectator of general classroom bullying. For the first time at school I was petrified of the consequences that I was about to face.

I walked into his silent office and there he sat down, took a pause and spoke.

'Langley's father, the Major General, would like the chance to talk to you.'

I was petrified as the housemaster dialled the number. The telephone was passed to me and I heard a clipped upper-class direct voice.

'General Langley here. My son James never really spoke much about things, but his mother and I have read his diary now and found out from there that you were his only friend. When everyone else refused to communicate with him, you were the only one to care about asking how he was. As his parents we are grateful for the kindness that you showed him and we will never forget this.'

I was speechless, shaking, and may have uttered a thank you as I put down the phone. I went directly to my study and was greeted by unpacked boxes ready to be emptied for the new term. I looked out of my window with London and its lights in the distance; I broke down and cried.

*   *   *

The clarity of my dreams during my time at school was amazing. I had one dream so often, it became quite a friend.

I am sitting alone at a table outside a bar in a piazza in the Tuscan hills in the heart of Italy. I have ordered my pasta and I am looking out whilst enjoying the shade from the midday sun. I see a boy soaking his head with water from a cold rushing tap. In the middle of the square there is a large fountain that resembles a tree with water shooting from its branches. Suddenly, without warning, the water stops. The boy looks at the tap bemused and the final drops from the fountain drip away forsaken in the sun when only moments before it was in full flow. I ask the lady in charge of the bar why the water has suddenly ceased and she replies that during the middle of the day in summertime, the main supply to the village is cut off. I finish my lunch and go for a walk around the town. As I reach the top of the hillside I see a line of trees shadowing a strip of land.

I walk towards it and find a gate which I gently open. Greeting me is the greenest green football field that you could ever imagine; lush grass, freshly painted white markings and pristine goal posts with their nets floating in the gentle wind. In the centre, and in each penalty area, huge sprinklers spurt water out, covering the precious turf.

Above all and with sacrifice, the people of the village protect this treasured piece of land with their love, passion and heartbreak for a game between two sides of eleven men and a ball.

* * *

I was the only boy at Montgomery to receive the football magazine *Goal* each week. We were encouraged to order *The Times*, the *Telegraph*, the *Daily Mail* or even the *Daily Express*. The papers were delivered by seven o'clock in the morning and laid out neatly on the table in the hall before breakfast. *Goal* flared like a solar storm; to love football at my public school meant you were in a minority. On arriving at the school I knew that football was not even played, instead it was hockey. Hockey, for God's sake. I should have known there and then, that this world was not going to fit easily into my life.

Soccer was my first true love. When I was only six, my bossy form mistress, Miss Holden, wrote in my school report: 'Samuel will not achieve much if he continues to be football obsessed'.

Well, my team's Tottenham Hotspur, based in north London on the Tottenham High Road, and that season when I was six, even the Spurs' goalkeeper, Pat Jennings, managed to score a goal in a game against Manchester United: how could you not be obsessed with a team like that?

It's a wealthy club that's extremely well supported. Spurs had majestically won the double of the First Division championship and the FA Cup, but that was the year I was born. They had won UEFA Cups and League Cups over the years, but never quite repeated the glory of that double-winning side and I lived in hope at the start of each season rather than confidence. My room, though, was covered with pictures of my favourite Spurs footballers, in between the beautiful girls. Every spare moment I diligently followed the comings and goings of what was happening in north London even though I felt cut off, imprisoned by conversation from other sports.

It was the start of January and I had decided to take the Saturday off and go and support the team. I had no games and would not be missed. Burford could cover at roll call. The usual clandestine dash to the underground, the tube into London, a change for the Victoria line, and then on to Seven Sisters. In the house there was by chance another Tottenham supporter, one of a few boys in there who actually liked the game. The Earl of Blythe, a yob aristocrat, two years older than me always nicked my copy of *Goal* and many times I found it damp and well thumbed besides the ground floor loo. I challenged him about his continual theft but he pleaded innocence and looked horrified at the mere suggestion. In fact, he told me to 'just piss off'.

'How would you like to come and see Spurs play West Ham this Saturday?' I asked the bespectacled spotty fan. The Earl readily agreed and although we didn't particularly like each other we were content to spend the afternoon supporting our common cause. When we were on the tube I saw something bulging from his jacket.

'What's that protruding from your pocket?' I asked.

'Just a couple of loo rolls,' he replied defensively and with an edge to his tone.

It was the tradition of the time that once a goal was scored, morons from the terraces would hold on to one end of a loo roll and throw the main bulk on to the pitch. It was meant to look beautiful in flight but in reality, it just looked brainless. Originating with the fanatics who stood on the terraces of South America, the British version of the ticker-tape splendour usually ended like Christmas lights in Blackpool, cold and unappreciated.

We lined up to get our tickets and made our way to stand at the Paxton Road End directly behind the goal. What greater joy than to enter a football stadium, walk up the stairs, find your place and marvel at the atmosphere?

The Earl of Blythe, as if in search of pheasant, sought out a good spot.

'Look at those guys over there,' he said, indicating a knot of burly Spurs supporters in their mid-twenties. They were mostly wearing sheepskin jackets or Crombie overcoats against the cold and the drizzle, with Spurs scarves tied on their wrists, and big flared Brutus fader jeans worn slightly short in the leg to show off their serious eighteen-hole Doc Marten boots.

A shock early goal by Trevor Brooking gave West Ham the lead and the Hammers held on to it for ages. The West Ham fans were taunting the home fans whenever things went a bit quiet.

After the half-time break, Spurs came out and started to take the game to their East End opponents. It was wonderful to see those wearing the white shirts glide across the January mud.

With the early rain we'd seen now relenting, the ball was booted upfield by Pat Jennings, the Tottenham goalie. Then the Spurs captain, Steve Perryman, walloped the ball hard into the West Ham area where it was deliberately handled by a defender. Penalty! Keith Osgood had no trouble from the spot: one-all. Then, nine minutes later, John Duncan for Spurs was played through beautifully by brilliant young attacking mid-fielder, Glenn Hoddle, and slipped it past the West Ham keeper to make it 2–1. A huge roaring orgasm of sound erupted around the stadium. Blythe was ready to seize the moment. He got hold of his loo roll and attempted to unfurl it gracefully into the sky. Unfortunately it never reached the pitch. The projectile barely unrolled but instead flopped without warning straight into the head of one of the hard men standing just a few yards in front of us.

'Oi! Which idiot threw that?' bellowed a menacing voice.

A huge hand rested on Blythe's shoulder, 'All right you, out of there.' It was a huge policeman and he was not kidding. He led the aristocrat out and I meekly followed. Blythe started to argue his case, complaining that he didn't know he had done something wrong.

'Look here old boy, there has been a mistake. Just let us back in the ground, and we will forget the incident,' his Lordship pronounced.

'You don't throw bog rolls around the ground,' grimaced the copper. 'And besides, it's for your own good; you've not done yourself any favours by chucking it at those hard boys directly in front of you. What's your name and address?' He took out his pad and licked his pencil.

'The Earl of Blythe, 115 Eaton Square, London SW1.'

The policeman looked at him quizzically. 'Listen, mate, if you're the Earl of Blythe, then I'm the Queen Mum.'

'Well then, you're my man.'

The policeman shook his head, got tired of us, and told us to be on our way and not to come back.

'Think of a better name next time, you nasty little yob.'

As we walked away, Blythe turned around and shouted 'Wanker', at the top of his voice and saluted with an over-extended V-sign.

The two of us then prepared to bolt down the Tottenham High Road. As we started to run, Blythe's shoe fell off and he had to sheepishly return and pick it up. The policeman was standing hands on hips over the dirty over-worn penny loafer.

'I'm sorry, officer; I didn't mean to say that.' The police-man growled and pointed in the direction of Seven Sisters tube station and we hurried away to the safety of our school without any fuss.

The journey home was antagonistic, not a word shared between us. Blythe annoyingly hummed a Demis Roussos number and I was holding in my anger that the buffoon opposite had ruined my day. As we crossed into the school grounds, Blythe looked at me and said, 'I've had enough of Tottenham. From now I am going to support Manchester United, they're the most aristocratic club in the country.'

'So much for loyalty, your Lordship,' I retorted. 'And you make a rubbish hooligan.'

*   *   *

I just didn't feel like joining the others, Burford, Grafton and Spit. They had arranged to meet some friends at a party in Earls Court; Grafton's sister Sophie was giving it. She was a ravishing seventeen-year-old who had the reputation of being the most beautiful girl ever to have attended Cheltenham Ladies College.

'You can give her a snog if you want,' he generously offered. He went to his desk to fetch a family photograph framed by an 'I love Walt Disney World' frame. Most incongruous for Grafton, but she was certainly beautiful and shone majestically between her two brothers. But for some reason I didn't feel like venturing into the heart of London that night. I wanted to be alone, solitary with my thoughts. I felt as if I were withdrawing; waking up in the morning not looking forward to the day, wanting instead to curl up into a ball and hide at the bottom of my bed. The institution was rubbing hard against my skin and I was beginning to feel uncomfortable with the drawn boundaries. So my friends gave up and made their plans and escaped into the night without me.

I was spending the night in my study as promised, alone

with my thoughts, with fleeting regrets that I wasn't in the heart of London making out with Sophie. I looked at my watch and the night was still young so I grabbed my coat and set off into town to look for somewhere or something to cheer me up. The town wasn't particularly large and still had a hangover from World War II with bombed houses still not rebuilt some thirty years since the end of the war. Christmas lights, no more than coloured bulbs hanging low from a long wire, welcomed all visitors. The High Street still had businesses with 1950's-style hoardings. The cinema had an art deco visage and the neon advertising that week's movies lit up half the town. There was an ice-cream parlour called Doletti's which again shone brightly and whose menu, especially the banana split highlighted in the centre of the window, would tempt anyone. They regularly changed the tempting concoctions on offer and each time I went by I had an urge to run in and consume half the menu. But it was dangerous, as masters and their families were regularly in there and the possibility of being caught, especially on a Saturday night, was extremely high.

I drifted away from the main drag and found an area near to the town's cricket pitch which remained unspoilt and glistened with pride in the heart of summer. But for now there wasn't a sound and no light except that of a distant pub that stood alone on the far side of the field. I looked suspiciously, fearing that it would be the perfect retreat for masters, but I put my trepidation to one side and ventured forth.

The Rose and Crown was a labyrinth of warrens, each with its own log fire crackling and burning strongly. The bar was in the centre room and had an old till marking pounds, shillings and pence; time had stood still in this enclave of drinking except for the jukebox that blared out Abba's recent hit 'Dancing Queen'. Laughs rang through the rooms, mixed with loud talk and opinions; it was England at its most familiar. Wearing my heavy coat, collar up, I made my way to the bar.

'Coca-cola, please.'

The barman gave me a suspicious look but his ruddy face and big brown eyes were comforting and welcoming. He poured the drink, asked me if I wanted ice and offered me some crisps on the house; I took salt and vinegar and sat alone in the room immediately to the right as I walked in. The offer of crisps was a first and I was comforted by his generosity. I could hear debates ranging from the Saturday football games to whether Jim Callaghan was doing a good job as Prime Minister and how they missed good old Harold Wilson.

'Brian Clough should be the PM. At least he would tell us straight,' slurred a drunken man sitting to my left.

For the first time in weeks I felt sanguine. Although alone, I felt at peace. I felt free and the prison that enclosed my mind seemed distant. I finished my drink and crisps and decided to stay. I returned to the bar.

'Same again?' the landlord asked.

I took my drink and went to the juke box to chose a record. I chose David Bowie's 'Drive-In Saturday' and returned to my table and just as I sat down caught the sight of the girl that would mark my life. She wasn't far away from where I was sitting and in fact, if I had tried, I could have heard the conversation she was sharing with her friends; but having been distracted I hadn't even noticed her until that moment.

She had the most beautiful face I had ever seen, thick golden hair, piercing clear green eyes, olive skin and a smile that could launch an army. I was struck down. I had fallen in love at first sight. I pretended not to look in her direction and, awkwardly, I sipped on my drink and played with the ice and lemon with my fingers; I tried to focus on everything else but this gorgeous creature. She must have known that I was trying to avoid her gaze as when I looked up for the second time, our eyes met and although I wanted to say hello or turn away or do something, I simply couldn't react: I was dumbstruck.

'Come on, you idiot,' I thought, 'do something.' I got up and made my way to the gents. I could hardly breathe. Staring at myself in the cracked mirror in the rather damp, ill-kept pub loo, I splashed cold water on to my face and ordered myself to get it together. I took a deep breath, straightened my hair and walked back into the bar. The jukebox was still playing, this time the Bay City Rollers blaring out their hit 'Bye-Bye Baby', contrasting to my state of mind. I immediately looked at her table but she had gone.

Where was she? Panic blanketed me. I was paralysed and in that split second I thought that I would never ever see her again. I went to the bar disoriented and asked for scotch on the rocks.

'I think you should just have another Coca-cola, don't you?' The landlord's deep voice calmed my panic. He saw that I was flustered.

'Just take it easy now. She's waiting for you.'

It must have been obvious that I was spellbound. I took my drink from the bar and bumped right into her.

'You're from that school, aren't ya?'

'If you mean *that* school, yes, but I am meant to be incognito. Is it that obvious?'

'It seems so,' she laughed and I fell into a state of rapture.

*   *   *

Her name was Lana. She had been named after her grandfather's favourite film star, the beautiful and sensual Lana Turner. Lana lived in the town, behind the cinema. Her father worked for a local building company and her mother was a housewife. She didn't have a boyfriend, which I found remarkable, but still I was able to discover this key fact within seconds of meeting. She had been clocking me for the last hour but I was so deep and alone with my thoughts that I had hardly looked up.

'You seem to have a great deal on your mind?' she asked.

I explained that no one listened to me at school and however hard I tried to express my pain, no one, not even my close friends, could hear my anguish. I had never expressed myself in that way to anyone, but here I was, within minutes of meeting, opening up my soul to a total stranger.

'I'll listen,' she said, 'I'll always listen.'

Lana's friends were impatient and made loud noises from their neighbouring table.

'Don't worry about them, they're just being silly. They were telling me to come over and talk in the first place.' And so we continued as if we had known each other for years, about everything and nothing, but I do remember at that instant I was happier than I had ever been before.

I was about to ask for her telephone number but just before I phrased the question, Lana reached into her bag and brought out a lipstick and scribbled the numbers that I will always remember. The lipstick was bright red, and although smudgy the digits were clear enough.

'You should call me; they do have phones up there, don't they?'

'For sure, it's not that archaic. Pretty medieval, but we do have running water so we can wash.'

'Well that's good, I don't like dirty boys.'

'Shame,' I replied.

'I'm going to go now,' she said. Her friends were insistent. I stood up to give her a kiss goodbye and she took hold of me and hugged my frame tightly to her chest, and then in an instant she disappeared. Her smell still floating in the air, the warmth of her hug burning my skin. I collapsed on to my chair and began to yearn for her immediately.

The sage of a landlord walked over to my table with a port in his hand. 'Here,' he said, 'have this one on the house. If you were older, I'd give you more. Enjoy yourself; enjoy the moment.'

'Her name is Lana and she has swept me away into a place I've never visited before. It feels like I'm swimming in a vast ocean.' I was looking up at the landlord.

'Yes, well. Just make sure you don't drown,' he replied dryly.

I stayed in the pub until closing time and then made my way into the darkness and back to school. I walked up the main road ignoring my usual circumspect route. I felt like a gun-slinger walking into a western town confident that no one could stand in my way; I felt invincible and high. I made my way to my room, kicked off my shoes and shook off my clothes and collapsed naked on my bed staring to the ceiling, thinking about what had happened. My euphoric spirit was jolted by Summerfield swinging open my door with a crash.

'So you're here? I'd heard that you had left the house and gone to London.'

I discreetly grabbed a towel and covered my body. He was drunk and even from a distance stank like a brewery.

'Go back to sleep, Alexander, I'll deal with you later,' he slurred and luckily didn't bother to walk into my room. If he had done so, he would have seen my jeans and coat discarded by my bed.

*   *   *

The following morning my friends greeted me with exaggerated stories of kisses and slow dances at the party in Earls Court. 'You don't know what you missed,' they all exclaimed and there were promises of another party the following week. I wanted to tell them of my night, about where I'd been, what I had experienced, but something inside me said this was my time, and not to be shared with a pack of hyenas who were devouring every short skirt they had encountered a few hours before. I spent the entire day with Lana's voice in my ear sharing every movement, every thought. Should I call now, should I call tomorrow? 'What's the right thing to do?' I kept asking myself; my instinctive nature was lost in a haze of infatuation.

Sundays at boarding school were the longest days, as after chapel there was very little to do. There was the library, a game of squash perhaps, or a table in the tuck shop. The Montgomery school tuck shop was open from early morning until six o'clock and familiar faces reserved their seats and spent the day munching on Twiglets and sandwiches. Parents would be seen wandering the grounds with their offspring looking generally rather awkward as they followed a good distance behind. I always discouraged my mother and father from visiting anyway.

The Italian restaurant I had taken Mr Preston to, stood alone as Sunday's treat on the school's property. Bursting at the seams, the chorus of upper-class voices pierced the sound barrier and the deluge of snobbery made me want to disown my rite of passage. Mr Baresi, the Italian owner, welcomed all mothers with 'Bella' or 'Bellissima' and led them to their table with the care and attention that warranted the extravagant prices. I watched how he operated and marvelled at his charm. We had a shared passion for football and many an afternoon I would pop into the restaurant for a chat and to enjoy a taste of Italian coffee.

That Sunday, I wandered up to the restaurant, eager

for advice on how I should make my next move in my first quest for love. The place was predictably full and Mr Baresi was hurriedly darting from kitchen to tables acting as the maître d', owner and generally a good egg. I tried to signal him from the street as he was in full flow. What followed were hand signals that neither of us could understand. This went on for far too long until Mr Baresi stormed outside.

'Alexander, che cosa?'

'I am in love, Mr Baresi.'

His mood changed instantly and his face softened. He leant towards me, sighed and then smiled and then sighed again, as if he were reflecting on his long turbulent love life.

'You come back at, say, five o'clock when I will be ready to pay my full attention to you.'

He then grabbed hold of my face and gave two huge slobbery kisses on either cheek. The restaurant's occupants froze with dumfounded expressions etched on their faces. He returned inside and shouted at the top of his voice, 'He is in love.' The crowd remained startled and silent; in Italy they would have cheered.

Mr Baresi was in the kitchen when I returned later. On seeing my lost face, he threw down his towel, poured a coffee, grabbed some biscotti and led me to a table.

'Girls, continue the drying. I have to talk to young Alexander, he is in love.'

The young girls, who had served drearily all day, giggled, cooed and started to smile for the first time since morning; the power of love held no bounds.

'You see, Alexander, there are two ways to play this. One, call immediately and tell her you love her with all your heart, or play it very cool and let her bleed to hear your voice again.'

I listened intently as if I were in the presence of a prophet. He spoke with admiration and a hint of sadness. Mr Baresi's love life was pretty complicated, and I understood that Mrs Baresi had left him some time previously. He talked and talked mostly about his woes and it was a good hour and closing in on my time to return to the house for roll call when I interrupted and said, 'Well, what shall I do?'

He paused, looked to the ceiling in search of God and said with a baritone scorn:

'Let her stew and wait; don't call her until the pain is so great for her that she is on the floor begging to hear your voice again.' He hit his thigh whilst emphasising the point.

'Thank you, Mr Baresi.' And after we embraced, I set off back to my house more confused than I had been all day.

*   *   *

The following Wednesday I visited Mrs Wheeler alone, as Grafton had flu and had been quarantined in the sanatorium. Mrs Wheeler as usual had the list of shopping waiting for my arrival. 'You seem to have things on your mind,' she said as she handed me the list. I told her that my life had looped, so she smiled and suggested we talked about it after I had done the shopping. I ran to the nearest store and bought her usual items in haste. I knew that my elderly friend would have the right advice. I sat down in front of her fire and told her what had happened on Saturday night.

'And you haven't called her?' she enquired.

I explained what Mr Baresi had advised and she looked on in horror as I recited his words.

'What a foolish man he is and you are a fool to listen to his rubbish. Get up from that seat, go to that phone and call her immediately. Come on, get moving.'

She was pointing and there was no room for argument, so nervously I moved towards Lana's heart.

I had her number safely in my back pocket, but even then I knew it. I dialled, slowly and precisely; it started to ring. Please, please I thought, don't let her mother pick up. It answered.

'Hello, is Lana there? I am sorry to bother you.'

'Who is calling? Samuel? I'll get her for you.'

The welcoming tone was a relief. Lana came to the phone. There was no mention of her not having heard from me. She was just pleased to hear my voice and I was thrilled to hear hers and we spoke easily and happily. Mrs Wheeler was across the room, pretending not to listen, doing her cross-word, but she was all ears. I asked Lana if she would like to come up to the school and see me. Without a pause, she agreed. We arranged to meet at four o'clock that Saturday outside the headmaster's house.

'I'll be there on the dot,' she said and my heart leapt. I put the phone down and virtually ran into Mrs Wheeler's arms.

'See, it wasn't that bad,' she said. 'Don't play games. Be honest with yourself and be true to your heart. Then if things don't go right at least the honesty will lessen the pain. You're an Aquarius: you need a girlfriend, because you're communicative but at the same time Aquarians get nervous. Overcome that and things will be good.'

'What will I do without you?' I said to Mrs Wheeler.

'Oh, you'll do fine, but try not to listen so intently to your Italian next time.'

Now I had to tell my friends and when I returned to school, there they were in their Corps uniforms gathered on the fire escape. I told them about my Saturday night and though I expected them to rib me, to laugh and tease, they in fact didn't. They were happy and each one shook my hand and patted me on the back.

'Hey come on, guys,' I said, 'let's not make this into a marriage. All I'm saying is that I met someone and I wanted you lot to be the first to know.'

So we laughed and toasted Lana with a puff from a cigarette.

*   *   *

The week moved as slowly as pouring treacle. I failed the Latin test, I failed the Maths test and I was nearly sent out of the Geography lesson for falling into a dream and only waking when asked a question. In fact I answered it in French thinking that I was in a History lesson; confusion was setting in. Saturday could not come quickly enough and when it finally arrived it was that perfect winter's day. Clear blue skies, brilliant sun and a crisp cold in the air. I played a game of squash, and ran up to the house as soon as I had finished. I showered, splashed expensive after-shave around my neck which I had stolen only weeks before from my father's bathroom and, for the first time in months, combed my hair. I waited, hands in pockets, on the street outside the house.

Mr Webster passed by. 'You look smart, Alexander; waiting for your parents?'

'No sir, for my girlfriend.' Presumptuous, I know, but he was half way down the street by the time I had answered.

At four o'clock on the dot, I saw this lone figure walk confidently to the left of the chapel by the library towards me. She was even more shockingly beautiful than I had remembered and her warm smile swept away any chill that I may have been feeling. We greeted each other tentatively, kissing lightly on each cheek, her citrus scent whirling through my head. Many girlfriends journeyed to the school on the Saturday and we seemed no different from others that were walking on the campus that day. We did not hold hands although I know we wanted to, but our bodies accidentally brushed each other as I gave her my guided tour. I was enthusiastic about the school for the very first time, explaining who the old students were and describing each building, its history and what went on in there. Although she had lived only a few miles away her entire life, it was her first visit.

Mr Baresi was busy serving an innocuous couple as we walked in for tea. He left their order standing as he rushed over to greet the two of us as if we were his own children. His customary welcome of 'Bella' was even more vocal than usual as he kissed Lana's hand and led us to the perfect table in the far corner of the restaurant.

'Order whatever you like, my darlings; today, my dears, your tea is on the house.'

We were hurried in our conversation. She asked about my family and so I described my life simply without exaggeration. I was the younger child, I had a brother; my older brother, whom I adored and worshipped, lived in New York City working in a bar. Tom had attended Montgomery and was an A-grade student playing for the 1st XI in cricket and eventually becoming a prefect. I was asked if I found his success difficult to deal with.

'I don't feel I'm living in his shadow at this place, if that is what you're asking.' I enjoyed and was surprised by her inquisitive questions.

'And your parents?' She seemed genuinely interested. I told her that my parents lived outside Oxford. My mother, quiet, compliant, a woman of few words and, oh, how beautiful in her twenties, smiling from old photographs, looking so fragile. My father always controlling, wanting it his way but at the same time generous and giving us everything we could possibly ever wish for. I had overcome the loneliness of being eclipsed by the different personalities in my family by being gregarious, extrovert and even more different.

As a family we spent our time in our country house in a hamlet called Dean and I couldn't wait to get there so that I could play with my friends from the local village. One afternoon my father said that I was beginning to sound like the locals and that I should go and have elocution lessons. How perplexing, I had thought, but I did, and that's why I talk posh now and Lana laughed and said, 'Well he better not meet me or else he'll have heart failure,' and so I took her hand for the first time and looked straight in her eyes and said, 'He'll adore you and think you are the most beautiful girl he has ever met.'

She replied, 'You small so nice,' and our lips touched.

'Enough of that,' said Mr Baresi, spoiling the moment by plonking the largest bowl of pasta in front of our eyes. 'Now eat and fall in love.' And we smiled and attacked the delicious food and for the rest of our time there said very little and yet spoke a million words.

After our tea, we walked hand in hand back to the house. And with roll call just moments away I pulled her close and kissed her mouth. A kiss that I will never forget, a kiss that said I loved her.

'Will I see you tonight?' she asked pulling away and we giggled in a way only young lovers can.

As I started to run down to roll call, I turned and said, 'I will be there sitting at the same table waiting for you.'

I joined my friends and our names were called out as usual, slowly and one by one. I couldn't wait for it to finish. I couldn't wait to tell my 'gang' about what she was like and that I had kissed her for the first time and that I was happy. But as roll call finished Summerfield called me over.

'Tonight I want you to be on duty for the prefects. You

will serve in the prefects' study from seven o'clock until past your bedtime at half past ten.'

'But I can't,' I cried.

'What do you mean you can't, you insolent boy? You don't have other arrangements, I believe. You will be there on time.'

There was and could be no argument. Throughout the long night I stood to attention in their study running to fetch their wants as the swine lounged in their authority. I thought of Lana sitting in the pub, waiting in vain and deciding at the end of the evening that she wouldn't see me again. I created many stories in my mind with a depressing uneasy theme. The conversation amongst the assembled prefects was both tedious and unrefined. They were an angry concoction, hating everyone but themselves with a smattering of racism thrown in for good measure. The occasional insinuation that I was homosexual caused this parliament of fools to burst into mocking laughter.

Homosexuality was widespread in public schools. Being found in a sexual liaison with another boy would, however, result in immediate expulsion and purported shame for the family. Although rumours about certain students spread, it was only that and it was rare that anyone was caught. I never understood the loathing and bitterness that was directed to those at school who found solace in another boy's arms but then again I was never threatened by those who were different or in search of their true identity.

After what seemed like the longest of nights, Summerfield sent me off to bed.

'And I mean go straight to your room. I'll be checking on you within the hour.'

He didn't in fact and, like the week earlier, I fell to my bed and stared at my multifarious collection of posters not with love in my heart but revenge. Summerfield was on to me and the stakes that evening had been set. He was determined to make my time at school more uncomfortable than it already was. Now I had to make the decision to fight back and that I did during those late milk-train hours with thoughts of my girlfriend left sitting alone in a pub on the opposite side of town.

*   *   *

The following morning on the Sunday I attended Reverend Landau's class. There were mutterings of anti-Semitism growing in the school, something that I hadn't yet experienced. Yes, the occasional sharp comment from someone or other but nothing too wicked. That week the papers had been full of the son of a property magnate who had left Montgomery suddenly and blamed it on boys picking on him because of his religion. It was big news and swamped the conversation that morning. One boy complained that whenever he walked into his house, coins would be thrown in front of him, heated by a lighter, and when he tried to pick them up he burnt his hand, to the laughter of all those watching.

'Why don't you just ignore the bastards?' I asked, 'and certainly don't pick up the coin. To do it once is fine but to repeat it could seem pretty witless.'

'You sound as if you are supporting them, those Nazis.'

'I am certainly not, but I do think that it's best to ignore those morons.'

'That's what they said before the war'

We discussed whether incidents such as these should be reported to the housemaster and the class was split but there had to be a line drawn and ultimately sitting back and letting it continue I certainly agreed would be a mistake.

'Anyway, you are not even Jewish,' swiped Cohen, making a reference to the fact that my mother was

Catholic. Once again I found myself being attacked by both sides.

My mind was elsewhere and I regretted not being more sensitive to Cohen's pain. I couldn't wait for the class to end and as soon as it did I decided to go into town without permission in search of Lana. The chance of finding her was slight, to say the least, as the pub on a Sunday morning was still closed. I walked towards the area where she had said she lived. I could not find her. Just before lunch I gave up and on returning to the school realised that all I had to do was call her number. I found a red telephone box with smashed windows and the stench of piss from the previous night. It was frosty and I could see my breath billowing through the air. I dialled her number, trying hurriedly to force the dial back anti-clockwise with my finger each time to be able to do the next number more quickly.

'I'm so sorry I didn't make it last night, the head of house has his fucking cunt eye on me and didn't let me out of his sight. He's a sadistic son of a bitch.' I hadn't even said hello.

'Do you want to talk to Lana.' It was her mother on the other end of the line; I nearly died of embarrassment. Laughing, Lana came to the phone.

'Forgive me,' I pleaded. And so she heard my reasoning and was far calmer than I had ever expected, especially as I had built up a maelstrom in my imagination.

'Let's see each other today . . . please?' and I promised that I wouldn't let her down again; a heavy vow for such an early stage in a relationship and also for someone so young.

And so we met at the same time, at the same place and this time we held hands as we walked by the scholastic buildings back to Mr Baresi's. The welcome from the overbearing Italian was even more warm than the day before except as I finished ordering a huge tea, Mr Baresi whispered in my ear, 'Today you will pay.'

Warwick was seated at the next table with his parents and glanced consistently in our direction sizing us up. They looked and acted in a similar way to their son, upright, slow, considered in action and all mean-mouthed 'That's one of the shits who made me suffer last night.' Lana turned and caught Warwick's stare. She growled and he looked uncomfortable and returned to the silence of his table.

'I wouldn't worry about him, he's just jealous.'

No, I thought, he is not jealous, he is envious. Jealousy is something one has but is afraid of losing whilst envy concerns something one does not have. And here I was with a wonder that most teenage boys would dream of having by their side.

I paid my bill and walloped a generous tip on top. Mr Baresi gave us a warm farewell and I decided to show Lana off to my friends. They were clustered in the woods having their usual smokes. I introduced them to Lana and within minutes they had all become her friend. She had a streak of 'tomboy' about her and captured their eyes and hearts before the hour was out.

*   *   *

I woke up with the worst sore throat, my body sweating and trembling. I simply couldn't move and on hearing the bell at half-past seven and the five-minute warning at five to eight, it was an impossibility that I was going to be able to join the lessons.

Grafton came running into my study, 'Where have you been? Summerfield is on the prowl and . . . God, you look awful.'

I asked him to tell matron. Every adolescent teenager had a crush on Mrs Mills, our matron. I had had little contact since my arrival mainly because I had remained healthy well physically anyway, but I saw her from afar and more often than not saw her in my sexual teenage head late at night. Mrs Mills must have been about forty, voluptuous, brown eyes, long black hair and not unlike Sophia Loren. Mr Mills was never mentioned, but rumour had it that the fool left soon after they were married.

'I'm poorly, matron,' I said, already starting to flirt. She took out her long thermometer, shook it and placed it slowly and precisely into my mouth. She looked concerned whilst her voice was soothing; I had a high temperature of 104. 'Well, we can't look after you here,' she said, 'you will have to go to the sanatorium. Don't worry, I'll make sure that the housemaster knows that you are sick.'

'Please look after me, matron, or should I call you Mrs Mills?'

She ignored my rambling and told to me to get ready for the sanatorium.

Weakly I dressed, pulled on my coat, wrapped my heavy long scarf around my neck and walked unsteadily with matron to the other side of the grounds close to the Field house. As I was escorted through the school I used matron's shoulder for support, the boys rushing to their lessons eying me with envy. 'You poor boy, don't worry, you will get better now.' She was the perfect tonic.

'Will you be with me all day, matron?' I asked rather pathetically. She would not, but would look in on me in the afternoon.

'You will still have Nurse Madget.'

I wanted to say that I didn't want Nurse Madget and stamp my foot, but thought better of it as I was beginning to sound desperate.

Nurse Madget was in charge of the sanatorium. It stood alone behind a row of trees, a vacant-looking Victorian building. I was led through a wood-panelled doorway into a room not unlike a hospital ward, with bar heaters hanging from the walls. It was a long, wide, echoing room with eight empty beds, four on each side. The beds had wheels attached to their legs, a hangover to when the sanatorium was an open hospital for the locals. I was the only boy on sick leave and the only patient.

The nurse's quarters just outside had a small television on a wooden table, a two-sided desk and a torn over-used sofa. A small fireplace over-laden with logs stared from the corner. It was like drifting back into another time.

'Nurse, this poor boy has a fever and a high temperature, look after him won't you?' Matron then turned to me. 'I'll send for one of your friends, who will probably bring up one of your naughty magazines.' For an instant I thought that she might be flirting but it was probably the fever speaking. I reached for her hand and she ignored it. Nurse Madget then led me to the end bed; she was the opposite to my matron, devoid of sexuality and masculine in all but her voice which was thin and high. I collapsed on a bed that was a hundred times harder than the one I usually slept in, but no matter. I was exhausted, frail and poorly.

The rest of the day was void of anything but for an intense fever. The nurse came in to serve some hot watery chicken soup which I immediately rejected. I looked at my watch and the day had left me behind as it was two o'clock in the morning I was feeling disorientated when I felt a tap on my shoulder. I turned to find Burford pensively looking down at me. He seemed distant.

'Why have you come to visit me now, in the middle of the night? You don't need to risk that, come and see me tomorrow during the day.'

'I just wanted to make sure that you're all right; I know how it feels to be so sick.' His voice reverberated into my ear and sounded different. I then closed my eyes and unable to continue the conversation drifted into my dream.

The next morning, matron's was the first face I saw. She took my temperature and it had remained high. 'You won't be going anywhere today, young man. I want you to try to rest and eat that.' She pointed at a full bowl of porridge.

'I will try, Mum, I mean matron.' She ignored my slip, put her hand on my forehead and gave me a beautiful smile. My breakfast was dismissed and I received a disparaging nod from Nurse Madget. 'You will eat at lunch; we have a nice cottage pie.' I groaned. I slept that morning and with no appetite lunch was delivered and promptly refused.

'You will have to eat soon or we will put you on a drip.' This was Nurse Madget's idea of humour.

Burford and Grafton arrived that afternoon laden with magazines, bottles of Lucozade and chocolate. They didn't stay long as I wasn't strong enough to joke with them about how matron had carried me through school the previous day.

'The whole place is talking about it,' crowed Burford. 'Tell me, did you shag her?' My mouth and mind were numb so that I couldn't even deny it or tell them not be so very silly.

'See, I told you he did,' and my two buddies left me to die.

The first sense of recovery began to set in when I gulped down a thick vegetable soup and heavily buttered bread. In the background I heard the theme of *Crossroads* twanging from the nurse's room. I got out of bed to take a call from my mother. She has always been softly spoken and it has always been a strain to hear her down the end of the telephone line.

'Are you watching 'Crossroads?'

'No, Mum,' my voice still weak.

'You really have to tell us when you're unwell, Samuel.

Your father and I have been most concerned we have not heard from you.'

My father was then handed the phone and, not asking how I was, went on about how he had once been in the sanatorium and from his description little had changed.

'Did you know that during the war it was opened to the town? Keep in touch now. By the way are you watching 'Crossroads?' were his parting words. I left the phone more exhausted than when I first stood up.

I wanted to call Lana and asked the nurse if she could spare two pence. Lana was not in, so I left a message with her accommodating mother explaining that I had been unwell but was slowly on the mend. As I walked back to my isolated bed I gave the nurse a smile which she blanked and continued to watch her favourite show. Forlornly, I crumpled on to my bed and stared at the empty beds and thought of all those who had been nursed in the room. I saw my father as a fifteen-year-old ordering everyone about as he does now and saw others either being homesick or enjoying the break from lessons.

I woke abruptly again in the middle of the night and it was Burford asking how I was and telling me everyone was thinking of me. I told him again not to be so silly and to go back to his house. 'You were nearly caught yesterday; the nurse came in just as you were leaving. Don't risk everything for this. I'll see you tomorrow afternoon.' The lights were suddenly switched on and the nurse looked in suspiciously.

'I'm sure I heard something,' she tutted, and she paced up and down the room with her eyes looking under each bed.

*   *   *

I still had a slight temperature the following day and matron, who was wearing a rather fetching blue suit,

102

suggested I remain in the sanatorium for another twenty-four hours. The magazines that had been left were devoured and by lunch time not only was I ravenous but in search of company. Nurse Madget carried in a tray of macaroni cheese, apple crumble with a heavy load of custard on top and an apple juice. Unhealthy food for the unhealthy boy.

'How long have you worked here for, Nurse Madget?'

'Longer than you have been on this earth.'

'Am I your most favourite ever patient?'

'No,' she said unemotionally and walked back to her quarters. I was bereft of conversation and boredom was setting in. I looked longingly at the door wishing to be surprised and then as if by magic Grafton, Burford and Lana walked in.

'Look who we found on the grounds.'

Lana approached my bed. 'I've missed you,' she said and she stroked my hair. Those moments I'll cherish, I cling to them, to have someone that near. She held my hand; Grafton had been to see Mrs Wheeler that afternoon and passed on a bar of chocolate as a gift from her. 'She said that she would send some healing.'

'Will it reach the sanatorium?' I giggled.

After what seemed like only minutes, the nurse appeared and asked my visitors to leave.

'I'll come and see you on Friday,' promised Lana, 'that's if you're still here.' She kissed me on my forehead. I waved my friends out of the door and then collapsed into the sleep of sleeps.

Missing out on my dinner, I was woken by the words, 'It looks like you're getting better.' Burford had reappeared in the middle of the night.

'Hey, listen,' I said, 'it's mad to come and see me every night at this time. Although I really appreciate it, you're bound to be caught.'

'Well, you're better and will be sent back to your house tomorrow. So we won't be meeting again like this. But I wanted to watch over you and make sure that you regained your health.'

'Thanks,' I replied. 'You're a great friend and your mere presence has each day made me stronger.'

I then returned to my dream. I dreamed of the school many years before. How bleak it was and how mere survival was an achievement. It was the turn of the century as a huge banner hung over the Old School greeting the twentieth century. I watched a fourth former run with delight along the main road noting the bright sun and soft wind against his face, his black tie blowing over his shoulder. He ran towards the school's swimming pool, an Olympic-size construction known as 'Pond'. I watched as he dived in into the cold water from the hot day and then to my horror I saw him sink to the bottom unable to move, cramped by pain. There followed a commotion and the lifeguard, probably the master on duty, dived in to rescue. The boy lay still on the concrete next to the pool. He was carried by two boys to the sanatorium and then I awoke.

There was the sound of Nurse Madget's voice. She had walked in eager to catch the intruder: 'I'm sure I heard some noise.'

'No, nurse, there is no one here but me, but thank you for checking,' I said. 'Anyway, don't you ever go to bed?'

She chortled and marched off.

*   *   *

The following day my temperature had returned to normal and colour had returned to my face. Matron remarked how much better I looked and said that it was time to return to the house. So I dressed and had indeed regained my strength.

'Thank you, nurse,' I said, but she did not reply as she was busy introducing another sick note to the sanatorium. What an unhappy person, I thought, but the fresh air blew away any negativity and my strides back to my study built up my strength.

The last thing I felt like was a cigarette but I knew that my friends would be sitting out on the fire escape smoking the smoke. Spit was in a corner, his wiry hair dropped over his eyes. He apologised for not visiting but he had gone back to his home in Bristol as his grandfather had died.

'He was a kind man and I'll miss him especially when I go to the football. I'll be going alone now'

I gave him a hug and explained that he needn't worry as I was well looked after.

'Burford even visited me every night, after lights out.'

Burford seemed perplexed. 'I never visited you at night time.'

We argued but he was adamant and I was confused. I shook my head and acknowledged that my fever must have been far worse than I had realised.

A week later on the Wednesday I was with Mrs Wheeler recounting my time in the sanatorium. 'Legend has it that the old place is haunted,' she said. 'A young boy died there after falling from a horse.' I paused, looked up at her and said, 'No, he died by drowning on a hot summer's day.'

*　　*　　*

The invitation arrived by telephone the following week. Lana asked whether I would like to join her family for lunch the following Sunday. I was only too happy to go and found myself knocking on the grey door of her terraced house.

It was her father who opened the door, a tall barrel-chested man, wearing a white shirt tearing at the seams, baggy jeans and an anchor as a tattoo on his forearm. He was daunting and a little terrifying. I was looking smart and indeed very clean, well scrubbed and settled in a spotlessly clean uniform.

'You must be Samuel or is it Sam?'

'It's Sam.' My voice was hesitant and my confidence had for that moment disappeared.

I was led into their warm overcrowded house. The gas fire was burning in the living room, two huge chairs, a grey sofa and a table laid out for our lunch. Lana bounced out of the adjoining kitchen and kissed me. 'Don't be so nervous, he is a big softie really,' and stuck her tongue out at her dad.

Her mother, young, tired and still beautiful, crouched over the oven inspecting our roast. Her smile resembled her daughter's and she welcomed me with open arms. 'What a handsome lad you are.' I was embarrassed and turned a little red. Lana led me away and we stole a kiss. Straightening my tie she told me to be calm. 'They ain't goin' to bite.'

We sat down to my favourite of roast beef and Yorkshire pudding. It was delicious and I ate very quickly, much to the amazement of Lana's father.

'What, do they starve you up there?'

'No, it's just if you like something you have to eat quickly because you can then pick up seconds before anyone else,' I tried to explain.

'Well help yourself then, there's plenty left.'

And indeed there was, so I crammed my plate with more roast potatoes, a slice of roast beef and the last remaining Yorkshire pudding. 'The food is awful and I eat mainly from the tuck shop or at Mr Baresi's, a mad Italian who has a restaurant near by.'

'All that money and they don't even feed you?' Her father didn't hold back. 'If I had that sort of money, I don't know if I would have sent Keith.'

Keith, Lana's brother, had not made an appearance at lunch as he had a late night and was still comatose. He was an apprentice welder and liked to play hard at the weekend.

'Of course we would,' argued his wife. 'Best education in the world, that school. Something we should all have. Don't you agree, Sam?'

'I suppose I do,' I stuttered. 'That sort of private privilege is all very well, I think, but this is definitely my happiest day ever since I got there.'

Lana's father smiled, contented that he thought he was in the right.

Lana's mother asked about my family but I played them down and spoke little of them as I was embarrassed about my background of wealth and so-called privilege. In truth, it was my first encounter with a girlfriend's family and although deliriously happy I found it not a little daunting.

I was beckoned to watch the afternoon game on ITV's *The Big Match*. Lana came and sat beside me and reached for my hand, which I retracted. To show such emotion in front of her parents was like walking into a different universe and something that rested uneasily on my shoulders.

'Don't be shy, you can hold her hand.' Her father laughed and I gave him a curious look. The main game was between Arsenal and West Ham. My knowledge flowed easily and for the first time her father and I spoke in harmony.

'Didn't know you boys knew anything about football.'

Lana elbowed her father heavily in the ribs and told him to lay off. He gave her a warm kiss on her head and asked for forgiveness. They clearly adored each other.

Lana left the sofa and coaxed me with her index finger from the door. Dad was still watching the football and mother was finishing off cleaning the plates.

'Want to come to my room?' she whispered.

'You must be mad; your dad would kill me.'

'Don't be silly, he's too busy watching the game.'

Her room was simple. A narrow bed with a light-blue cover and a desk with books scattered. A picture of her parents with large smiles started from a picture frame shaped as a love heart; it sat alone on a side table by her bed. There were no posters on the wall, just a small drawing in a wooden frame. It showed a seashore at night with waves crashing against a high wall, on top of which stood a pub with the light streaming from one of the windows.

'It reminds me of something but I am not sure what.'

I turned to her and there she stood still, perfect, and time had stopped. I pulled her to me and we kissed and kissed and kissed again.

* * *

Keith had emerged from a long deep sleep. He barged into Lana's room and we pulled away from each other.

'Don't you ever knock?'

He didn't respond, looked up and then slouched out of the room.

'That was my brother, he doesn't say much.'

Keith had spiky black hair and looked a bit like one of the Sex Pistols, now famous for swearing on television. It was hard to tell whether he liked me or in fact whether he liked anything.

We rushed downstairs and the football was still blaring from the television. Keith was sitting next to Lana's father. No sooner had her mother finished washing up than she was preparing tea. I went into the kitchen and asked if I could help, but she shook her head and asked me about my time at the school. She was interested and seemed to know more about its history than I did.

'I've lived in the town all my life and when I was a kid my parents used to take me and my little brother for walks around there. You're the first actual student I've met though.'

I smiled and listened intently although all I really wanted to do was to take her daughter and continue kissing her as before.

'What would you like for tea?'

I told her that I must be hurrying along as roll call was only minutes away.

'You are very welcome to visit us any time,' were Lana's mother's parting words as I was leaving. I thanked her, shook her father's huge hand and said farewell to Keith, who did not respond. Lana led me to the end of the terrace.

'It wasn't too terrifying, was it?' I held her and we kissed again.

'I'd better get back; I don't want to spoil this special day by being late.' I walked away and looked back and she hadn't moved. I grinned and she smiled back. I was falling madly in love.

*   *   *

The first half of term was slow and difficult. The house seemed to be overshadowed by a storm cloud that was ready to burst at any time. Even the most gregarious of us seemed to be extra quiet and we followed our routine without question. Summerfield, who was forging a sinister friendship with his new best friend, fellow Prefect Warwick, gave me space and those weeks were trouble-free.

Half-term greeted us quickly during Easter term as it was only ten weeks long and therefore the shortest of all of them.

I travelled with Andrew Grafton to the East End during that half-term. We headed for Whitechapel Road to visit the pubs where scuffles took place regularly and to taste the air of the corner of London my ancestors on my father's side had originally fled to. Although evidently under age the publicans didn't seem to mind and we got increasingly merry throughout our East End tour.

As soon as we rambled into one pub close to the London Hospital we should have known we were heading for trouble. The room went quiet as soon as we opened the heavy door and eyes followed a merry Grafton with cigarette hanging awkwardly from his mouth walking to the bar. I followed closely behind but it was clear that we were strangers. And how. Grafton asked for a Guinness, I asked for a Pernod with ice and a touch of water. The landlord, heavily pock marked face and with no hair, served with a shrug. The air was heavy with a dense smell of cigarette smoke. I was telling Grafton in a boisterous, haughty voice that this was the district where my grandfather's family, the Alexanders, had once lived and where the likes of my Uncle Louis would be at home today, what with the signed black-and-white photographs of boxers like Henry Cooper and Alan Minter on the wall behind the bar, all signed with 'Best wishes'.

I have always had a close connection to boxing. My Uncle Louis had a natural talent for the sport and at a young age was tipped to reach the very top. Although my father had gone to Montgomery School, my Uncle Louis, his elder brother by ten years, had gone to a minor public school in the north of England, due to 'a mix up in the admission papers', according to Uncle Louis. There were rumours that he avoided taking the entrance exam as he had little chance in achieving a high enough mark to be accepted.

He was a property man by trade who accumulated a large portfolio of property in Cromer, Cirencester, Bournemouth, Ramsgate and Cheltenham – a heterogeneous selection of towns but he seemed to be doing very well from it.

Each time he was out on the town with a beautiful starlet

his name was mentioned in the national press and a school comedian would cut out the offending article and pin it to the main noticeboard. Although he was regularly in the gossip columns, little was known about this wealthy man, with his navy-blue cashmere coat and his swept-back dyed black hair.

He wasn't married and I found it hard to understand how a man with this handsome face, endearing smile and wealth had never met his true love. I had thought for the first time marriage was not destined for everyone.

'How come you've never married, uncle?' I would impudently ask.

'Never had the time,' would be his non answer.

And that was my Uncle Louis, a man of secrets which as a teenager captivated my eager curiosity.

'What is your favourite movie, Uncle Louis?'

'The one I saw yesterday,' he would reply.

'Do you have a girlfriend, Uncle Louis?'

'Last week I did.'

Yes my Uncle Louis lived in his own world and his inquisitive nephew had no chance of breaching his inner sanctum.

Meanwhile, in the back room of the pub there was the usual pool table and an intensely competitive game was in progress. Grafton and I wandered in to get a look.

I forget the other man, but remember Sean, who was not tall but wide and clearly horribly strong. He smelt expensive with an aftershave that said, 'I am illegally rich so mind your step', and his suit although beautifully tailored reflected a heavy appetite. Sean was popular as the gathered drinkers kept shouting his name and willing him to slaughter his opponent. He played with the cigarette glued to his hand, not taking a drag. He hit the balls with pace and when he missed a shot, spoke critically to himself and slapped his side, geeing his whole body to pot his next shot. I wanted to distance myself but I also kept edging towards the table to gain a better view drawn by his mere presence.

Sean was about to pot the black to complete his victory and win a huge wad of used notes which was piled above the fireplace to the right of the table. My enthusiasm and stupidity got the better of me and as I leant over to witness the black fly into the top left, I knocked over his pint of bitter which spilt over the baize-covered table and swam slowly to three of the six pockets.

The room went instantly quiet and faces froze in terror as I saw an unshaven old man shake and gulp the air. The fear was more intense in that pub than the smell of nicotine and it took me a few seconds to realise that it was all heading in my direction.

Sean looked at me in my ill-fitting public school tweed jacket. For a split second I saw pity in his eyes which I thought would be my let off, but sadly that was just wishful thinking. He put down his cue on the wet stained green baize table, straightened the sleeves of his shirt and walked towards my face. In one quick definitive movement, he grabbed my throat and pushed my head into the wall with such ferocity that I thought I was going to be decapitated. In fact it was performed so cleanly that I rather admired his prowess. Strange to admit, but sadly true. Then with his other hand he took the cue off the table and swung it behind his back in preparation to slam my face or if I were lucky my shoulder. At that point I didn't think luck was weighing heavily on my side so I tried to close my eyes and prepare for the moment of execution. I was so terrified that my eyes wouldn't obey my instruction and they just blinked uncontrollably. The venom spurted from his mouth as the cue headed towards my skull. And then a miracle happened when a big black hand stopped the slaughter of my face by grabbing the cue and throwing it to the other side of the bar.

'Do you know who this is?' yelled my rescuer. 'Do you know who the fuck this is?' he repeated.

'Who the fuck am I?' I thought.

'That's the boss's boy.'

At this point Sean turned as white as a blanket of freshly fallen snow.

'I am sorry, I didn't know,' he said as he straightened out my crumbled green tweed. He offered me a beer immediately but I refused and asked for my Pernod to be refilled; confidence had returned with speed. I then offered Grafton a short which he readily accepted. Grafton, I should point out, instead of saving his erstwhile buddy had been heading to the exit with remarkable haste. A major characteristic of the public school boy; if a fight looms and it does not directly involve you, get the hell out of there.

We spent the rest of the night cheering my dear Uncle Louis, Sean regularly going to the bar refreshing our drinks.

'I am sorry about the spillage on your beautiful pool table,' I said, looking straight at the menacing landlord.

'Don't you worry, my boy, it is just a pleasure to have you here.'

We closed the pub that night, full of promises that we would return. Jimmy, my saviour, a middleweight from Doncaster who once fought on a bill at Wembley Arena, even drove us right to Grafton's front door out in St George's Hill near Weybridge.

'Your uncle did me a good turn when things were rough. I will always be grateful to him.' And then he clenched his fist, faked a punch in my direction and drove back to the East End.

*   *   *

Hung over and elated, I called my father the next morning, gossiping that his brother had powerful East End friends.

'I think you must be confused, Samuel. Neither I nor Uncle Louis would never get mixed up with those types.'

I shook my head, not for the first time, in disbelief. I knew what had happened the previous night and it was clear that Louis was an angel . . . of sorts.

*   *   *

I was rarely picked up from school, instead I normally had to make my own way by tube to Paddington and then on to the main line to catch the Oxford train to Charlbury. The journey had become my friend and a good friend at that, especially as it was taking me away from the boundaries of my school.

In all it took two hours door to door and wearing my jeans and putting my feet up gave me that sense of liberation. I once was so tired that I fell asleep as soon as I found my seat at Paddington. The train jolted and I awoke startled.

'Are we at Oxford?' I asked.

'Young man, that's the most stupid thing I've ever heard. We haven't even left Paddington yet.'

On reaching my stop, my mother would be waiting by the ticket barrier, smiling and welcoming. The station was unchanged from the turn of the century and the station master, a Mister Herbert Burrows, looked as if he had been at the grand opening.

'Welcome back, young man, how is school?' I would lie and tell him everything was wonderful and he would beam and eccentrically give a salute as if he were reporting for duty.

'At ease, Bert,' I would utter.

Mother hugged me in an awkward clumsy way, but that was my fault.

I fell into the BMW and we took the fifteen-minute car ride to our house just outside Chipping Norton. I loved the house and my room especially, with all my hidden delights. My Subbuteo five-a-side table tucked under my bed, and posters of David Bowie in Aladdin Sane guise and Brigitte Bardot draped over a Harley-Davidson. But my favourite was Raquel Welch in a bikini looking like wolf fur in the movie *One Million Years BC*. Such a favourite that I'd bought another copy to take to school. Ah, the hours I spent imagining what she would look like with it off. And then it struck me that Lana was like a younger version of Miss Welch and perhaps that was why my love was so instant. I stared at my exquisite poster and sighed with satisfaction. I played my records at high volume and was unaware that Mother had been calling me down for lunch.

*   *   *

She finally knocked on my door, 'Aren't you coming down?'

I mumbled that I would be down in a moment but went to the loo to have a read. The small loo near the kitchen was my favourite. Small, with sea-green wallpaper and narrow, it had *Playboy* magazines piled by its side which although read a million times still seduced my fascination. *Playboy* was part of the furniture in the house but remained in the downstairs loo and my father's bathroom, although even older issues were stacked in the airing cupboard on the top floor.

'Mum, why do we hide the *Playboys*?' I asked, sitting down to lunch.

'We don't hide them, they are your father's and it's his decision to hide, I mean place them wherever he likes. Anyway, he buys them for the political articles, not for the girls.'

I grinned and turned to our cook Violet, 'What do you think, Vi?' I asked.

Violet was round, happy, very warm and loving. A black South African, a refugee from the apartheid regime in her homeland, she and her husband Harold ran the house.

'Don't be so naughty now, young Sam, you can see your mother doesn't want to talk about it.'

So I left it at that and gave Violet a loving kiss on her cheek to her embarrassment.

'You are my favourite,' she whispered and returned to the kitchen to serve up my favourite lunch of chicken with peas and mashed potato.

Mother asked about school but I was vague and the conversation was stilted. Poor mother, so heavily dominated by my father in both conversation and space, was lovely but so timid. She was slightly more confident when my father was out of the house but virtually all conversation was prefaced with a sort of an apology.

'I don't mean to give you a hard time, Samuel, but you must keep more in touch with us, we hardly hear from you.'

I apologised and said that I was distracted but would in future make more of an effort to call.

'Are you beginning to enjoy yourself there?'

I had been there for over two years and this was the first time my mother had really asked me if I liked school.

'I find it difficult, Mum, I really do.' My mother listened with an understanding expression stuck to her beautiful face. The eldest daughter of aristocrats from northern England, she was honest, quiet and dominated throughout her life by powerful oppressive men. My maternal grandfather, who died when I was still very young, had the reputation of being short-tempered and overbearing. My father was very much the same. In fact they were very alike except my father was Jewish and, from what I heard, this made my father unacceptable in the eyes of my mother's parents.

'Did Grandpa disapprove of Father?'

'Why do you ask that, all of sudden? But, no, absolutely not,' she replied.

'I thought they didn't like the fact he was Jewish.'

'How silly you are. No, it didn't bother them. It probably would have been worse if he had gone to some secondary modern. But he didn't. He went to your school, the best school in the world.'

'You're not a snob, are you, Mother?'

'I am absolutely not. But maybe my parents, your grand-parents, might have been.'

We continued to banter but it wasn't that much fun as my mother rarely rose to the bait. But underneath it all was the image of Lana and my desire to ask her home for the weekend. In truth, I was nervous of how they would accept her accent or whether they would embarrass me. I decided that I would wait for my father's return and make my decision at supper.

The day grew dark early and I spent the majority of the time holed up in my room playing my Subbuteo soccer game with an LP I had bought during my last holiday of Liverpool fans singing their songs. It was called the 'Kop Choir' and it was forty-five minutes of thousands of Scousers shouting their favourite football chants. It made the sound in my bedroom resemble a full stadium and with my added com-mentary it entertained me for hours until there was a knock on my door.

'What's that bloody noise?' said my father, home from the City. 'Sounds like a bloody pub.'

'Hello, Father; good to hear your voice again.'

Supper was ready and I followed my father to the dining room. 'Just popping into the loo, Father.'

'You leave those magazines alone. Don't loiter,' he ordered.

He was in a scratchy mood and what made him think I would be reading those magazines anyway? I sat down and Harold started to serve us.

'Fine to have you home, Master Samuel,' welcomed Harold.

My father asked how school was going and I told him that as expected all was fine although I did also recount the grim start to the term when we'd heard the news of Langley's suicide.

'Didn't he share with you that first term?' my father asked. I nodded.

'You never liked him, did you? I remember in the brief time I met him, he seemed an unattractive young man. I knew his father; a stuffy so and so.'

I was aggravated. It didn't seem right to criticise the dead but that was my father's manner, dismissive and candid.

'Have you heard from Tom?' asked my mother, piping up from the other end of the table.

Thomas James Alexander, my adored and worshipped older brother was six years older than me at twenty-two. He had gone to Oxford straight from school and for some reason missed his gap year and now he was working in a bar New York City. I missed our long conversations about anything and everything. He seemed to have steadiness surrounding him that I could only imagine possessing. He was the favourite with my parents and I always felt a nuisance, as if I had arrived as a mistake and was never welcomed. Tom, as he was known by us all, couldn't put a foot wrong in the eyes of my father and with this in mind I saw my opportunity.

'I received a postcard only this week, father, and Tom asked whether I couldn't join him for a week in the Easter holidays.'

My father paused and with his usual idiosyncrasy when pondering the lay of the land let out a huge sigh and said, 'I think that would be a very good idea, spending some time with your brother. I'll buy a ticket and you can leave as soon as the term is finished.' He yawned, had a final bite of his treacle pudding and left the table.

My mother saw the satisfaction embracing my face. She leant over and took hold of my forearm and squeezed.

'Go and join your father in the library.'

'I'd rather not,' I replied.

'Please. For me.'

And so grudgingly I made my way to the library. My father was in a world of his own, sitting in his favourite brown leather armchair reading the *Evening News*. He peeked up for a moment and saw me staring at him from the sofa. He asked if there was something wrong. I shook my head and he returned to his world.

I shot upstairs and immediately rang Lana to relay my news; I promised that one day I would take her. We discussed whether she would come down to visit for the weekend but I thought it best to avoid the collision with my father for the time being.

'He has some business colleagues coming down so the timing isn't very good and my mother is going to visit her sick sister, my aunt, and may want me to go along,' I lied, and didn't feel good about the fact, but I was trying to protect her from any potential onslaught. I think she understood but sounded disappointed.

'I miss you,' I said and was about to tell her for the first time that I loved her when my father yelled from downstairs, 'Get off the bloody phone.'

'I'll call you tomorrow; I'd better go now, I am being hassled.'

I went to bed that night, my head full of dreams of New

York City and the beautiful face of Lana, with the music of *Hunky Dory* floating over my warm soft welcoming bed. School at last seemed a long, long way away.

In the morning I walked down our drive and made my way into the village to find my local friends. They were as usual playing football on the recreation field and they all greeted me like the long-lost friend that I had become. Recently I had caught myself drifting away, preferring to stay at home in with my own company rather than rushing to the football field to play a game. There was once a time when I returned home from school that I would rush to see my local friends even before I had said hello to my mother, but not now.

I was moving on, and in conversation had less and less in common. They talked about the disco in the local hall, I talked about our sexy matron; they talked about the darts championship in the White Bear, and I gossiped about my delinquent friends at school. And it was that day when I realised that we had strayed from each other and our friendship was for the time evaporating.

'How were your friends?' asked mother as I returned for lunch.

'I don't think we have much in common any more. I was a bit bored, to be honest.'

'It's about time,' barked my father. 'I never understood what you saw in them.'

*   *   *

Sunday lunch was not unlike many other families in middle England. Roast beef and Yorkshire pudding, apple crumble and arguments. Aunt Florence, known by all as 'Aunt Flo', was in attendance, as was Uncle Louis.

Aunt Flo, the younger sister of my mother, was loud, forceful, bossy and quite the snob. She always treated me with a sense of dismay and tended to talk to me slowly as if either I were thick or I wouldn't understand or perhaps a bit of both. 'You wouldn't believe it, but that son of Michael Sanders has gone and had a tattoo done on his forearm,' she tittle-tattled. 'Have you ever heard of anything more revolting?'

'You wouldn't believe it, but Samuel had his ear pierced just before Christmas,' moaned my father.

'Oh, tell me it's not true, Samuel!' She looked worried, as if I had committed a heinous crime.

I admitted my naughty excursion to Aunt Flo, who for the rest of lunch looked intently at my left ear lobe. Anything with the hint of a working-class action dismayed my entire family and I know that's why such a trivial business had affected my father and aunt so strongly.

'People like us just don't behave like that.'

Poor Aunt Flo was so different from my mother, full of conversation, opinionated, but her romantic life was a disaster. Married young to a British aristocrat based in South Africa, she'd discovered her newly acquired husband in bed with his secretary on their second day of honeymoon. Since then, from what I had heard, her damaged heart never healed and a strong wall surrounded her eccentricity.

'How's Tom?' she asked. My father's demeanour instantly changed and he informed the gathering how well my brother was doing in New York.

'I miss Tom,' Uncle Louis chivvied into the conversation. Everyone's favourite, my brother was, but their talk didn't really bother me as he was my favourite too.

It was the first time I had seen Uncle Louis since my excursion to the East End and the fortuitous meeting with some of his nodding acquaintances. Uncle Louis was warm and understanding and without fail slipped a fiver into my hand and would whisper, 'Spend it wisely, my boy,' but when I mentioned that I had visited a pub down in Whitechapel and made friends with a group who seemed to know him, his mood changed.

'What were you doing down there? I would be surprised if you met any friends of mine.'

'Is it true you knew the Kray twins, Uncle Louis?' Silence consumed the table. 'Well, that is what my friends from this pub told me. Please tell me it's true.'

'I did come across them once,' Uncle Louis surprisingly confessed. 'I had a share in a club in Portman Square and for the opening night we had invited all the high-falutin members of society. I walked into our office one day and read all those who had accepted. On the list were Ronnie and Reggie Kray and I immediately asked how their names were on the list. Well, I thought they can't come, so I made my way down to their pub, the Blind Beggar on the Whitechapel Road. As I walked in I saw them with a group sitting at a corner table knocking back the beers and the vodka. They were very civil and welcoming and agreed not to attend the opening night as long as their arch-enemy from South London, a man called Charlie Richardson, did not attend the event either. Don't worry, I told them, that lot were not invited. We shook hands and I left happy with my work. The night of the party came and it was huge success, Henry Cooper, ex-champions, film stars, beautiful models, you name them they were there. But later it was reported that Charlie Richardson had been at the party.'

I was amazed; my Uncle Louis had never spoken about this before.

'Anyway, the Krays heard about this, added three and three to make seven, and sent me a gift in the post.'

'And what was the gift?' I asked, bursting at the seams with excitement.

'Two dead fish in a shoebox. This meant that within a

very short time, I would be joining the fishes at the bottom of the River Thames.'

My mouth fell to the table. 'Uncle Louis, you old rogue,' I thought. My father tried to change the subject and Aunt Flo tutted disapprovingly. I pleaded with my uncle to finish off his story.

'Well, nothing really, I rang a policeman friend from Scotland Yard, and he arranged police protection. The twins were arrested the following day for a murder committed in the exact pub I had visited them in. They went on trial and they were found guilty and sent to jail. And believe me, young Sam, if I had known what they had been up to, I wouldn't have gone to their pub, not for a million pounds.'

'You're my hero, Uncle Louis,' I sycophantically drooled.

As Harold came in to clear the plates, Aunt Flo brought up the suicide of Langley. 'What a terrible tragedy. Did you know him, Samuel?'

As I was about to answer, my father interjected: 'They shared a room together in their first year. But I can't remember them getting on.' It was becoming my father's habit to answer any question that was directed at me.

'Can we just change the subject?' I said, and used this as an excuse to get up from the table. As I left the dining room I overheard my mother tell the gathering that I was still very upset about the incident and for Florence not to bring it up again. I think I heard Aunt Flo say something like 'poor Samuel'. But I was heading to the loo to get some space and to read some magazines.

Uncle came to see me before returning to London. 'If you're a good boy,' he said, 'I'll take you to a fight before you leave for New York.'

'Thanks, Uncle Louis, I would love to do that. But I leave for New York straight after school breaks up.'

'Oh, we will work something out soon, don't you worry. And young man, let's not bring up that boxing again. It upsets your father.' He chuckled, and he handed me a crisp blue five-pound note. 'Got yourself a nice girl yet?'

'Yes, uncle,' but before I could carry on with my news, Louis was heading for his Bentley which would take him back to the City to continue his coveted life.

Later, I was called from my room to say goodbye to Aunt Flo as well.

'Let me see that ear of yours.' It had been on her mind ever since my father mentioned it. She studied the evidence carefully and whispered, 'You're such a naughty boy.'

'You don't know how naughty, Auntie Flo.' She then slipped me a nice new ten-pound note and squeezed my nose with affection. Fifteen pounds and counting, soon I would be able to take Lana for a posh dinner.

The following night my mother dropped me back at school. My father had said his goodbye that morning and promised that he would arrange the tickets for my journey to New York. He would write to my brother and tell him what day I would be arriving. Little was said with mother as we headed up the dark A40 road.

'Have a good second half to the term, my darling,' and she gave me a small peck on my cheek and handed me a twenty-pound note.

As soon as I walked through the house door I was greeted by a sharp command. 'Oi. Go and change into your uniform, Alexander,' ordered Warwick. 'Roll call in five minutes.'

I'd left my bed unmade and clothes were thrown from one side of the room to the other. It seemed I had shot out of school before half-term without a care in the world except to escape as quickly as possible. I found my trousers tucked into my bed, my shirts all marked round the collar with dirt, and my tie draped over my light. Annoyed that I hadn't taken my uniform home to be washed, I dressed expeditiously ready to report for duty.

Spit put his head round the door, 'Come on or else we will be in trouble before the second half of term has started. And I would put some aftershave on if I were you, you stink of fags.'

The smell of cigarettes had lingered on my clothes for the week I had been away; another important reason to take your stuff home when you can. I was learning the rules of keeping an ordered life, but it was very slow going.

*   *   *

'You have your top button undone,' barked Munro, the head of school and one nasty piece of work. Indeed I had my top two unfastened and this was strictly against the rules.

'Right, you are school fined. Report to the school prefects' study directly after chapel on Sunday.'

I had had little contact with James Munro, but his reputation has gone before him. He had been top boy for two terms and controlled his pack of prefects with a heavy hand. There were twenty prefects and when walking the street we mere mortals would have to salute them as a mark of respect for reaching their lofty position. They swaggered, hand in pockets, and relished their power. Summerfield and Warwick were part of this caucus and fitted perfectly.

'Dear me, school fined. That's a pain,' Grafton reassuringly surmised. 'Make sure you are spotless: clean clothes, clean hair, clean nails.'

'Oh God,' I uttered, 'It's not that heavy is it?' Grafton nodded.

'Don't be late by a second and don't answer back after you are lectured and you hand over your five pound fine. If they catch anything wrong, you will be fined again and will have to report back the following week. Huddleston, you know who I mean – the son of that American porn king – was school fined week after week for nearly two terms until he had the good sense to offer some back editions from his father's output to the head of school. No, this is not good news,' he concluded.

Spit spat, Burford tossed back his curls. I had lost Uncle Louis's fiver very fast and had no *Playboy*s for trade.

I thanked them for their confidence, and dragged on a cigarette. I sat, not particularly worried, blowing smoke rings into the March air.

*   *   *

On the Wednesday at my usual visit, I asked Mrs Wheeler what would happen on Sunday with my school fine, but it didn't seem to register with her and I took this as being a good sign. I spoke about Lana to her as well, and Mrs Wheeler invited her to join us for tea the following week.

I hadn't seen Lana since half-term and we arranged to meet at the local Wimpy bar. Many of the tables were full of old dears gossiping about this and a lot of that. I held Lana's hand and spoke about my half-term and the news that I was going to visit my brother in New York.

She seemed disappointed that she hadn't been invited to my house but I explained that it wasn't the right time and that I didn't mean to offend, but meeting my father would be more like a trial than a celebration. I leant over and kissed her full on the lips and place the outside of my hand on her cheek. I wanted to tell her that I loved her but the words were stuck somewhere in my chest so I let the moment stray and walked over to the jukebox and played George McCrae's 'Rock Your Baby' – I smiled, gave a little jig and returned to the table.

'You've been invited to Mrs Wheeler's next week. She wants to meet you.'

She seemed more nervous about that than any invitation from my family.

'I hope she won't tell me anything bad.'

I told her not be so silly and I ordered my third banana milkshake.

* * *

It was Sunday and I had to be spick and span and on my best behaviour. My charm wouldn't win the day; even the most charming man in the world couldn't talk his way out of this situation; if laces were undone, waistcoat marked, or, say, tails crumpled, then the fine would be repeated and humiliation the next Sunday would follow. It was only on Sundays that we had to wear tails. Black of course, white shirt, usual mourning black tie, black waistcoat, grey pin-striped trousers; a picture of the classic public school boy.

There were three of us who had been fined that week. I hadn't seen or met the other two before. They both looked a type, the type that would inevitably be school fined and although tidied up, they still had an intrinsic stain of dirt swathed over them. I noticed one had a mark on his trousers but chose not to point it out as I had taken an instant dislike to him.

The prefects' room was oak-panelled, with three large bay windows at one end and a thick foreboding desk strategically placed in front. The head of school sat centre with two of his cohorts either side. The others sat on throne-like chairs in a long line. In total there were twenty prefects. There was no expression on their faces and the only light came from the portrait of the former headmaster James Balfour who had an odd grin bearing down on the proceedings.

Each of our names was called individually. Walker was first, and in he went and out again all within seconds.

'What happened?' I asked.

'I paid my fine and they told me to get out. Easy when you know how.' I smiled and wished him well through gritted teeth.

Banbury was next and he took longer and raised voices were heard. I had my ear scooped to the door and heard the head of school shout: 'How dare you not see that mark on your trousers. Pay your fine and make sure that next week you are spotless.'

'Does that mean I am school fined again, Munro?'

He was sent away and for a moment I felt guilty. 'Oh, well,' I thought.

'Alexander,' my name shattered the silence. I swung open the heavy doors and faced my opposition. All lounging where they sat, legs spread, special coloured waistcoats, and each face as ugly as the last. I walked to the table, sureness in my step. Munro glanced down at me; he looked intimidating on the raised platform discreetly set behind the desk.

'We had a meeting with the headmaster last week and we decided that the school should rid itself of the scum that is festering.' He spoke precisely. 'You are the scum we were talking about and we want you out.' The other prefects murmured in agreement resembling the manner of the House of Commons. 'And what is that growing from your nose?'

Overnight a nasty red ripe spot, like a carbuncle, had grown at the tip of my nose. Known as a shagger in school language, the onslaught of acne can be a devastating blow in confidence for any teenager. They appear uninvited, unwelcome and a boy's worst enemy.

'It must be a spot.'

'Then get rid of it and we will then get rid of you. Now get out.'

I paid my fine and want to write that I snarled and said something extremely witty back, but that would be an untruth.

Instead I put down my Uncle Louis's note and walked neatly out of the room avoiding the deliberately out-stretched legs of my torturers.

I strode back to my house and immediately inspected the spot that had emerged on my nose. I decided that it would be an impossibility to meet with Lana that day. How could she find such a sight attractive? So I called her house and made the excuse that I had been ordered to stay in my room and therefore would not be able to see her until Wednesday. Vanity ruled that day.

Mrs Wheeler had prepared the most delicious tea, thin sandwiches, cucumber, smoked salmon and mustard cress, followed by scones with strawberry jam, clotted cream, and chocolate cake. There was Earl Grey tea with cold milk and a small plate of sliced lemon in case the milk was not to our liking. She had made a tremendous effort and I was full of gratitude.

Lana followed within minutes in her school uniform. She wore a tight blue jacket with a lion crest sewn to the front pocket, red and blue tie, grey pencil skirt and black high heels. Most fetching it was, and I whispered in her ear to wear it again next time and she pushed me away in mocked shock. I introduced Mrs Wheeler as my dearest oldest friend and before I could say Lana's name I was shoved into the kitchen to boil the kettle so they could have some time alone together. I had asked about the shopping but I was told to sit down and enjoy what was on the table. The food disappeared very quickly and we listened intently as Mrs Wheeler recounted again her love affair with a boy, not dissimilar to me apparently, sixty years before.

We were both fascinated to hear about her 'gift', as she described that when she was young she would hear voices echo and see flashes of light around her bedroom. At first they were distant but as years went by they become clearer. Then her instinct would overtake her as soon as she met someone new and she would have premonitions if she dared to concentrate.

At first she apparently placed an advertisement in the local newspaper: 'Clairvoyant: know your future for as little as two shillings'. All sorts used to visit her usually in search of reaching their loved ones who had been lost during the war.

Mrs Wheeler did not pause and spoke quickly and excitedly. It was as if she hadn't told these stories for years and that she had rediscovered them in the attic of her memory. The dust was blown away and we were the welcome participants in her secrets.

I walked with Lana back to her house a mere ten minutes from where we had just been sitting. I adored her even more for the courtesy and interest she paid to my elderly friend.

'She gave me this,' and Lana opened her hand to reveal a pendant. 'She said it was magic and helped dreams come true,' and she clasped it tightly.

'You are my dream come true,' I purred and we kissed passionately for many minutes until I felt a tap on my shoulder. It was Keith on his way back from work.

'Got a light?' he asked.

I searched in my pocket and lit his cigarette.

'Cheers,' and he moved on into the house. Lana giggled and I looked blank. 'Blimey, I think he likes you.'

'What makes you think that?'

'Because usually if he caught someone kissing me, he would smash them in the nose.'

The following weeks were kind and floated by with a lucky star hanging directly above me. I surged ahead with my academic work and for the first time since my arrival managed to galvanize some high marks in a spread of tests. All the masters wore a look of grudging surprise when they handed back essays to me with an A marked on them.

'Much more like it,' and 'I didn't know you had it in you', were common observations from my uninspiring teachers but it did not harm, it only made me more determined to work harder and add a slice of confusion to their set opinion.

The prefects clearly had immense dislike for my sort but never over those weeks rebuked my appearance and one even jovially added a 'good morning' as I hurried to class. At first on returning from half-term I thought that dark clouds were again setting in but I was wrong. Langley's suicide still wounded the house, and Summerfield and his troops seemed to keep their distance. My clandestine meetings with Lana were able to continue without a hint of trouble.

Perhaps that lucky pendant did have the promised power?

*   *   *

My tickets to New York had duly been purchased by my father and as soon as term had finished I had rushed down to Oxfordshire to prepare for my big journey.

I had managed to steal a few moments the last afternoon of term with Lana in our usual café but I was torn between missing her and my excitement for visiting the United States for the first time and to spend a week with the brother that I loved and that I missed.

*   *   *

My mother dropped me at London airport and I caught the 9.55 Pan Am flight to the land of movies and opportunity.

I sat in the last row of the aircraft close to the loo which I did not find particularly disturbing as it reminded me of school. I sat between the largest of women who squeezed into her thin seat and a cute religious freak who was going out to America to join a group that called themselves 'The People's Temple'. The large woman smoked incessantly. As soon as the 'no smoking' sign was switched off, the inhalation began and even if you did not smoke then it felt like a pack vanished into your lungs before the jet had even reached the Atlantic.

'After you have seen your brother you should come and join me, I'm heading west to California. You're exactly what the People's Temple are looking for,' declared the freak. Although clearly psychotic, she was rather attractive. The banter and the madness in her eyes had a penetrating effect on my being.

'You are *far* too young to be tied down.' I had bored her with stories of Lana and it became clear that she wasn't interested in my rambling and anyway believed in free love.

'And what might free love be?' I asked.

'Making love to anyone you take a fancy to.'

I spluttered my tepid coffee over the large lady. I was trying to work out the connection between being a hippy and swinging but at that time couldn't find the link. Her reddish knotted hair lay over her semi-see-through tee-shirt, her pert nipples protruding.

'Your tongue is hanging out,' she pointed out as my eyes wandered away from her face. She moved her hand towards me and slowly rubbed my leg. I was transfixed and wanted to stop her but just couldn't or didn't want to. She went to my flies and started to unzip them; her hand disappeared into my trousers and I groaned like an old man trying to bend over. My large friend to my left looked down at my crotch and made a loud tutting sound which sort of put me off.

'Why don't you get your cute little butt up from that seat and follow me to that little cubicle,' the hippy whispered. I was a few feet away from joining the mile high club, losing my virginity and cheating on Lana before I had even crossed the Atlantic. Hippy crept past and made her way to the loo which was literally the row behind us. I had to make a quick decision. A group of Hasidic Jews had gathered in a neighbouring aisle and had started to chant; one with curls hanging to his shoulders glanced at me and shook his head. The guilt of it all made me dizzy but still I rose from my seat, clambered over my fat chain-smoking neighbour and made my way to the small cubicle. The stewardesses were not looking as I knocked on the door. It folded back and my saucy hippy beckoned me in. It was a tight squeeze yet room enough to get into a great deal of trouble, but just as we were about to kiss the plane bumped violently and the 'fasten your belt' sign flashed on. A knock followed with a strict instruction to take our seats immediately as the turbulence was now in full flow.

'We'd better sit down,' I suggested.

'Ignore it, cutie pie, and make love to me.' She jerked her leg between mine. Another harsh knock on our door and a flash of madness in her eyes and I was sitting in my seat with my belt strapped on.

The plane touched down soon afterwards at JFK and my heart started to pound as New York City and the United States waited outside the hatch door. As I took my first step on American soil, I knew this exciting land would have so much to offer me. I waved a fond farewell to Lucy, the girl I very nearly lost my virginity to, and carried my bag through customs and into the arrival hall.

There waiting I found this exceedingly beautiful, tall slim girl holding a sign with the hastily written name of Alexander on it.

'You look so like your brother. He wanted to welcome you but he had to go to work to make up some time, so here I am.' Her name was Suzy and she was Tom's girlfriend and had the sweetest of natures. We caught a checker cab into Manhattan and my first glimpse of the famous skyscrapers impacted my psyche with their height and authority, and the Empire State Building settling in between illuminating the sky, dominant above all others.

My brother lived on Hudson Street on the corner of Perry, downtown in the west village of New York above a newsagent and close to the White Horse Tavern where Dylan Thomas hung out and mused, and poisoned himself with alcohol. The 'common' part of his building was dark stone and cold and not dissimilar to my house at school and yet his apartment was bigger than I had expected. It had a room waiting for me, beautifully tidied, warm and welcoming.

Suzy and I spoke easily to each other. 'You must have done this,' I said. 'I have never even seen Tom pick up a sock.'

'No,' she lied, 'we tidied up together as your brother wants you to be comfortable.' She made coffee on an over-used stove and although jet lag was beginning to set in I was as excited as I had ever been. We sat down and she told me how she had been Tom's girlfriend for over a year and that it had been love at first sight in a bar called Fanelli in the heart of Soho, not too far from where they now lived.

'Your brother served me a Guinness and we have been together ever since.'

She was a model and although coy about her success it was clear by magazines littered through the apartment with her face staring from the cover that she was successful.

I spoke of Lana and took out a photograph taken days before in a passport photo booth. Although already creased I was comforted by carrying it close.

'It was love at first sight for me as well but as yet I haven't admitted that to her.'

'You sound just like your brother; he only confessed after we had been going out for nine months.'

'It's a family thing,' I explained. 'None of us show much emotion.'

We laughed together and I could see how she had touched my brother's heart. Time was passing by and she picked up the phone to see where my brother had got to. As she put down the phone she told me that my brother had left the bar an hour earlier.

'He should be here soon as the bar is a fifteen-minute walk.' And just as I noticed a sense of worry sweep across her face and a biting of her lip, the door swung open and there stood my handsome older brother. He had lost weight and his features were more chiselled but his embrace was heartfelt and he whispered 'I've missed you' into my ear.

We fell into the city and he hailed a cab that came crushing to an emergency stop. 'We are going uptown; I want you to taste Manhattan at its brightest and its biggest.' He turned to the driver. 'Take us to Fifth Avenue and Central Park South, the Plaza Hotel.'

'Que?' the cab driver answered.

Tom laughed. 'No one speaks English here and that's part of the beauty of this city, you don't know which country you're going to meet.' The cab beat the land speed record chasing along a bumpy, unkempt Eighth Avenue missing other vehicles by inches.

The Plaza was a huge wedding cake of a building made famous in my eyes by the Beatles who stayed there on their first night in America. My eyes looked to the sky and building after building stared down at me with lights streaming out on an army of faces hurrying along the sidewalk chasing after their dream. There I was in the heart of Manhattan, heart pounding, giddy with the most exciting metropolis my young eyes had encountered.

We had an early dinner in the Palm Court with a portrait of a curious character called Eloise staring down at me. She caught my imagination and Tom explained how Eloise had been created by Kay Thompson who had performed regularly in the Plaza during the 1950s and wrote the story in her suite in the hotel after each show. The book became an instant success and merchandise sold immediately and there was even an Eloise ice-cream parlour in the lobby of the hotel. Miss Thompson was even given her own suite for a while, in return for the publicity that had been stirred.

'Why have you chosen this hotel to share our first drink in the city?' I asked.

'I spent my first night at the Plaza when I arrived in New York and I want you to share the same treat. There is a room waiting for you upstairs but just for one night. Tomorrow it is back down town and slumming it with me.'

He handed me the key and told me to get some rest. 'I have a new job and I am working at lunch tomorrow, so come to the restaurant called the Black Sheep. It's near where we live on 11th Street and we can spend the afternoon together.' He handed me the address and I squeezed his hand and kissed his beautiful girlfriend good-night.

My room was vast and decorated in a comfortable garish English furnishing but no matter, it was heaven compared to my school study and its surrounding walls. I fell heavily on to the soft bed and although exhausted, and my stomach full, ordered room service of a BLT and the biggest plate of fries, and switched on US television for the first time. I spent the next hours glued to the commercials being interrupted by programmes. I was happy that night, so happy, and fell asleep with the television blaring loudly as jet lag took its toll.

My sleep was short and I woke up at five, ready for the new day. I watched a black-and-white movie, *Arsenic and Old Lace,* starring Cary Grant, and again ordered room service for a breakfast of waffles with maple syrup and a huge banana milkshake. I looked out of my window and saw Central Park for the first time stretching as far as the eye could see, hundreds of acres ready to be explored.

'Never walk there at night,' warned the Italian waiter who delivered my food. 'You will be dead within seconds; at night the evil walk that piece of land.'

I had a hot bath and wrapped myself in a substantial towelling robe before getting dressed to catch a cab downtown. As I was leaving, I turned to my room and promised myself that I would return one day with my own cash in my pocket and my ravishing girlfriend to keep me company; I took a deep breath and sucked in the air and marched on to the bustling streets.

My ride downtown was faster than the one coming up and my exhilaration was compounded by an overweight Jewish New York cab driver coughing and wheezing. Before we reached our first block we were discussing world politics, music and my education. 'Why is a nice Jewish boy like you being sent away from home to a boarding school? You should be at home helping to run your father's business,' he shouted from the front as I sat squeezed in the back with a thick, seemingly bulletproof sheet of glass separating us.

'Hey, boychick,' he continued, warming to his theme as he chewed and spat on a thick cigar. 'There are lots of

Jews here, more than in Israel, you won't believe how many! But heck I don't believe you are one, you're bustin my chops. That voice belongs to Laurence Olivier not Jerry Lewis.'

I laughed and was about to say that an accent can hide anything but I couldn't get a word in, and in our twenty-minute journey, I had received a guided commentary on the city.

On reaching 11th Street, I tried to hand over my crisp green notes.

'Hey, don't worry, kid, have this one on me. I just had the classiest Jew in my cab and I am going to dine out on that. Enjoy the city.'

And with that he hurtled away in search of his next unsuspecting customer. The city seemed to be growing and getting better and better and I saw each block, each corner, as if in its own movie, taking shape in Technicolor and wonder before my very eyes.

*   *   *

The Black Sheep was on the corner of 11th and Washington and resembled from the outside an old English country restaurant. My brother was behind the bar. The restaurant was half-full and yet consumed with loud conversation. He pointed to the end table and signalled me to sit down. I watched as he worked and noticed how withdrawn, tired and thin he seemed but I put it down to my weary jet-lagged state and dismissed any concern.

I ordered a bowl of vegetable soup and a cottage pie as I waited for my brother to finish his shift. The weather had transformed from the night before and what seemed like spring now resembled the middle of winter.

'The weather changes like my wife's face here in the city,' the cab driver had charmingly explained. 'One moment it is in the high 70s and the next day it can drop thirty degrees.'

So this is a city of extremes, I reflected, and I would not be wrong.

As soon as I finished my hearty lunch, my brother's coat was on and we left to walk through the meat-packing district that had been cleared from its early-morning work. The raw odour of freshly killed animals still manifested and animal blood blotted the sidewalk. We walked slowly and carefully in step to avoid the red stains. We turned into Gansevoort Street and on to Hudson, and then we doubled up to reach Tom's apartment.

We spoke about our lives or should I say I spoke about mine. My brother had left Montgomery before my arrival there and knew and experienced the pitfalls but had survived the full term. His reputation as an A-grade student hung over me. Not every day but made guest appearances when academically I had not reached my potential.

He listened intently and heard my pain and confusion with intense discipline.

'I don't know if I can survive, Tom. I'm ready to snap and my only joy is hanging out with my delinquent friends and my desire to spend my time with Lana.'

'Then hold on to that and play the game. I found it as difficult as you but I kept my anger in check and avoided trouble whenever I felt it was threatening.'

I always listened to him and invariably tried to act on his advice, but knew it was going to be difficult and although our conversation was placating, I pondered that perhaps we were a little more different than I had realised. He spoke of his life in New York and how liberating his days were. We spoke of our father and Tom admitted that Dad's adoration had suffocated his ambition.

'But you are the one he adores, his eyes light up every time you walk into the room or your name is mentioned.'

'Well perhaps that's the problem; I'm not as perfect as he thinks.'

The tie between the two was from my perspective as good as any father–son relationship. They went for long walks together and I would see them laugh and be tactile with each other. I would stare alone with my head resting on my hands from the drawing-room window as the two went off to the local pub to share a drink with each other. I was never invited as I was told I was too young, but knew that my father wasn't interested in what I had to say. There was no hurt, though, only acceptance.

*   *   *

Suzy was in the apartment draped over the sofa on the telephone. As we walked in she quickly sprang to life and ran into Tom's arms.

'I was worried about you,' she said. He told her that she should not be concerned and went into the kitchen to make us all a cup of coffee. There was no question that she over-reacted but Tom nudged my shoulder and said, 'She is a little possessive.'

Jet lag finally claimed me as a cross-Atlantic victim and so I crashed on my bed to be awoken by my brother's voice hours later.

'Come on. We're off to a party, your first in this wild city.'

I jumped up, had a hot forceful shower that I had never experienced before and was about to shave the small part of beard that was sprouting from my face when my brother ordered me to hurry up.

We caught a cab into Soho and made our way to a loft on Prince Street. The room was heaving with androgynous people, and Diana Ross's 'Love Hangover' blared out from each corner. I made my way to the bar where a hustled barman poured drinks as fast as they were ordered. I asked for a vodka and orange and swigged it down as if I were drinking milk. My brother was nowhere to be seen so I drifted into a corner and watched the theatre unleash itself in front of my virgin eyes. Suddenly I was approached by a seductive temptress, older than me by many years. She yelled above the music. 'What are you doing here?'

'I'm here with my brother at my first party in New York.'

'Are you now?' I think she or he said, smiled and passed me an over-sized cigarette which I thought was slightly odd but being the English gentleman I did not refuse.

'That's the second first you will experience this evening,' she purred, her long fingers stroking my neck.

I felt dizzy, light and happy and everything immediately seemed loud and frivolous. I had come out of my shell and with another inhalation I made my way around the room talking, hugging any stranger that crossed my scattered path. I had my head resting on the shoulder of a rather large hairy man when I noticed my brother. I held him tightly.

'Can I dance with your beautiful girlfriend?'

He smiled. So I took the beguiling Suzy by the hand and led her to the dance floor. Rhythm was not my speciality but I seemed to find the beat in the music whereas before I had never captured it. I took my shirt off and started to swing it over my head. I began to sweat like a marathon runner. Onlookers who were behaving just as outrageously stopped what they were doing and turned in my direction clapping and encouraging my performance. Within minutes my shoes and socks were off and so were my trousers and just as I was about to reach for my underpants, my brother's arm pulled me away and dragged my body out of the party.

As it was bitter outside and I had virtually nothing on I sobered up mighty fast.

'Tom, I think that I just had my first smoke. I think it was drugged.' My clothes were recovered and Tom and Suzy escorted me home, walking through the now empty streets with the occasional loose sheet of newspaper keeping us company. The steam from below the pavement made me feel that I was in a place of wonder and I thought how extraordinary this city was. I complained that they were being over-protective but they didn't listen to my wittering and, looking at my watch, I saw it was three o'clock.

*   *   *

The next day I woke to find the apartment empty. Tom had gone to work and there was a note from Suzy asking to meet me at P. J. Clarke's on 55th and Third Avenue. P. J. Clarke's is a New York institution with a bar upfront and a restaurant behind. I found Suzy with two of her friends sitting at a corner table.

'I hear you had quite an evening last night,' remarked a dark, mysterious, ravishing Italian-looking girl. I explained that I was not myself and apologised to Suzy for my behaviour. She smiled reassuringly and told me not to be silly. In walking into the bar I'd noticed an old-fashioned phone cubicle. I excused myself and with my hand full of change made a call to Lana to tell her of my excitement. I piled in the quarters and luckily she answered the phone but as soon as I had said, 'I'm having a fantastic time,' my time had run out and the conversation abruptly ended. I shrugged my shoulders and with Sinatra's 'My Kind of Town' ringing in my ears I returned to the table.

The girls were giggling but stopped when I approached and then the fabulously beautiful Chiara asked the question that immediately resonated with hidden meaning:

'So was the girlfriend happy to hear from you?'

'She was . . . I think . . . but the line went dead before I could ask her anything, let alone tell her what I had been up to.'

'Don't you worry, she may have just been happy to hear your charming voice.'

I had no idea whether she was joking and it irritated but it did not matter, I just enjoyed looking into her deep dark brown eyes.

Tom had to work all day and night so Suzy asked what I would like to do. I had no idea so I looked for the right answer, but in truth all I wanted to do was immerse myself in the city and have an adventure with the Italian beauty sitting to my right; Lana seemed a distant three-thousand miles away at that moment.

'I'll look after Samuel,' and so without any hint or suggestion, Chiara had taken control of the situation. I looked to Suzy for reassurance and her angelic smile gave the green light. I was deliriously happy and slightly intoxicated by the grace and allure that surrounded. Even Karen, the third member of the beautiful trio, a dark Puerto Rican girl with the darkest of eyes, the whitest teeth and short jet-black hair who said little and smiled more, was becoming one of my best friends.

All three loved my accent and asked me to 'Just say anything' and cooed in unison when I uttered various *non sequiturs*. Oh, if only life were as easy as this, I mused.

*   *   *

Lunch continued to well after four o'clock and there were not many times I had felt happier. The bill arrived and the girls split it with clean fresh greenbacks and refused to take my money.

Suzy excused herself to call Tom and when she returned to the table, her mood had changed and the glow that radiated from her face had turned to a grey concerned veneer with a splash of sadness.

'I have to go; I have an appointment and I am *late*.'

'What about Tom?' I asked.

She was flustered, 'I'll call him later, have a fabulous time.'

And with that she grabbed her bag, kissed me on the forehead, pushed a spare set of keys into my hands and hurried through the bar on to the streets of Manhattan. The two remaining girls spoke with their eyes and the table for the first time since I arrived went silent.

'She is always forgetting something,' explained Chiara. 'The agency has given a strong warning about her punctuality. Next time she is out.' She pointed her thumb to the door and Karen nodded in agreement, but something didn't seem right, as if they were hiding something.

*   *   *

Chiara was living an uptown girl existence in an apartment on the 48th floor on the corner of 79th Street and Park Avenue. We had bade our farewells to Miss Puerto Rico on the corner of 55th and 3rd and hailed a cab to our next destination on Lexington Avenue, opposite Bloomingdale's.

It was a model casting agency and like a prisoner who had been locked away for years, my desperation on seeing so many breath-taking girls in one place couldn't be hidden; I was insatiable and my tongue fell heavily from my mouth and could not be retrieved.

Chiara introduced more and more gorgeous friends, all tall, with long legs. When they offered their hands to say hello, I mumbled in a language crossed between Turkish and Swahili, neither of which I spoke. If I had to choose the winner from amongst the girls, it would have been impossible.

The role was for a desirable waitress serving a new pasta sauce so Chiara with her Italian looks was optimistic that she had a good chance of being cast. After a long wait, which was not long enough in my view, we left the office and walked back on to the bustling street.

*   *   *

The doorman gave Chiara a warm welcome and before I knew it, I was hurtling skywards to her apartment.

'We are going to have fun tonight, young Samuel, we are off to party at Studio 54,' she purred.

'Can we leave out the "young" in that sentence, please?'

She apologised and began to run herself an oil-drenched bath.

'You can come in and talk if you want to.' I could hear the bath filling and the smell of the oils sailed around my body.

'I'm OK, thank you; I'll wait here in the kitchen and make myself some coffee.'

And not for the first time I began to feel guilty as Lana's face swept across my eyes. I searched for the coffee and the coffee maker, desperately opening each cupboard and wasting as much time as possible, avoiding the temptation that sang only feet away.

And then just as I had finally made the coffee I did not want, I felt the presence of Chiara behind my shoulder. I turned to find her in a shocking red dress so savage in its appearance that it seemed to eliminate any resistance that I may have been storing.

'So are you ready?' she asked.

'For what?'

'To go out and party.'

As the elevator went down, I stared at her, not a word being said; it was at that moment I knew that the red dress would slip from her body with my helping hand.

*   *   *

The crowd outside Studio 54 was not unlike a rugby scrum. The multitudes had gathered and were desperately waving at, probably at that moment, the most powerful man in the world. Yells, screams, shrieks all mixed into one to gain the attention of a baby-faced assassin called Marc who with the mere wave of a hand granted someone their dream or by a shake of head destroyed it. Marc took his very own time signalling to friends and the cool alike to walk to the rope and be let through. The herd of neediness would have put most off but the crowds grew and grew and the push became more intense. Chiara stood motionless in the middle, not a wave or a signal to the referee; I held on to her hand. The moment of recognition came and Chiara and friend were beckoned like the Emperor choosing his favoured in the Coliseum. We walked to the thick rope and those around murmured disappointments and sighs.

I turned to one who had yelled jealous abuse: 'What do you expect? She is a beautiful model, for God's sake.'

To which he replied, 'What's she doing with you, then?'

I ignored his insult and followed my Italian beauty into the club like a puppy.

*   *   *

'Car Wash' by Rose Royce greeted our arrival into the old theatre cleared of its seats to make way for a huge dance floor. Large unforeseen objects lowered themselves from the ceiling as I was trying to find my rhythm. I was virtually knocked out by a huge liquorice-type object that instead of falling to the floor fell directly on my head. But who cared? I was dancing with a young Sophia Loren and losing my mind in a whirl of freedom and happiness.

Chiara had left the dance floor and I continued to dance with whoever dared to get near.

'Having a good time?' I yelled to my new exotic skinny

black dance partner. She ignored my question and moved gently away with a fixed smile on her face. Diana Ross was grooving to one of her own hits and an over-excited public schoolboy was not going to destroy her groove. Chiara dragged me off the dance floor laughing her head off. It was that glorious time of life when whatever you did was seen as charming or cool by your companion.

We made our way up the stairs to the dress circle where alcoves of large cushions beckoned us to sit and watch the debauchery heading off in all directions. I could see a huge animated figure of a man-in-the-moon hung over the dance floor. When a large hanging spoon came to rest under its nose, the man-in-the-moon lit up. 'What was that all about?' I wondered.

Chiara meanwhile was rolling what looked like a cigarette but from experience the other night, I knew would be something more testing. She took a deep inhalation and then to my complete surprise turned the spliff around, grabbed my mouth and blew smoke into my lungs. I left my body and flew into the air, luckily finding myself back in my shoes moments later. Her smile beckoned me to her lips and with not a moment's hesitation I kissed her passionately. And there we remained in each other's arms kissing and touching each other for hours. I was high with her soft lips and ravenous mouth and the drugs in my lungs. I wanted to devour her and any thoughts of my life outside Studio 54 were as distant as the real moon which shone wondrously above the Manhattan skyline.

We crawled out on to a still intense avenue and hailed a cab. 'I should go downtown,' I said with no real conviction.

'No, you're to stay with me tonight, my darling one.'

The conversation was over with those words; it had not even begun and the image of my darling Lana lay coldly in the streets of England far from Chiara's seductive warm

New York apartment hanging like a branch over the Big Apple.

I was sober enough to feel as if I fitted into my body; only an hour earlier I was convinced that my body had been removed from its head and was gyrating alone on the packed dance floor. I politely offered to make a coffee but there was no answer. Chiara had disappeared into the bedroom. I searched like I had done earlier, wasting time and trying to avoid the inevitable not because I didn't want to launch the rest of my life that night but because I was petrified.

'Where is my darling?' The words shattered my composure or the little of it.

'I am here just pouring milk,' I responded weakly.

And then she appeared with not a piece of clothing standing by the bedroom door. She was a wonder, as perfect a body as I could have ever imagined. My hand started to shake and my mug of coffee started to slurp over my hand and drip on the expensive white carpet. 'Put that down now, you silly boy. You haven't done this before, have you?'

'Of course I have,' I replied but it was no use as she clearly did not believe me. She walked towards my unconfident but horny body, took my coffee-drenched hand and led me to her bedroom. Oh, how I wanted her and how I was ready to be taken by this beautiful confident full-breasted girl. I pulled my clothes off after struggling for what seemed an eternity with my boots. She felt and kissed me gently and whispered Italian in my ear and in an instant I was inside her, my virginity lost in the heart of Manhattan.

I was so excited that if it weren't for something I had read in *Mayfair* only a few months earlier at school, it would have ended before it had begun, which in fact it nearly did anyway. The 'Quest' section of the mag had advised that if things got too exciting for you too quickly, you should simply think of anything but sex. 'Think of something dull to take your mind off things,' it advised. 'Try, for example, to list the tube stations starting from Sloane Square and going on from there.' But the tube line had little interest for me so for some strange reason I started to order fish and chips. Was it to be haddock or plaice, and maybe with a portion of mushy peas? I had just about chosen cod with fries when I lost control.

'I am so very sorry.' My apology was genuine with a smidgen of humiliation. Chiara smiled and I am forever grateful that instead of laughing and making me feel ashamed, she held me tightly and told me not be so silly. 'Perhaps be slower and more gentle my sweetheart.'

I felt relieved that there might be another chance to prove whatever I was trying to prove. So minutes later I was touching her peach-like olive skin with hands that moved gently across her extraordinary body; her ambrosial scent making me feel unsteady. That night drifted into the morning. Chiara was the perfect first teacher; understanding for the excitable child and encouraging at the same time. It was the first lesson and I wanted to learn and become a good student but with the overwhelming emotion of considerable happiness, guilt began to set in and Lana's voice started to swirl around my head and so even on my first night of sex, I was shrouded with guilt. Damn it.

I glanced at the clock that was blinking red numbers. It read three o'clock and I rubbed my eyes to check again. It was three in the afternoon and I was alone in a wrecked bed, bottles empty strewn on the floor and a note pinned to the pillow.

'I had to go to an appointment. I got the pasta job. You are my lucky charm, see you later my sweet angel x.' I immediately reached for the phone to call Lana but after dialling a couple of numbers, I gave up, replaced it and pulled the sheets over my head.

My mouth was dry, my head was thumping. I dragged myself out of bed and poured myself an orange juice which I slurped down in one extravagant gulp. I went into the bathroom and caught site of someone who resembled a tramp. It was me. So I ran a shower and stood under the rushing water to sober up. As I walked out, the phone was ringing and without thinking I picked it up. It was Tom who asked how I was and said he wanted to see me. We arranged to meet at six o'clock at his work and the two of us would then go off to dinner. 'Let's just spend some time together.' His words reverberated down the phone.

I caught a cab which as usual hurled itself downtown, dodging the craters lodged in the road. Like a pinball I was thrown from side to side but I did arrive safely and paid off my potential killer.

Tom was nowhere to be seen. He had left work an hour earlier and left no message. I wasn't particularly surprised by the fact, I simply thought he had made his way home, so I walked up to Hudson to his apartment and rang the intercom. There was no answer and so I pressed again and again but no one was answering the door. I sat on the stoop and waited, thinking and hoping and expecting that Tom would appear at any moment. It was a clear fresh night and the street was busy. The White Horse Tavern just a few yards away was full, as were the tables outside.

It was seven o'clock when I saw Suzy walking nonchalantly towards where I was sitting.

'You don't have a key?' she asked.

'No and I had arranged to meet Tom at work but he wasn't there.'

Suzy looked puzzled and then a sheet of concern covered

her face, so much so that I asked her what was wrong. She hesitantly put her key in the overused lock. It wouldn't turn and Suzy become more and more angry. 'Come on you bastard, work.' It was now that I knew something was seriously wrong but words were lost at this moment as the door finally relented and burst wide open.

Suzy darted up the stairs, her spilling bag adding to the insanity of the situation. She then searched for the right key for the front door and hands shaking finally found the one that fitted the lock. She turned the key and burst in; I was right behind.

Tom was slumped over the loo, arms falling to one side, his face resting on the seat. His bedraggled hair swept over his face. On the floor a lonely syringe had fallen, and nearby was a strip of foil paper opened and slightly burnt. I was frozen in shock by a sight so far from my reality that the truth could not be digested by my brain. Suzy pulled him away and laid him on the floor, face up, eyes closed. She screamed, 'Call an ambulance,' and I rushed in search of the phone but found myself going completely in circles as I had no idea where the thing was.

'Where is it?' I humiliatingly asked. She pointed to the window which overlooked Hudson Street and I noticed the swirl of yellow cabs outside busily looking for a fare. I dialled 999 but the line did not go through. I tried again and again but still no response. I started to panic, and cursed and cursed again.

'Can't seem to get through,' I shouted to the bathroom. Suzy came rushing out and grabbed the receiver without a word. She dialed 911 and started to ask for an ambulance. I left her and pulling myself together walked into the lamentable bathroom. And there I saw my beautiful brother lying flat on the floor, looking towards the ceiling. His skin was off-white, a grey, smoky colour that made him age by years; his lips had turned from a healthy red to an air force blue shade. It was at this instant, this sight that I grew and changed as if a conductor hovering over my head directed my destiny with his baton and pointed my journey to speed into a different direction along the highway. I believed he was dead and I searched for God and started to cry with excruciating pain.

Two paramedics arrived who immediately set to work. Tom's breathing was at least now audible but depressed. I watched, transfixed and horrified by the drama as one of them tried to find a vein so they could give him some sort of a narcotic antidote. I then saw my brother's arms ravaged with habitual use. Finally they found one in his thigh and waited a minute and then found a more suitable vein and gave him another dose. And the miracle of his recovery took place within minutes.

'Hello there, I gave you something to spoil your trip. You wasted your money.' I couldn't believe what the paramedic had just said, but he had just saved Tom's life as my brother seemed to be regaining his faculties, so I let it go. Tom was just about beginning to make sense when the ambulance crew arrived to take him to hospital.

I thanked the paramedics and they could see how shaken I was.

'He needs help. By the state of his arms he is a habitual user. He will continue to take more and more heroin until it kills him, sad but that's the truth.'

It was then, and I mean only then, that the whole barbarity began to dawn on me. My older brother was a junkie, a heroin addict. We followed my brother down with his stretcher and sped to the neighbouring St Vincent's hospital where he was dashed through the Emergency Room doors and delivered to a bed where a doctor checked his pulse, looked into his eyes and placed a stethoscope on his chest.

Tom survived that long night. He had been moments from death but his heart was strong and was regaining its regular beat. Oh, that night when many of my dreams were shattered. I slept on the bench in the melancholic corridor outside the ward. A Samaritan had covered my body with a harsh but warm blanket and I slept deeply, ignoring the intense wailing of other patients that echoed through the long hall. I dreamt of my brother that night; we were meeting the night before a battle wearing the uniform of war, and sharing a drink in a tent with the rain lashing down outside. I was concerned my brother would not survive the following day.

'You will come back tomorrow; you will survive, won't you?'

'I promise you, I am going nowhere.'

My dream ended abruptly when Suzy brought over a cup of coffee and hugged me so very tight. Her eyes were red, her face lined overnight.

'Go and see him,' and she pushed open the door and there he lay, head raised on a number of full pillows. My eyes welled and I knelt down and planted my head on his chest.

'I didn't want to lose you,' I whispered. He put his hand on my head and messed my hair. 'I promise you, I was going nowhere.'

I had many questions but they would wait. And so I sat by him with not a word spoken.

Chiara, who earlier had retrieved a key from Suzy when visiting the hospital, had food waiting when I returned to the apartment. Thomas had been advised to stay for observation at St Vincent's for the day and Suzy remained stoically by his side. Poor dear Suzy, it was clear that she had been riding a roller coaster over the last few months but she, although somewhat beaten, was still relatively strong. I admired her spirit but above all I admired her love for my brother.

'I suppose you knew my brother was a drug addict?' I asked Chiara.

'I knew,' she replied calmly. 'He had promised Suzy that it was over, that he had given it up for the last month or so, we believed him but . . . '

'But what?' I interrupted.

'But he lied, not only to his girlfriend, to us his friends and to himself, and I'm sorry for that.' She then pulled me towards her and we started kissing passionately and we fell to the floor where we made love in a passionate torrent of tears and anguish. After it was over I looked straight into her eyes and wept not only for Tom but for me and for my parents who were going to be so wounded that their son and heir was so very sick.

The phone rang and I picked it up like a gun-slinger drawing on his weapon. It was my father and his voice took my breath away.

'Everything all right?' was his opening line.

'Of course. Why shouldn't it be?' My reply was far too aggressive.

'Are you enjoying yourself?' he continued.

I told him that I was and when he asked about Tom I said that he was at work and would be working late.

'Tell him, the old man rang, and Sam, try to spend some quality time with your brother, he will have wise words and advice for you.' I continued my faltering act and then sent my love to my mother and gently replaced the phone. I sat down shaking at the conversation I had just seemingly carried off. Chiara moved towards the chair but I brushed her off; I was tired and wanted to be alone.

*   *   *

Thomas on returning was naturally distant. I wasn't sure whether it was good to be around and spent time in my room, door closed, reading and feeling low. When I went to the kitchen to fetch a Coke, my brother would be gazing out of the window, lost in his thoughts.

Chiara took me to a movie and held my hand throughout. It was a relief to get out and Chiara's affection was a welcome reminder of the gentler side of life. *Annie Hall* had been released the day before and the buzz reverberating caused lines to be formed outside the movie house. We queued and my confused state seemed to reflect Woody Allen's persona projecting from the large screen.

The movie was the perfect tonic and my sense of humour was returning. We found a restaurant on 4th Street and ate a pizza that melted in the mouth. I spoke of my family and Chiara asked about my father.

'Your brother seems to be fearful of your papa.' I shook my head and was adamant that she had got it completely wrong; in fact I grew very angry at the suggestion. I didn't like the insinuation that my father was at fault for what was happening to Tom.

'Calm down, my lovely, it is only what I see.' I shook my head and as she stroked my face I smiled. 'Stay with me tonight. I think Suzy and your brother should be alone, don't you?' I was not going to argue. I needed her warmth, her beauty, and I followed my Italian friend uptown and back into her bed.

I awoke in a chaotic room; sheets strewn across the floor, a blanket the sole survivor from the bed covered my nude body, an empty bottle of wine fallen from the table to the ground, a stain of wine ruining the white carpet. Chiara had already left for work, but a note was pinned to the pillow with the words 'Angelo mio, mi sto innamorando di te'. My Italian was vague to say the least, but I recognised something about 'love' and swaggered to the kitchen. The smell of coffee covered the room and I poured it into a deep cup and then the memory of the last twenty-four hours came flooding back to me. I hesitated about returning downtown to my brother's apartment but it was my last full day in New York. The weather had changed overnight and from the cold of yesterday it had leapt high into the 70s.

Suzy was at work when I arrived and Tom was alone, staring again into space with the television on at full volume drowning out any sense of pain. I lowered the volume and turned to my brother. Colour had returned to his face and although still frail, he had regained a certain amount of strength. He stood from his chair and started to open his heart.

'I tried to tell you the other night that I was weak, but you weren't listening. Everyone has always expected me to be number one, an A-grade student, top of my class, head boy and first in the race. Well, I was never that. I might have been on the surface but in fact I was always waiting for someone to tap me on the shoulder and recognise that I was a phony, that I didn't belong.'

'But that's just how I feel,' I replied, 'but I finish bottom of the class. I am not an A-grade student and I don't star in the school play, and I am still expecting that tap on the shoulder.'

Thomas smiled and gave me a clinch and whilst doing so I heard the tremor of my brother crying for the very first time. His pain blazed through my skin and I held him close, taking on the role of an older brother.

*　　*　　*

We went to lunch on Bleecker Street and for the first time he admitted his addiction. How it had begun by simply getting high on marijuana, which instead of having a

156

calming effect made him closely analyse his own existence. And from there he was offered some cocaine and became addicted to the whole process of taking the drug. Scoring down in Tribeca, rolling up the note, making excuses to go to the bathroom and snorting up. He made new friends and shared his secret with just them. Unfortunately they were serious drug takers and it wasn't long before he was taking heroin and chasing that very first high. 'I am always looking to repeat that moment but I suppose I never will.'

He continued to explain how he managed to pay for his habit.

'I spend all my hard-earned money on the drug and I have borrowed cash off my girlfriend and anyone close. Things got so desperate that I rang father to advance me some cash. I made an excuse that I had got my girlfriend pregnant and needed funds to deal with it immediately. All that has gone on the drug.' Suzy had found out from a friend that he was taking the drug. 'I was able to hide my habit from my own girlfriend. I lie and lie again. I never did before but I do and I know by admitting that now it is my step on the road to recovery. You see Sam, I want to get better.' He did look thin and as he was talking a ray of light shot through the glass front of the restaurant and shone brightly against his grey skin; he looked a hundred years old.

His candour took my breath away and I listened hardly moving, my eyes looking directly into his as his confession and atonement flowed. He took the occasional break to sip the glass of water which was freely filled by our waitress.

'I'm planning to go to Narcotic Anonymous meetings and attend my first tonight. Six o'clock on 4th Street.' He asked if I would go with him. Of course I would and I was pleased to see that when his steak and fries arrived, he devoured it like a wild animal that had not had a kill for some weeks; at least he had reclaimed an appetite.

The meeting on 4th Street was crowded but we managed to find three seats that seemed to be waiting for us on the very first row. Suzy had joined and there we sat listening to the tales of others whose lives had been devastated by their addiction; families that had been decimated, friendships that had been ruined and health that had sunk into the abyss.

'My name is Thomas and I am an addict.' My brother was invited to introduce himself to the gathered and he didn't resist the offer to speak. He told the audience that this was his first meeting and that he was here because he wanted to get well and was shamed by his behaviour to all those that were close to him. The encouragement from the room was overwhelming and I could see how others who had shared the same experience could be an island of support.

After the meeting, many ran to the comfort of a cigarette and milled outside discussing their lives with newly acquired friends. Tom did not want to hang around and so we left in search of a restaurant to share my final night in New York.

We went uptown to Mortimers, a haunt overflowing with former English public schoolboys, the type that I had left behind only a few weeks before. Round tables close together and a crescendo of noise saturating the long room. It was not unlike Mr Baresi's back at Montgomery but of course far more expensive. My brother was full of energy when only twenty-four hours before he had faced his own death. He was excited, well – so I believed – with the second chance he had just been given. He was full of optimism and as the dinner flowed I saw light return to his eyes and the shadow of death that had lingered seemingly drift away.

Chiara joined us late as she had spent the day filming

her pasta advertisement. She covered my face with kisses as she arrived and I sat looking gormless and turning very red. 'I think you are in trouble there,' my brother whispered and nudged me hard in the ribs.

Dinner was remarkably happy and full of laughter and conversation. How memorable: Chiara's wondrous smile, Suzy's warmth, and my brother's effort to put his experience behind him. I loved him that night probably more than I had ever done before. It was the sort of evening when even bad jokes seemed funny. Chiara grabbed the bill as it was placed in the centre of the table. I resisted and tugged at the strip of paper. I wanted to treat my brother and my new friends as I still had pocket money that my parents had given in case I needed 'extra'.

'No, my darling one. You are my talisman and today I made a pile of money for serving a plate of spaghetti Bolognese.' We laughed and toasted the future. We then stumbled on to Lexington Avenue and gave each other hugs as if we would never meet again.

My plane was leaving at nine o'clock the next morning and so Chiara decided to stay with me downtown. I was slightly drunk, emotionally exhausted and wanted to be alone, but Chiara's warm body was irresistible for some-one who had recently discovered sex. I had little sleep as the appetite of my Italian vixen was unquenchable and before I fell into a dream the alarm went off, signalling the end of my trip.

I left to catch a cab to JFK. I gave Suzy a kiss goodbye and she whispered, 'Thank you'. Chiara passionately grabbed my waist and staring straight into my eyes said 'Angelo mio, ti amo.'

My brother and I walked slowly to the corner of Hudson and Perry Street to wait for a cab. The wait was not long as a yellow cab screeched to our feet.

'I love you,' I said. 'Here, I have three hundred dollars left and I want you to have it.'

My brother took the money without hesitation and also grasped my hand and said, 'I don't know what I would have done if you had not been here, I love you and will always love you; don't ever forget that.' And so I got into the back of my cab and it sped off along Hudson Street towards the airport.

I looked behind to see my brother returning to his apartment; but his head was down and so he didn't see me staring through the rear window. I would never see my darling brother alive again. Within six months he would be found dead, lying face down on the filthy ground in a public lavatory in New York's Penn station.

*   *   *

The summer term was a beacon on the desolate landscape of school life. During the longest days, the sun greeted us most mornings and the warmth helped sweep away any grumbling that had haunted my school career.

My mother dropped me off at the house and kissed my cheek, 'Be good, my darling boy'. I looked straight in her eyes and promised that I would and then turned and walked towards to the main house door. The noticeboard displayed the news that I would be moving two floors up on the new side to the very top of the house along the tight corridor to Room 408. It had always been my favourite. It had the sense of being miles from anyone or anything. Alone, perched like a bird's nest sitting contentedly on top of an old oak tree.

*   *   *

The period between my return from the United States until the time my mother drove me along the M40 was short and full of a desire for the first time in my life to return to the sanctuary of my boarding school. I wanted to avoid questions about my time in New York. It was Father, to my astonishment, who had been waiting as I walked in the terminal arrivals hall. I was so amazed by his presence that I hardly recognised the tall figure in a light blue coat waving as I looked straight into his direction. 'Over here, you silly boy.'

My father had never picked me up from anywhere; he was what is known as a semi-absent father. Evident at home, but absent from anywhere else. I immediately thought he knew what had been going on in New York and I dreaded being interrogated because if anyone could see through my lies it was inevitably my father.

'What are you doing here?' were the words that I greeted him with. He smiled and took hold of my bag, another first. The relatively short drive home was drowned by Radio 3 but my father was in a jovial mood and seemed genuinely pleased to see me. He asked about Tom but just because my answers were monosyllabic, they didn't arouse his suspicion; it being my usual behaviour. He drove too slowly in the fast lane and there was continual hooting from other cars, but my father didn't seem to notice until I asked directly if he could move lanes. 'Why? What is their bloody hurry?' he replied.

By the time we reached home we had listened to the entire recording of Elgar's First Symphony. My father, one hand on the wheel, the other oscillating and conducting like Sir Adrian Boult.

My father revealed that when Elgar completed this work, he wrote, 'there is no programme beyond a wide experience of human life with a great love and a massive hope in the future.'

'Listen to this, dear Sam, when you feel a little down. It

is full of optimism.' I nodded, dumbfounded by Father's words; perhaps he did care after all.

*   *   *

My mother was warm and gossiped about Aunt Flo falling over her wheelbarrow in her garden and breaking her left foot. 'Don't laugh, Samuel, she's very poorly.'

My father was chuckling but my mother ignored the two of us and simply shook her head at the lack of sympathy her family had for her dear sister.

At supper, shepherd's pie and green peas were gulped down in seconds and I spoke about New York with excitement and untruths. I was drunk with jet lag and with school calling within eighteen hours I excused myself from the table and took a deep breath and called Lana. Her brother picked up the phone. 'She's out.'

'When will she be back?'

'Don't know,' he unhelpfully replied and before I could say any more, the phone was down and I was left with the dial tone buzzing in my ear.

*   *   *

By the time Grafton and Spit came crashing into my new study, I still hadn't spoken to Lana.

'You lucky bugger,' they both cried in unison. The room, like all things that fit perfectly into one's life, was coming together like poetry. Posters seemed to fit in on my walls like a masterpiece in a museum, well sort of. Raquel Welch in a two-piece fur bikini posed above my bed guarding me from the dark forces that were sure to threaten. My bed tucked into one corner with my desk on the other side and the iconic poster of the blonde rubbing her bum on the tennis court overshadowing it. My desk had once been Tom's and his deeply carved name resonated from the centre. I looked at his carefully designed name and as if stunned by a jolt of electricity I turned away.

Spit had already lit up and was blowing half the smoke of a Marlboro cigarette into the room and the other half into the darkening sky. The window overlooked a building site of the new central dining room, to be named the Main Hall, and could be opened wide and was perfect for edging out and having that discreet ciggy. Unfortunately Spit was anything but discreet. A disused chimney in Room 408 remained and was another perfect place to blow smoke up and to hide the countless butt ends that were bound to emerge throughout the term.

It wasn't long before Troubles and Burford had found my haven.

'You lucky sod,' cried Burford, falling on to my newly made bed, curly dark hair falling over his eyes, 'you have the best room in the house. Not only is it perfect for hanging out but also prefects are never going to be bothered to walk up here. You are lucky and so are we.'

And we all laughed together, practised blowing smoke rings into the air, and cheered on the coming term.

'How was the Big Apple?' asked Burford and just as I was about to tell them some lies the bell sounded for our first roll call. The five of us trooped down to the hall to answer our names and hear the opening speeches from the housemaster Mr Webster and Summerfield, still our sadistic head of house.

The procession of authority marched in to the packed hall. First Mr Webster, coughing as he walked, Summerfield following in step. He seemed to have grown during the holiday and his podgy face was redder than I remembered. He looked at the floor as he walked with his cohort Warwick following closely behind, if not a bit too close. And in a flash it hit me; Warwick with his heavily groomed jet-black hair, pristine uniform and stretched stature was in love with his senior prefect. I knew it and I couldn't understand how I hadn't noticed before. I would hold on to this recognition and place it carefully in my top pocket; I knew it would come in useful one day.

Matron was part of the ensemble and as she passed I smelt her and swayed with the force of her essence. I sent her a smile and she caught it and sent one back. Matron was my secret passion. I wondered whether she would see a difference since I lost my virginity and decided to test it first thing the following morning. There was part of me that believed printed on my forehead were the words 'I am not a virgin' for all to read. I just hoped Lana couldn't see it.

*　　*　　*

'Boys, quiet please.' The housemaster began his welcoming speech. His Scottish chords sounded more stretched and worn than they did even a few weeks before. It gave the impression that he was slightly drunk.

'This term we will be moving to the central dining room, which as you know has been in the process of being built for the last two years. By June it will be completed and the school has the privilege that a member of the Royal Family will be here to open it. A proud day in our history and a splendid honour to have such a visit in The Queen's silver-jubilee year. Nearer the time I will announce the roles that we will all play on that special occasion, until then food will be served as usual within the house.

'The summer time is a period where we can all enjoy the good weather and the longer hours,' he continued. 'Go out and enjoy yourself but do not, and I repeat do not, enjoy yourself too much.' I gave Burford a quizzical look, and Summerfield then stepped in, virtually pushing the housemaster to the ground; again it was clear that Mr Webster was uneasy on his feet.

'Thank you, housemaster,' he drawled. 'Other than some notable exceptions,' he glanced in our direction, 'the house behaviour improved last term. Let's have more of the same therefore. I promise each and every one of you, though, that those who step over the line will be dealt with in the most severe fashion.' I coughed nervously.

'Let us welcome this term's new boys.'

The house turned towards four pubescent individuals cowering in the corner with the onset of acne. They then had to, like I was made to once, stand on the table and sing individually the first verse of 'Men of Harlech'.

> *Hark, I hear the foe advancing,*
> *Barbed steeds are proudly prancing,*
> *Helmets in the sunbeams glancing*
> *Glitter through the trees.*

A letter would have arrived during the holiday instructing the new boy to learn the four lines. Each struggled through with high petrified voices; when they finished, the entire house thumped ferociously on the table as an act of encouragement for what they had just been through.

The house was dismissed and as I was walking out of the hall, Warwick followed me.

'We are watching you, Alexander.'

'Well, thank you for those welcoming words. You really are a treasure,' I replied and trounced off towards the telephone. With luck it was not in use and so I rang Lana and finally we connected. I was so happy to hear her voice and was eager to tell her everything about my trip. What was the point in lying, if you couldn't tell the truth at this early stage of the relationship surely the rest would be a lie; wisdom far beyond my tender years, at that moment perhaps. I promised myself to tell her about Chiara after meeting Mrs Wheeler on the Wednesday.

'I have missed you, I can't tell you how much,' she cooed.

On returning to my room, my friends were recounting their holiday tales to each other. Burford had fallen in love with what sounded like a kooky art student from his local town. On my sixteenth birthday we got engaged,' he announced rather formally.

'But haven't you only known her for two weeks?' I was surprised.

'It doesn't matter. When you have found the one, there should be no question of how long you have known each other, and anyway I plan to tell Mr Webster as soon as possible so that I can get free time to go and see her.'

There was a disbelieving stunned silence but we ignored our instinct and all gave our friend a cheer.

I wanted to tell them about Tom and even about Chiara but it was not the time and when asked about New York, I went on about visiting Studio 54 and how high the sky-scrapers were.

As I was falling asleep I noticed the stench of cigarettes staining the air. If I wasn't careful, punishment would come crashing down before the term had even begun. With punishment would come restrictions, and escaping these walls would become much more difficult. I made a decision there and then, that if smoking were to feature in my room of all places, the chimney would have to be used and by one person at a time. The window would be kept wide open all day and even at night; another bonus of a summer term. With these pressing thoughts swirling around my head I drifted into dreams of my brother looking healthy in New York and Chiara and Lana meeting in the school tuck shop and becoming the best of friends.

*   *   *

166

The first wake-up bell of term after weeks of sleeping in late greeted the body like a powerful left hook. In unison you could hear the house moan.

That summer, I had started life's long sentence of shaving. It had happened overnight; last term maybe once or perhaps twice I stroked the hairs above my top lip but now it seemed a much more considerate state of affairs. I had bought a set of the latest disposable Bic razors from JFK and an American shaving cream Edge, thinking that it suited my image. Yes, that morning I certainly needed a shave and managed to cut myself at least twice above the top lip and numerous times around the neck which gave the perfect excuse to visit matron after my breakfast of strawberry yoghurt and a tepid cup of milky tea. Strands of loo paper were stuck to my face covering my cuts as I trawled up the cranky stairs to see matron. A queue had formed on the first day of term and I waited impatiently behind five hypochondriacs.

'Oh come ON, will you,' I shouted.

'Just be patient, Samuel, your time will come,' purred our gorgeous matron.

Finally my time arrived and matron looked quizzically at my torn face.

'I am not sure you need to shave that rigorously, young man,' declared matron. 'Maybe just there, and say once a week.'

She was sliding her index finger on the vermilion border where the pink part of the lip meets the flesh-coloured. I felt more than a tingle of excitement and wanted to take her fingers and to start to suck them but I resisted or rather my mouth froze and I projected a face of confusion. 'Don't rush yourself; from the men I have known, shaving is said to be a laborious, torturous regime. The longer you can put off this agony, I would suggest, the better.'

She peeled away the paper stuck to my face and her deep seductive eyes pierced my tired ones and I gave her an embarrassed smile. 'Thank you, matron,' and with that I left, thinking of having sex with her on the fur rug which lay at the centre of the Surgery Room.

*　　*　　*

Mr Harris had been my form master since I first arrived but we were greeted with the news that poor old Bomber had fallen gravely ill during the Easter break and would not be returning. He had been at the school for forty-five years.

'A very decent man,' my father declared when I had mentioned that he was not only my form master but my History master to boot. I never really got to know him, he was truly past his sell-by date by the time I arrived at the school and he shouldn't have been allowed out to water his garden, let alone teach a class. He had the odd habit of making up nicknames for all us. Mine was just 'The' after Alexander the Great; I suppose he thought that the nickname 'Great' could go to my head. Charles Ash, who sat at the next desk, was known as 'Cigarette', and Rupert Cook, who sat to my other side was called 'Fanny,' after Fanny Cradock, a popular female TV cook of the time. A good man, who even to his last days had a fine sense of humour; his academic ability when I arrived was of some concern, though: he believed that Glasgow was the capital of Scotland. Senility had clearly set in.

Waiting for us as we trooped into our form room was a Mr John Davie, another Scot with wired red hair, a handsome sharp face not unlike Sean Connery and built like a prop forward. He gave each and every one of us a distinct look and made an introduction. 'My name is Davie, Mr Davie to you, and I will be your form faster and I am

168

taking over from poor Mr Harris for your History. I know that you will be taking your O levels this term but you don't have to worry, I am right up to where you have studied and I will help with the final push before your exam.' And with those words I was reminded that I had done no homework in any subject during my holidays. I was about to be in major trouble. How could I have forgotten? Exams were just round the corner.

'OK, let's get down to it. I have in my hand the multiple-choice part of your paper, which should take at the most thirty minutes. Alexander, hand them out, please.'

I walked round from desk to desk slowly looking for any excuse to duck out and playing for time.

'Hurry up, boy, we don't have all day.' Mr Davie was losing his patience. I glanced at Grafton and gave him a lost look; he did not seem much more confident.

'Half an hour, and it starts now,' Davie clicked on his stop-watch as if we were about to set off on a race.

The first question covered dates around the period of the English Civil War.

'What year was Charles I executed? – A.1637; B.1647; C.1721; D.1649.'

Well, as they say, you do have a one-in-four chance and miracle of miracles I knew this answer as he had been executed on my birthday, 30 January, and I knew it was 1649. So one out of one. I put up my hand to impress our new teacher. He approached softly so as not disturb the other boys.

'Sir, if I know the exact date should I put that down?' I pointed to my answer to show exactly what I meant and also to show my new master what a bright, clever boy I was. But he was more experienced than I expected.

'That won't be necessary, laddie.'

He turned and impatiently walked away. The following

questions needed more than luck or distant connections with birth dates and by the end I was virtually rhyming 'eeny meeny, miney, moe'; a tactic in the history of multiple examination that usually leads to certain failure.

'Time's up,' was called by our officious new form master and we were dismissed to our next lesson.

'How did it go?' I asked Grafton as we strolled along with our arms full of books.

'No problem. Most of them were A. From the first question to the last.'

He seemed most pleased with himself but as question one's answer was D and that I knew, I did not think that his smug smile would last very long. I sped through the first group of lessons without any more tests and ran back to the house to cram three weeks of homework into forty-eight hours. I banned anyone from visiting for either a chat or a fag break and dived into my books to swot and write a number of essays. No sleep that night, only work, and when the morning bell sounded I collapsed on my bed, only to be woken by Spit who had covered at roll call.

Mr Davie marched soldier-like into the classroom and the noise which was reaching fever pitch suddenly died down.

He unpacked his worn briefcase and held the collection of papers from our test in his gargantuan hands.

'This is a load of rubbish, an absolute load of tripe with one exception. You boys will have to get down to some serious work.'

Gloom filled the room and I thought to myself that at least I was not alone and that my class comrades were just as idle.

'Alexander,' he looked down at me and I prepared for the worst, 'You are the only boy who has emerged from this car crash with any credit. Well done.'

Stunned? I was bloody stupefied.

'Thank you, sir, I just try to do the best I can.'

The class immediately turned on me and threw paper pellets and erasers in my direction.

'How dare you all behave in such a way? Hard work has never hurt anyone. Alexander should be applauded, not be the subject of such scorn.'

I thanked him and wallowed in the praise that was bestowed upon my lucky head. The form was put into detention on the Wednesday afternoon and I was put into 'Coventry'. The boys couldn't figure out how I'd achieved such high marks but if I'd told anyone that it was a mixture of luck and desperation, few would have believed me. No detention for me on Wednesday, just the waiting arms of delicious Lana.

*   *   *

Post was laid out neatly by one of the staff on a big red table by the house entrance. I didn't receive much mail as my father never bothered and my mother preferred to use the telephone. But as I made my way down to the dining room a postcard with John Lennon's face stared out at me.

I knew immediately it was mine. 'We miss you, Love, Tom.' Next to his name were thick red lips printed from Suzy's mouth with her name scribbled underneath and a big X. It warmed my body and I was overcome; I broke down and cried uncontrollably. I ran down to the basement of the house that stored the large and noisy boilers and fell to my knees. David Burford saw my dash and followed. He crept behind and tapped my shoulder.

'Are you OK?'

I turned and said nothing but my eyes were red and he could see I was deeply distressed.

'If you want to talk, I'm here.'

His offer was what I needed and we agreed to meet after his corps and my Wednesday afternoon with Mrs Wheeler.

My scrambled holiday work was handed in on time and the impending disaster was diverted for the time being. I was dizzy all day waiting to see Lana again. I had decided that I wasn't going to admit anything and only hoped that Lana saw no deception in my eyes. It was a coffee earlier in the day with Mr Baresi which persuaded the truth to remain firmly in my heart.

'Never, and I mean *never*, tell the truth,' he implored, 'Even if she catches you in bed with another girl, just tell her you were discussing your homework.'

I asked Mr Baresi if he had ever been caught with another woman. 'Yes, many times, but I did what I just advised you, young man, denied everything.'

Mr Baresi's wife had still not returned with his children and it was becoming clear why she left in the first place. But still I took his advice and as I was leaving he said, 'Just because you are with another woman, it doesn't mean you don't love your wife or in your case, your girlfriend.'

He spoke with a knowing heavy heart.

*   *   *

'You look as if you have been in a war and I am not sure who won.'

Mrs Wheeler's greeting was on reflection predictable. I was piling heavy shopping into her small fridge and refusing to acknowledge what she was on about, but it was no use. I couldn't lie to her and she was also psychic. I ripped open my soul and the tale of New York came tumbling out, Tom, Chiara, everything. She sat me down and her comforting words added wisdom to my adolescent years.

'You don't have to tell Lana,' Mrs Wheeler advised,

seemingly in agreement with Mr Baresi. 'You will only hurt her and the blow will be hard for the girl to understand. Just enjoy being with her and we will see what happens. But for the time she need not know.'

She cupped my face in her warm hands and sent me on my way. I turned back to the door as I walked on to the street but it had shut and Mrs Wheeler had vanished. With renewed strength I ran along the pavement to the Wimpy bar where we had planned to meet on the stroke of four o'clock.

I was early and the restaurant was empty. I chose a table by the window and gazed out waiting for her to arrive. She was late and I started to look at my watch with concern and then all of a sudden she ran in out of breath and drenched by a freak rainstorm.

'I'm so sorry, I hate being late,' and she put her arms around me and gave me a kiss. She was hurried in her speech and garbled with her news, but I presumed that this was nerves and our separation over the last few weeks. It made us feel as if we were reliving our first date. Her hair was wet and her skin dripped with the rain. I explained about Tom and how I was trying to deal with it. She listened carefully and tugged on my fingers when my voice started to break with pain. I felt little guilt; my overriding sense was that I was happy to be by her side once again.

'It's my Mum's birthday on Saturday,' she told me, 'and the parents are having a party. They would like you to be there. That is if you want to?'

I said that nothing would stop me.

I walked her to the bus stop and waited for the bus to arrive. Although a long queue was forming and impatient travellers made disapproving sounds, we kissed passionately and noisily.

'See you at the weekend,' she yelled from the platform of the moving vehicle and we waved each other goodbye.

* * *

Lord David Burford was the son of a wealthy aristocratic landowner based in the Midlands. His older brother lived in Washington DC and by reputation was one of the great playboys of the western world. He had married the Swedish Ambassador's daughter at the tender age of nineteen; and from what Burford reported continued to have affairs with diplomats' wives throughout the capital. We both shared a love for our older brothers; they had also been at our school at the same time.

His younger sister had recently run off with a reggae artist in Jamaica, much to the disappointment of his father and amusement and support of the brothers. I had spent a week the previous summer in their large house surrounded by beautiful grounds.

'How much land do you own?' I had asked Robin, David Burford's older brother.

'As far as the eye can see,' as he looked out of their large drawing-room windows. The sound of Bob Marley and the Wailers drenched the corridors of the house and the younger sister, who had yet to run off with her new friend, walked around with bare feet and a cigarette hanging from her full lips.

His mother was not dissimilar to mine, quiet and slightly put upon by the rest of her family. Dinner around the table although very English resembled a large Jewish family, full of fights, arguments and debate. During this particular dinner, Robin was in trouble as his wife, a Swedish beauty called Jaclyn, refused to talk to him. His behaviour the previous evening had landed him in trouble as he had made a pass at an Italian songstress on a crowded dance floor. His poor wife, who was probably surviving a marriage by the tip of her fingers, yelled at him across the table.

'I don't mind you cheating on me, but do you have to screw them in front of my eyes?'

With that she picked up an apple from a fruit bowl on the sideboard and threw it viciously at his head. It landed with such force that it sputtered from his skull on to the table. She stormed out, but without a nod to what had just happened, the conversation proceeded as before.

'He is always getting into trouble,' laughed Burford, 'And I am planning to be as naughty as him.'

These words from the summer before seemed pertinent when Burford knocked on my door to see how I was coping. It was the third time that day I had revealed what had happened in New York the previous week.

I had promised myself that no one would know, but letting go of the story was helping.

Burford listened, but it was clear that he had his own problems.

'She's pregnant,' he said.

'Who's pregnant?'

'Zara, the girl I am engaged to, and I don't know what to do.'

For someone who had always walked with the air of confidence, his shoulders had slumped and his bright handsome face was scribbled with worry. He said that the easiest thing would be just to arrange an abortion but Zara would not even discuss the issue.

Confusion had set in and there was nothing I could advise. What started as an evening where I admitted my problems turned out to be Burford's show; he was clearly upset and angry.

Tired, I strolled down to roll call the next morning,

waiting for the new day to begin. I noticed immediately that Burford wasn't there.

Summerfield came up to me. 'Where is your bum chum Burford?' he asked. I shrugged my shoulders and was told that I should go and look for him.

I was full of fear as I climbed the stairs to the other side of the house. The memory of Langley was still so close that I opened his door full of trepidation. What was I going to find? Burford was so bemused the night before and so down. His bed had not been slept in and it was evident that he had not been there all night. I left his room and decided to go straight to the housemaster. Mr Webster was hurrying to his first lesson.

'Sir, I think Burford has run away from school.'

The housemaster immediately went into action. He returned to the house and I was to follow. He called Burford's parents but they had not heard from him. He called the local train station but there had been no sighting. He then called the police and I heard the words, 'We have a missing boy,' pass down the phone. I was sent off to lessons and told that I would probably be called for a police interview later that day.

That afternoon I was facing two local policemen making notes and asking questions.

'We understand that you were talking to David Burford late last night. Can you tell us what you were talking about?'

'He was upset and he thought his girlfriend was pregnant.'

'Why didn't you mention this before, you silly boy?' rebuked the housemaster.

I muttered some excuse, but in truth my growing instinct was just to say nothing. I was asked whether I knew his girlfriend's full name and told them I knew it was Zara, but that was all. Before I had even left the office, the search had begun in earnest.

After forty-eight hours, it was printed on the front of the papers that he had been found sleeping rough on a farm near Cambridge. A photo of a dishevelled-looking Burford was printed. He had a blanket drooped over his shoulders and was surrounded by police; there was a small portrait of Zara to the right of the article. I was in the middle of reading the exposé of their love story when there was a knock on my door. Burford had returned to school and looked tired. He mumbled on about how difficult life had become and spoke of love consuming his being.

'I needed to see her.' The boy who only a few weeks before resonated the air of a confident Casanova had now been struck down and paralysed by a petite seventeen-year-old.

In the following two weeks Burford left the school without permission five times and it reached a point when no friends could be heard; he was not listening. I noticed his parents arriving at the headmaster's door and thoughtful discussions followed. In the end it was decided that Burford could after Saturday have the weekend off, so in fact he would become a weekly boarder and be allowed to see his girlfriend regularly. It was a liberal decision from the school and it gave me hope that although there were stringent rules, decisions could be made to suit the individual.

The freedom allowed Burford to return to his old self. The swagger was restored and the joy that had been squeezed out was replenished. Zara lost their baby at three months and instead of mourning, Burford was relieved and liberated by the turn of fate. He never asked about Tom and although I cared for my friend, I was angry that his life revolved around him and only him. I never met Zara during that term and when any of us asked when she was going to visit the school, the subject was instantly changed.

*   *   *

The house photograph is traditionally taken during the first few weeks of the summer term at the same spot: in the centre of the garden at the rear of the house. The photograph is then hung in the dining room as a record for posterity. My father can be seen quite clearly from the years of 1941 until 1945 and my brother from 1969 until 1973. They look remarkably similar except the pose, my father standing proud whilst my brother with longer hair slouches over the shoulder of a friend. They both became head of house, and so they ended up sitting next to their housemaster in their final year. I was never going to end up on that seat; that was known on day one.

'What are you doing?' I asked Burford. He was in the process of putting on a deep red lipstick.

'I think it will make my lips look more full.'

I shook my head in wonder and made my way to the garden. Juniors sat cross-legged on the grass and prefects with the masters and matron sat on chairs on the first row. The rest of us stood by seniority in the rows behind. And how dear matron looked that day; with blue jacket, a pencil skirt and high black stiletto shoes. She now looked like Claudia Cardinale.

'How beautiful you look, matron.'

'And how handsome you look, Samuel.'

I blushed, straightened my tie and walked to my allotted place. I stood between Troubles Winter and Spit Nimmo Smith and a harassed photographer stood under his old-fashioned standing camera and counted, one, two, three, and as a collection we smiled and the bulb flashed.

As it was happening I noticed out of the corner of my eye

Grafton, who was standing along the same row, hold up a model of Frankenstein. As soon as the flash went off, he lowered the evidence. Two more shots and the whole process was completed and we returned to class.

Two days later after roll call there was an announcement by the housemaster.

'On developing the film from the house photograph it was seen that a stupid boy had spoilt it by behaving irresponsibly. The boy in question has been dealt with and we will be sitting again on Thursday afternoon. House dismissed.'

We shuffled away from the wrath of the hall and smirked until we reached my room. Grafton was the only one not smiling. He had been pulled in front of the housemaster for that minor offence and had been placed on a final warning. A final warning is a hair's breadth from expulsion and for the slightest breach of school rules, you are expelled. A sigh of disbelief galvanised our room. We looked at each other with astonishment that something so trivial could lead to so grave a punishment. There was silence but within minutes we had all regained our confidence and led by Grafton we joked at the world we found ourselves in, and promised it would not get us down.

*   *   *

The follow-up photo was finally taken at a different location next to the school library, the reason being that it enabled the housemaster to see the assembled house group from the reflection in the window to his right. Indeed you could just make out in the finished house photo that his beady eyes were looking off at the window rather than at the camera; he clearly had no trust in his house.

*   *   *

It was the middle of the night and from the crow's nest of my room, I was still able to hear the crescendo of noise reverberating from the streets below. I rubbed my eyes and peered out of my window and saw a group emerging from the local town running riot through the school streets. There were about twenty of them with lengths of wood and bricks in hand and the abuse that was falling from their mouths made any class war seem very much alive.

I quickly got dressed and made my way down to the bottom of the house. The whole house was wide awake and excited by the potential war that was brewing only a few yards away.

'And where do you think you are going?' asked Summerfield, already dressed in his army fatigues.

'I thought I could help,' I replied.

'If you can help, then we certainly are in trouble. Now go back to your room.' Head down like a child who could not have his favourite sweet, I sulked my way back. I took up position and peered out of my window. Below were two roaring factions. On one side the town with weapons in hand, on the other the school led by Summerfield, many dressed in army uniform, their posh accents trying to placate the threatening mob. The town's leader from afar seemed familiar and it took a few moments to realise that the lanky individual was indeed Lana's brother Keith. I took my life in my hands and made my way to the street below.

'Lads, lads, this is madness. Leave now, be on your way. I am one of you,' I pleaded. Keith gave me a disbelieving look and so did Summerfield. I was standing between the two sides and after a moment's silence, Keith and his chums charged towards me ferociously and I turned my back and sprinted for my life in the opposite direction.

After a short chase the townies turned and engaged with the rest of the school contingent in a fight so bitter that it was drenched in cuts, blood and class distinction. I watched from behind a wall as fists and bricks were thrown and bodies tumbled to the ground. Within minutes, swirling blue lights were seen heading towards us with screaming tyres resembling an episode from a TV cop-show. Our visitors ran in different directions heading to the relative safety of their town.

The battle hadn't gone on long enough for there to be a winner but the marks on the faces of some of the prefects seemed to reflect the fierce fighting that had taken place.

The 'flying squad' assembled us and I saw Summerfield talk earnestly into the ear of one of the officers.

'I understand you knew one of them,' said the copper, who seemed familiar, and then it dawned that it was the same man who had led the hunt for the stolen painting.

'I thought I did,' I replied, 'but when I got closer I could see that I had made a mistake.'

He did not believe a word and turned away and we were all ordered back to our rooms.

'I was only trying to help,' I said but Summerfield was not listening and I was 'roomed' until the end of the week. Being roomed meant that you were confined to your room except for lessons and meal times. All posters were stripped from the wall, the radio could not be played, so no Nicky Horne's 'Your Mother Wouldn't Like It' on Capital Radio, and no visitors were allowed to come to visit. A boring, tortuous punishment and totally unjustified; my anger seethed.

The protagonist was Keith and he had seen me and I had seen him, but I wasn't going to admit anything and during the lonely days that followed I thought deeply about what had caused all their anger. For they were not acting out of joke or a bit of fun or even boredom on a Wednesday night; they were acting out a pattern that was forming throughout the country. A heavily drawn line in society had always been prevalent in the United Kingdom and had reared its ugly head in front of my eyes; the class war based on the division of society through control of its institutions and wealth. There was a sense at the time that the country was losing its hold and its self-respect and had lost its voice on the world stage. Class distinction had ended up firmly and violently on our doorstep and it needed the coming generation to reclaim their calm and not revert to violence which at the time was spreading from the football terraces on to the High Street.

I was unable to use the phone, so I wrote to Lana making no mention of her wayward brother and explaining that although I had been in trouble, I planned to go to the party at her house on Saturday night. 'I will be there no matter what for I miss your skin, your mouth, your voice,' I scribbled with a leaking pen. And indeed I did, for those hours I spent alone in my room, seemed to encapsulate my adoration for Lana. I felt lonely and in desperate need of affection.

*   *   *

As timing would have it, a letter arrived for me meanwhile with more scent sprayed on it than a Parisian bordello. Chiara had sent her love and had at the same time sent her essence to the entire house. I read her letter furtively and with a sense of guilt. I was more interested to hear about Tom than her yearnings for my body. Tom seemed to be on the mend and she described that she had dinner with him and Suzy the previous evening and he had gained weight and 'regained his smile'. I was relieved but my heart remained heavy and wanted to be near to my brother but that was not to be. One other concern was her promise to visit soon.

'It looks as if I have been booked for a job in London and soon I will see my darling in his school uniform.'

I had this sinking feeling instinct that my good time in New York was about to bite me firmly on the bum.

*   *   *

Summerfield had inspected my room on the stroke of eight o'clock on the Saturday. He was intoxicated and slurred his words as he cursed my existence. From the previous pattern this would be the last time he would check and so as he closed my door I confidently dressed, ready to disappear into town.

'Where are you going?' asked Spit. I explained that I was to see Lana and join a party of middle-aged ravers and before I knew it Spit had changed into his mufti and was keeping me company as we dodged between the bushes on our escape from across the school boundaries.

Summer term meant that it was more difficult to remain unseen but there wasn't a soul about that warm evening and fortunately we didn't see another human face until we reached the town. We stopped at a local off-licence to buy a cheap bottle of wine but were refused by the owner: 'You must be joking.'

'But it's not for us, it is for my girlfriend's father.' He hurried us out of the store and so we stopped at the local newsagents to buy some Turkish Delight. 'Why have you bought that?' asked Spit as we walked down Lana's street. 'Well, we can't turn up empty-handed, can we?' I replied.

Lana's father greeted us both with a warm, overbearing hug. I introduced my friend.

'What did you say your name was?'

'My name is Nimmo Smith but you can call me Spit.'

He laughed and led us into his living room where a group of mums and dads were sharing a drink and laughing at

183

naughty jokes. Although still early, the alcohol was freely flowing and the majority if not all of the gathering were intoxicated; everyone was having fun and it put to shame some of the drab teenage events I had recently been to. I looked for Lana but at first I could not see her and then I turned to the door and saw this flawless creature approach.

She said nothing and gave a fresh warm kiss on my lips. It was one of those moments, a moment that was so perfect, that it would imprint itself deep in the psyche. The heartbeat was spoilt by my friend pushing us apart and taking Lana's hand to cover with kisses.

'Hello Lana, I don't know if you remember me but I'm Spit.'

'I can see why,' she replied.

I was offered a drink and accepted a gin and tonic which was virtually all gin and a spoonful of tonic; without warning it went straight to my head. My merriment fitted naturally into the gathering. Spit was simply very drunk and slurred his words as he cornered a London cabbie, advising him on the best route from Harrods to Maida Vale.

All I wanted to do was grab Lana by the hand and ravish her in her bedroom. The drink must have affected my facial expression because when I was directing my eyes towards the door she went to the other room and brought back a plate of pasta. As she handed over the heavy plate, I whispered in her ear that I wanted to make love with her immediately. In fact I was shouting and silence had descended on the crowded room. I smiled embarrassingly and unsteady on my feet took backward steps to the bathroom close to the kitchen; I quickly locked the door and hung my head over the sink and purged my ugly behaviour. Within an instant I felt better, an anchor returning my body and control to my mind. I found some mouthwash in a cabinet and splashed cold water on my face; it was my first clue in life that drink might not always be a friend. I walked out very different from the person who had previously disappeared and I took Lana by the hand and led her away. We fell on the bed and I felt her desire burn through my soul. We started to kiss more passionately than ever before and I believed that this was going to be the moment for us to make love for the first time, even though the neighbourhood was only feet away. I lowered my trousers and lifted her skirt; she willed me to be inside her. But then as life goes, there was a bang on the door and without waiting for an answer Keith barged in. He had bleached his hair white and from his ear safety pins hung down to his shoulder. He wore a white T-shirt with 'Anti-Nowhere League' printed on it, PVC trousers and a spiked dog collar strapped round his neck. I quickly straightened my clothes as Lana moved away.

'Knock will you?' rightly moaned his sister.

'Hello, Keith,' I said.

'Hey, sorry about Wednesday but my fight wasn't with you. It's the scumbags you share your life with.' He acknowledged the fact that I hadn't turned him in and mouthed 'nice one, mate' as he left the room. I was so much in his good books that he didn't even punch my face for trying to have sex with his sister in his own house.

Lana looked confused and immediately looked for answers. I described the other night and Lana was outraged. The passion she'd had quickly drained from the room and I cursed my bad luck.

Spit was now plastered and talking loud gibberish to anyone whom he encountered. It was clear that it was time to leave. The party was still in full swing and the music was blaring and T. Rex songs were being sung. I thanked Lana's parents, who were busy having a very close dance, and waved my girlfriend goodbye.

I didn't want to leave, but I knew I had to. It felt like I was returning to prison and as I left the house with Free's 'All Right Now' blaring out into the night air around me, I sensed freedom seep from my body.'

As I walked and Spit staggered, we just avoided Mr Oxlade who was taking a late stroll with a surprisingly attractive nubile woman; they were embracing and were so involved that he missed us walking close by. The warm air remained although it was drifting past midnight and we climbed up a fire escape with little sound. I tiptoed up the stairwell to my room but on opening the door I found Summerfield lying on my bed with cane in hand looking in my direction.

'Ah, Alexander, where the hell have you been?' he sneered.

'I had a stomach ache and have been to the bathroom.'

'What? For the last three hours, in your mufti and smelling of cigarettes and drink?'

'You have been lying here for three hours?' I replied.

I'd been caught and yet for some reason I was relieved and felt the shackles slowly break from my arms. Although late, we walked to the housemaster's door and Summerfield banged pathologically at the door. Five minutes later a sleepy Mr Webster appeared. He seemed worn out and looked as if he had been attending the party I had just left.

'Can't this wait till morning, Summerfield?' he asked.

'No, sir,' insisted Summerfield.

Mr Webster listened as the head of house pulled out notes describing the times he looked into my room and the times when I was nowhere to be seen. The conclusion was inevitable; I was to report to the headmaster the following morning after chapel.

'Can I go to bed now?' asked Mr Webster.

Summerfield smirked and I returned to my room knowing what was to happen the following morning.

It was a short meeting with the headmaster, straight to the point; there was no courtesy, no wasted chat. I was placed on a final warning.

'I am disappointed. After showing Mr Preston round the school and making a strong impact and therefore making a good impression, I had hopes that you would reach the very top here. From this point it will be more difficult.'

I left his office wounded but not dead. Summerfield had struck a near fatal blow but the truth was that the incident encapsulated where my head was at that time and there was a sense of relief that my school life was heading to the light at the end of the tunnel, hoping though that it was not an oncoming train.

The phone rang and rang and I hoped it would continue to ring forever.

'Hello?' my father's voice said resonantly down the phone. My confidence disappeared and I stuttered as I explained my meeting with the headmaster that morning. The disappointment drowned the phone line.

'What am I tell your mother?' I had an answer but I let it go.

'Young man, now from this point, don't you let our name down,' and the phone went chillingly dead. I replaced the receiver and looked to the sky. My father in his indisputable fashion had cut me in half and left my corpse to be circled by the vultures.

I walked away from the red phone box and headed towards Mr Baresi's to claim a cup of strong coffee. On my way I caught sight of Summerfield across the road. He turned towards my direction and flashed the devil's smile. I ignored the blaze and walked on to the echo of his sadistic laugh; I didn't have the strength to retaliate . . . for now.

*   *   *

187

Andrew Grafton was my first friend at school. He was the boy who put his arm around my shoulder and advised me not to react after I had been thrown out of my first lesson. He wasn't a gossip, he was someone with few words and few friends but I liked him and enjoyed spending my time in his dark company. He walked with a secret, heavily marked on his sleeve, that was impenetrable to all he encountered.

The younger of two boys, he had an elder brother Nicholas, who had been expelled for drinking the year before we arrived. The boys, and their lovely sister Sophie, had been brought up alone by his mother near Weybridge in Surrey. His father had cleared off when Grafton was seven; he was an alcoholic and regularly beat up his wife in so violent a way that 'once my Mum couldn't leave the house for a week as her face had been so brutally marked.' He must have been very young to witness such horror.

His mother adored her children and she came across as a strong, caring, beautiful woman who would do anything for her boys. It was his grandfather that had left a trust to pay for his education. His mother worked at the local hospital as a psychiatrist and passed her week paying for her children's lives; Grafton never went without.

Grafton was short with her, though, and bossed her around. Once when she walked into his room where we were listening to records, he turned round and snapped, 'Next time, knock on my fucking door.'

He had gradually withdrawn further inside himself over the previous two terms. I no longer spent as much time with him and during our Wednesday community service after-noons we no longer met for a clandestine cigarette in town.

After a term he hadn't returned to Mrs Wheeler and instead was asked to visit another old lady in the street by the railway station. He rarely ever bothered to visit the poor soul and often on those afternoons he would catch a tube into London and disappear; I wouldn't ask where he had been.

It must have been three o'clock when I was woken from a deep sleep by the sound of the fire alarm. My first thought was that there had been no warning of a practice and what a bore that it was happening now of all nights when all I wanted to do was disappear deep into my dreams and not deal with the reality of my school troubles, my final warning spinning around my head.

Warwick rushed into my room, 'This isn't a practice. Get up, you sod.'

The corridors were full of running teenagers not behaving in an orderly way, more like passengers on the Titanic running to their safety after the ship began to sink. Smoke had started to fill my side of the house and when we reached the house garden many of us were gasping for air. Looking back we could see smoke pouring out from one room in particular and a few flames licking the window frame. A fanfare of fire engines with bells ringing arrived at the scene. Ladders were drawn and hoses unrolled and connected to hydrants immediately and efforts directed to where the heart of the fire seemed to be. Gallons of water were pumped toward the floor that seemed most vulnerable.

Mr Webster huddled the boys together and called out our names and this time, unlike the previous occasion, we replied directly and vigorously.

'Where is Grafton?' Mr Webster asked calmly.

Grafton was nowhere to be seen and then panic set in. I ran towards the house instinctively, wanting to find my friend, but I was pulled back by a member of the fire brigade and four of them dashed past into the house in search of the missing boy.

189

I was still lying on the deep squelchy grass when Burford had come over and pulled me up and whispered. 'Don't worry, he'll be OK.'

The wait was interminable and whilst the heat and flames were settling there didn't seem to be any movement coming from the door where the fireman had disappeared. And then suddenly two firemen carried a sixteen-year-old boy with singed pyjamas and coughing his lungs out into the cool early morning fresh air. He was gasping for breath; it was Grafton and he was alive.

A huge well of noise grew and we broke into applause at the extraordinary sight that greeted our tired eyes. He was laid down and an oxygen mask was fixed to his face as two ambulance men brought out a stretcher. I walked towards him as he was being stretchered away and told him that everything would be all right. He did not react and we were left to mill in the garden for another hour before the fire was finally sealed.

Spit was already off having a fag by the tennis court, blowing smoke rings into the burnt air. I sat with him and as if reading aloud an obituary from the morning paper, he reviewed Grafton's life.

'I never liked him; he was a cold son of a bitch.'

'You're talking as if he's already dead.'

'As far as this school goes,' he said, 'I think you will find he already is.'

In all, three rooms had been damaged, two floors below from my study.

I asked Mr Webster whether I could go and visit Grafton in hospital.

His lungs had sucked in a huge amount of smoke and he remained in observation. 'No,' was the housemaster's curt reply and three days after the fire we were still unaware on the health of our friend. Rumours were awash and then when gossip had reached fever point, Mr Webster addressed the house.

'You will hear, or many will read in tomorrow morning's papers, that the fire in our house was started by Andrew Grafton. He has admitted his guilt and has been expelled. There will be press around the school and once again I will ask you not to comment on the story. When a boy sets light to his school the world wants to know about it.'

We were dismissed and with a sense of perplexity, I walked with Spit, Burford and Troubles to the fire escape. As we left the hall, I bumped into Summerfield and under his breath he muttered, 'Good riddance to burnt rubbish'.

I was moments from punching his stupid head with my willing fist, but I didn't as that would have been a lame way to be expelled. So once again I swallowed my anger and sped by.

'Don't run, you little shit,' he shouted.

We all discussed how removed Grafton had become and how he would sit alone with his dreams while the rest of us gossiped. He seemed introspective, withdrawn, and it was only now it was clear a Stygian cloud had been hovering above him. The loneliness of the institution had now been set and each of us in that room were dealing with it in our own way. There was no one in a position of authority that was able, or probably willing, to hear our cries. Our tanks were running on empty and on the road that lay ahead there was no sign of a gas station.

I stayed in the following Saturday which was probably the right decision as the prefects regularly burst in my room like the Gestapo to check on me. Even when I had finally fallen asleep, Summerfield opened my door and kicked over the wastepaper bin, snorted and made a hasty exit. I returned to my sleep to again to be awoken by a jab in my ribs; I turned around ready to slam the perpetrator.

'Hey, it's me.' It was Grafton looking seemingly fit. He had returned to the school that only a few days before he had tried to burn down.

'Come on, get dressed,' he said. 'Let's go into London.'

'Are you mad?' I replied; he shook his head. Here I had my friend escaping from his life outside, to the school that he once did everything to flee. How strange the maze of life can be.

'My Mum was understanding and probably a little disappointed but she hasn't told me so. She has been more disturbed by the continual hassle from the newspapers. They want to hear my side of the story.'

The story was predictably front-page news in the downmarket papers. Grafton's family were described in lurid, unpleasant detail. They had tracked down his absent father who after he had left the family was living in California as the manager of an English bar in Santa Monica. The *Daily Mail* had printed a photo of his father pulling a V sign at a group of reporters. He looked like an older version of Grafton and had the headline 'Was this the Problem?' printed above the grainy black-and-white image.

It was reported in the *Daily Mail* that no charges were being brought but did not give a reason.

'I think they didn't want the publicity to be extended into a court case. Anyway I would have ratted on how Dickensian this dump is. Not sure if the *Daily Mail* or *Express* reader would enjoy reading that the public school institution was fucked up; they might well have puked up their cornflakes.'

I listened intently as hate and delusion spat from his mouth.

He told me how he had piled all his books into the middle of the room and set them alight. The paper ignited immediately, followed by his bed and then everything else in sight. He had staggered into the corridor, nearly overcome straight away by smoke, and by then the alarm bell had been set off and boys were heading with panic to the exit. He remembered collapsing and then the next moment he was lying in the housemaster's garden looking at the dark sky.

'Were you that unhappy?' I asked.

He looked at me, paused, and said: 'Yes.'

I didn't join him on his idea of going into London and explained that security was heightened since the incident and it would be inevitable that I would be caught.

I wanted to ask if he had considered the danger he had placed everyone in, but it was clear that he was not yet ready to face up to the responsibility of his own life, let alone that of others. I hoped he would find the answer he was desperately seeking.

'There is something you should know, Sam. When I bunked off my community service visits I used to head into Soho and hang round a gay place there, and well, just talk to people; to men.'

'Why didn't you tell me, Andrew?' I said. 'I wouldn't have thought anything different of you or scorned you. You were the first friend I made here, and who cares what you are into?'

The school was indeed homophobic but mainly because many of its inmates were at it with their neighbours and felt a sense of shame for being involved.

I said my goodbye and Grafton shook my hand firmly in a very English manner and left my room, head held high, shoulders slumped. I would never ever see him again but I recall his sadness and deep sense of isolation; he was a desolate soul.

*   *   *

Wednesdays had become my favourite day of the week. Not only were the lessons easy and relaxed but also my afternoons were spent in the company of the warmth of Mrs Wheeler and my customary meeting with Lana.

That Wednesday the heat was suffocating. England was scorching and in front of our eyes it seemed as if the top of the grass was glowing. At morning assembly we were at last granted permission to remove our blue blazers and take off our ties, a sure sign that summer had truly arrived.

I had rung Lana that morning and we arranged as usual to meet at 'our' café after seeing Mrs Wheeler.

'I'll make it short, so I'll be with you earlier than usual.'

Everyone had a smile on their face that day. People were hurrying on with their lives and there was a spring in everyone's step. Oh, how different England would be if our temperature was warm and the sun was out. I noticed the cinema doors wide open, encouraging passers-by to enjoy the afternoon show but even with a hastily written placard stating 'WE HAVE AIR-CONDITIONING', the foyer was eerily quiet.

I passed the fishmonger's and Mr Weeks there, who regularly supplied Mrs Wheeler's kippers, gave a heart-felt hello.

'See you later, I expect,' he said and I walked on looking forward to spending the whole afternoon with this warm and happy feeling glowing inside. I reached Mrs Wheeler's a little earlier than usual and knocked on her door with the rhythm of 'we shall not be moved'.

There was no answer and so I knocked again with the same enthusiasm and anticipation. Again there was no answer and so I took a few paces back from the door and hands cupped around my mouth I shouted out, 'Mrs Wheeler, Mrs Wheeler,' but everything remained tranquil, not a sound, no cars passing by, just the stillness of a summer's afternoon on a terrace street in a suburban town. The silence was broken by an elderly neighbour with a walking stick who came out from his door.

'You won't be finding her, she was taken off to hospital this morning and it looked pretty serious if you ask me.'

I was stunned. 'Where would she have gone to?'

'They would have taken her to St Thomas's; everyone ends up there,' he said cheerily. He pointed to the main road and without a thought I rushed off to the hospital, without stopping, three miles from where I was standing.

Originally a military hospital, its purpose was to train army nurses and doctors and to treat military patients to ensure their swift return to duty. It was a magnificent building and echoed of times gone by when our hospitals were built with grandeur and as a statement of the might of the Empire. This didn't help me find the main entrance though, and I wasted minutes looking for a member of staff to direct me in the right direction.

Mrs Wheeler had had a severe stroke and lay critically ill in a public ward surrounded by nurses and connected with tubes.

'Are you her grandson?' a kind-looking nurse asked me.

'No, but I have helped to look after her and she is a friend, a dear friend.'

The nurse left me at her bedside and I gazed down.

Mrs Wheeler seemed so helpless when only a week before she was robust and full of life. Now I heard her breath weakening and she had a look that was glazed and not focused; her life was diminishing quickly in front of my eyes.

I held her weak hand and she managed to smile. The nurse offered to call the school and inform them where I was and that I wanted to stay to care.

I made a call to Lana's house from a phone just outside the ward but she had yet to return from our prospective meeting in the café. I left a message with her mother about what had happened and apologised for not being there.

My voice was shaky but my resolve was strong. I returned to the bedside and spoke to my dear friend although she clearly was drifting away; I thought that she heard my words though.

The nurse brought me a cup of tea and regularly checked her heart and watched the monitors. And then without warning, Mrs Wheeler took a deep breath and blew harshly into the air; it was her last act on earth. Her head turned and I knew that she had died. I calmly called for the nurse and a doctor came running to her side.

There was nothing more to do. I walked away unflustered and out of the ward. Waiting as I pushed open the swing doors was Lana. She looked at me and did not have to ask the question. She put her arms around my shoulders and held on and gave me the warmth that at that moment I so desperately needed.

I was unsure what to do next but a nurse explained that Mrs Wheeler had a sister who was on her way from Dorset and that she would take the responsibility of dealing with the funeral and the other aspects of her completed life.

'You don't have to worry, young man, everything will be dealt with,' and with those words it seemed as if I was dismissed. I walked out of the hospital with Lana and although it was now nine o'clock at night, it was still bright and the heat of the day still lingered.

*   *   *

I was passing Mr Rose after morning lessons when he turned and said, 'I'm sorry, Alexander, I understand that the lady you'd been visiting died yesterday and you were there to witness the whole sorry event.'

I had my hands in my pockets and I was staring at the pavement. The funeral was to be on the Friday at 11 and I would be excused from lessons so that I could attend, if I so wanted.

Although the weather had been near to perfect that past week, on that particular Friday the rain was heavy. By the time I reached the crematorium my umbrella had blown inside out and with no raincoat I was soaked through. A small gaggle of friends were waiting outside a plain-looking brown brick building, talking amongst each other about how bad the weather was accompanied by the rain fizzling in the trees.

I went to the bathroom and tried to dry myself up; I had a comb in my pocket and straightened out my hair and looked reasonably respectful.

The rain had now ceased and I stood alone waiting for the whole process to begin. A small, frail figure approached and introduced herself as Mrs Wheeler's sister.

'I want to thank you for being here and also want to thank you for being with Ethel on her final night.' I shook her hand and realised that it was the first time that I had actually heard what Mrs Wheeler's Christian name was.

I felt embarrassed as others amongst the congregation came over to shake my hand and once again when I turned to seek some support, I saw Lana walking towards me in a sober black jacket, white shirt and tight skirt. This was not the time to feel aroused but all I wanted to do was take her.

She held my hand and I held hers tightly, whispering that I was thankful and thrilled to see her. As we walked into the grey uninviting chapel and found our seats out of the way, a gentleman I did not know approached and asked whether I would read a lesson; I looked at Lana and she smiled and nodded as a form of encouragement and so I accepted and was given a Bible. I was asked to read Ecclesiastes, chapter 3, verses 1 to 8:

To every thing there is a season, and a time to every purpose under the heaven: a time to be born, and a time to die; a time to plant, and a time to pluck up that which is planted; a time to kill, and a time to heal; a time to break down, and a time to build up; a time to weep, and a time to laugh; a time to mourn, and a time to dance; a time to cast away stones, and a time to gather stones together; a time to embrace, and a time to refrain from embracing; a time to get, and a time to lose; a time to keep, and a time to cast away; a time to rend, and a time to sew; a time to keep silence, and a time to speak; a time to love, and a time to hate; a time of war, and a time of peace.

There were few gathered, in fact they were precisely ten. The coffin lay plainly in front and I was angry that I had not thought to order a wreath of flowers to place gently on top. I stood and read my lesson confidently and precisely. As I left the platform, Beethoven's Fifth Symphony was piped through the speakers to fill the empty space.

'It was her favourite piece of music,' her sister whispered.

And then we stood and my eyes were transfixed as a button was pushed from back stage and the coffin moved towards an exit directly in front. I had only seen this happen once before, in *Diamonds are Forever*, and with Beethoven's most famous distinctive four-note opening I got the most uncontrollable giggles through deep grief and could not stop myself from buckling over. Lana jabbed me in an attempt to snap me out of it, but it was no use and I made a dash out of the chapel into the fresh air. I caught my breath and sobered up as my fellow mourners finally joined. Each of them was no younger than seventy, and they shook my hand and reassured me that Mrs Wheeler would never be far away.

'I'm sorry; I don't know what got into me.'

Lana looked at me with her bright green eyes. 'Don't worry, I think they all thought you were overcome.'

I looked to the heavens and apologised to Mrs Wheeler for my behaviour and then said my goodbyes and walked away from that black, uninspiring place.

I turned to Lana. 'Let's make love.'

*   *   *

Four feet high, every letter in thick white paint on each side of the main building. 'MUNRO IS A WANKER', 'STASH YOUR DASH', 'DON'T WALK AWAY . . . FUCKING RUN'. Not the most intellectual group of phrases, but the ramifications rocked the foundation of the old place.

I had a sense that something was different. There was an eerie silence, a slow pace on foot from most of the boys mixed with stifled laughter.

'Have you seen what's happened?' asked Burford. I shook my head and he pointed at one of the daubings. It had been painted near a statue of Queen Elizabeth I and what I immediately noticed was how aesthetically pleasing and how well proportioned and balanced the letters had been painted; strange but true.

Mr Cripps, the odd-job man, who walked around every day come rain or shine wearing a workman's brown coat, was carrying a ladder with a bucket. His assistant Jock, a new signing to the school, was helping and had a squeezy bottle of Fairy Liquid or something of that sort in his hands. Jock had a face that looked it had been pushed in by a heavy punch. His eyes were always glazed and if you said hello he just grunted. I was not sure if he had a brain. We watched as Cripps climbed the ladder and Jock held the bucket and the scrubbing started to remove the evidence that tarnished the old building. I smiled at the comical inefficiency of the two, who looked more like Morecambe and Wise than anything else, as I walked in good time for my lesson. O level examinations were only weeks away and I had a great deal of work to do to achieve the grades that were expected of me.

In all fairness I had changed gear over the last few months and my concentration was far more considered in class. I was pleased with the way things were progressing. Even with my outside school proclivities, I was confident that, come the results in the summer holidays, I would be looking smugly at a reservoir of A grades.

As I walked into class, everyone was talking about what had been written.

'What does "Stash the Dash" mean, Alexander?'

I didn't know why von Nadelheim thought I should know, but I answered him.

'Hide the dope, silly,' I guessed.

'Oh, I see.'

'Of course he knows,' said Khazandar. 'He was the one who did it.'

The whole form in unison looked round and started to stare. I shook my head and told them they had the wrong guy but I could feel the animosity and it surprised me how protective they were towards the school. Mr Yates strolled in whistling 'Penny Lane' and our lesson on the population density of the United States began.

I spent the following forty minutes carving 'Stash the Dash' into my wooden desk and as the lesson drew to a close I was busy sculpting the last 'h'.

'What is the population of Los Angeles, Alexander?'

asked Gripper Yates. His side-burns now virtually reached his mouth. I had no idea, I was so concentrating on my handiwork that I had drifted into another stratosphere. He walked up and looked at the desk and the pair of compasses held in my hand. I had been caught causing school damage.

'I suppose you are proud of yourself?'

'About what, sir?'

'About this.'

He was pointing at my three words now recorded on my desk for posterity. He ordered me to come back to his class that afternoon.

By the time I had returned to the house for lunch, Mr Cripps was still hard at work scrubbing the painted letters away, but he looked as if he was having little success as the paint had dried deeply into the old limestone walls.

I sat at lunch and Troubles drew on the atmosphere that had engulfed his class.

'They all think our little group were the ones that did it.'

I concurred that my form thought the same and it hadn't helped that I had been caught writing some of the very same words on to my desk.

'I am bound to be placed in a long detention,' I lamented.

Mr Yates was waiting with hands behind his head, and legs stretched out on his desk. He was angry and called me a fool. In his hand he had a sander, a square, and a plane to smooth down the wood.

'I wanted to send you to the headmaster for such an irresponsible act, but I know you are on a final warning so I have decided to deal with this myself. Go to the desk with these tools, smooth it down and make it look as good as new. And don't ever cause damage like that again.'

*   *   *

I was grateful for his balanced perspective on my ill-conceived behaviour; he had spared me a lengthy punishment but at the time I did not thank him.

My skill at carpentry was deplorable; at prep school it had taken twelve weeks to prepare a small wooden box which in fact I never finished as each time I banged in a nail, the wood would split and I would have to start over again. Even when I tried to varnish the finished product, finally completed by the woodwork master, it was as smooth as the Lake District, as the splodges of lacquer made each side unbearably uneven.

The fairness of the punishment encouraged me to go about trying to do the best job possible, planing the desk over and over again until all signs of my morning's work had disappeared. Gripper returned to inspect and clearly not particularly enamoured by my work, he dismissed me.

'Hey, Alexander,' he called as I was walking out of his classroom. 'You have white paint on your jacket.'

I looked around panic-stricken.

'Just kidding,' he said with a hearty laugh and placed his Sherlock Holmes pipe into his mouth. Ever since that afternoon I have always had a penchant for pipe smokers; it makes me think that whoever is smoking the strange contraption is a fair and decent man.

*   *   *

As I walked along the street, past the library and Mr Cripps still working hard with his removal devices, I was seized upon by six members of the rugby 1st XV. I was pulled away from the main thoroughfare to a place not far from where the house photograph had been taken weeks before. And there these strong over-blown rugger thugs purposefully laid into me, punching and kicking me to the ground with such vicious ferocity that I felt the boots go deep into my body striking my kidneys and blood spurted from my forehead making my face seem like a Jackson Pollock painting. One after the other they took their turn, adding verbal insults whilst I just froze in fear and shock, taking the sadistic and relentless punishment. I was drifting in and out of consciousness and I am sure I even called out for my mother.

Welland, the prop forward, grabbed hold of my collar twisted it and hissed words into my face.

'Don't you ever deface our school like that again. If you do . . . next time you will be dead.' And then with a final kick in my balls, they walked away.

In the weeks that followed I thought of brilliant retorts, but at that moment nothing came out of my mouth except for a few drops of blood. I lay there for a seemingly endless five minutes and then carefully and painfully picked myself up and made my way back to the house.

As I was slowly climbing the stairs I bumped into matron who looked at me with incredulous care. I placed my arm around her and she supported my devastated body to her quarters. She sat me down and asked to have a good look at the wounds. I removed my jacket deliberately and threw my ripped shirt to the ground and there we could see the bruising and hate that I had encountered.

She reached for some dressing and patted my skin with this cold liquid that soothed the pain and eased my mind. As she was doing it, she tutted and purred and conveyed tremendous care that I was comfortable and warm. I found her unbearably ravishing and although I was experiencing as great a pain as I had ever done I still couldn't resist fantasising about having sex with this beautiful ample-bosomed woman. I grew excited and she could see that I was hard and that I was longing for her. She slowly stripped away her top and unbuttoned her skirt; she wore no lingerie and the sight of her naked body bore proof that God was the creator and the leader of mankind; what a time to become a believer. Matron took my hand and placed it between her legs. She was wet and I fell to my knees and started to kiss her. She tasted so pure, so rich; she moaned but probably not half as much as I did. She whispered, 'I want you inside me,' and I then heard an insistent voice loudly penetrating my ear drum.

'Samuel, Samuel, wake up, you're making the most awful noise. Are you in such terrible pain?'

Whilst matron was pouring oil over my wounds, I had crashed out.

'You poor thing, it sounded as if you were having a nightmare.'

She then made a call to the housemaster and excused me from roll call. 'I'll have dinner sent up here and you can take it easy and we can watch a film on the television.'

'Thank you, matron,' still shocked from my beating and my erotic dream.

The sight of fish fingers, baked beans and a splash of cabbage did not particularly excite my stomach but matron carrying it on a tray certainly excited my groin. I was now in a great deal of pain and was suffering. The initial shock was wearing off and I realised I had taken quite a beating. Matron placed the tray gently on my knees and sat opposite asking what the hell had just happened.

'They thought I painted the graffiti and without trial, I was found guilty and punished.'

'And did you, Samuel?'

I sighed, 'No, matron; it wasn't me.'

She spoke little of her life and I suppose I found it appealing that her secrets remained hidden. She was undoubtedly seductive but I always noticed a hint of sadness flash across her face and this made her even more desirable.

'You can stay with me and miss your prep, if you like?'

'If I like?' I was choking with excitement, 'Yes please, matron.'

I was taking on the role of the vulnerable and I think it was working.

She leant over and switched on her television set whilst I stared and salivated at her deep cleavage, pretending that I was looking at a dull picture hanging behind. She caught my eyes lowering.

'What a lovely picture, matron.'

She had this habit that when I said something inane, she would simply ignore it and carry on with what she was doing.

'Now starting on BBC2 is *Brief Encounter*, starring Trevor Howard and Celia Johnson,' stated the very English announcer. A puff of smoke covered the screen and the film began.

'You are going to love this; it is impossibly romantic,' squealed my matron. And so we sat watching this doomed, unbearable love affair. I started to well up virtually from the first frame and then began to really cry. Matron, who must have seen it countless times, was drenched with tears and grabbing for the Kleenex throughout the romantic, tortuous drama. I thought of Lana and how our young love affair with clandestine meetings was controlled by my restrictions at school. I thought of matron sitting close, her breath occasionally touching my face, much older and insufferably untouchable.

As Trevor Howard placed his hand gently on Celia Johnson's shoulder for the last time, I assumed I would die.

'You are a sensitive soul, Samuel,' and my matron held my hand for an instant and then as if checking herself suddenly moved away.

As the end titles rolled across the screen, matron stood

up and looked at her watch, straightened her dress and said that it was time for bed. I was about to ask which bed, but I resisted.

'You seem somewhat better now, Samuel. Sleep well.'

'Thank you, matron. I suppose I'd like to be duffed up every day, just so I can spend the evening with you.' I then kissed her gently on her cheek and returned to my study still in pain.

*   *   *

It was that perfect English summer's day. The sun had burst through my window and its heat had roused my tired body. It was only half-past six in the morning and immediately I grabbed my books and started to revise for the exams that were now only two days away.

My friends had been banned from my room and our smoking and gossiping ritual had been transferred back to Dunsmore Wood, which had now changed in the years from the occasional few having a puff to dozens. My bruises had begun to retreat and heal but the ache remained vital inside.

I had arranged for Lana to visit and spend the afternoon watching the 1st XI at cricket. The Saturday lessons were consumed with more revision and as I walked to class I saw the white marks were still on the wall. Mr Cripps continued for days trying in vain to clear the evidence.

'Haven't given up then, Cripps?' I jested.

He didn't see the joke and by now nor did I. 'It will come off, if it's the last thing I bloody do.'

Lana arrived carrying a picnic basket and blanket and we sat under the large oak tree. A slight wind blew through the air and kept us cool from the heat that was increasing with each hour. She was wearing a white T-shirt and a short blue skirt which would flutter with the wind and reveal her legs; they had been kissed by the sun and she had a gentle tan.

Montgomery won the toss against their opponents from a public school in Oxford and chose to bat. They took full advantage of a docile pitch and were soon smashing the ball to the boundary as if it were only a tennis ball.

My files and books were scattered over the tartan rug whilst we stole occasional kisses. Montgomery continued their onslaught, and although I had countless distractions, I was revising and making an inroad into the library of facts especially in Classics and History.

'And what do you think you are doing?' Warwick asked strutting along the boundary with his evil comrade Summerfield.

'Revising and enjoying the cricket with my girlfriend.'

'How sad she must be to have a boyfriend such as you,' Warwick insulted as Summerfield smirked.

I rose to my feet but Lana also stood up and pushed me to one side. 'What a revolting and disgusting creature you are,' she cursed just inches from Warwick's face. 'And you,' looking directly at Summerfield, 'are particularly repulsive.'

'And you, my dear, are a common little tart,' sneered my head of house.

I went to hit him, for after countless terms, long weeks, slow nights I had had enough and I prepared to smash my knuckle into his ugly face. But Lana didn't allow the revenge to happen. She pulled back my body and told me to let it go, 'Don't react, they're not worth it.' And the two laughed and walked on.

'They are trying to get you fired from the school,' Lana spoke with concern.

'You mean expelled.'

'Whatever I am trying to say and I'm sorry I can't find the right word, but don't let them, they're just wankers . . .

You poor boy, having to share your life with people like that.' And she stroked my cheek with the warmth of her hand.

I shrugged my shoulders and realised that this continual bantering and bullying had created a numbness to my surroundings. There was a part that was sensitive to my life, to my ambition, to my friendships, but there was another side which had become permanently and incurably cold, disengaged and detached.

Montgomery had amassed a huge score and by the time the Oxford side had lost two early wickets, the game was as good as over. Spit had come over and apologised to Lana for his robust behaviour at the party. He sat with us for a few minutes talking about nothing and then a little more about nothing. I remember seeing Lana smile with the afternoon sun setting and the sound of cricket as its backdrop with the smell of newly cut grass. It made another of those perfect moments that you want to wrap and cherish forever.

We had intended to visit Mr Baresi but time had drifted and roll call wasn't far off. After our confrontation earlier in the afternoon, I was not ready to risk being late. We walked towards the house, neither of us wanting our time together to end. As we passed the art school, I pointed to where the painting had been hidden.

Lana then took my hand and we walked inside the building which was still and empty. As we spoke the vastness of the corridor created echoes and for no obvious reason we told each other to keep quiet. We walked into the main studio that was cut in half by a long worn wooden table. Either side there were oak easels with a multitude of brushes crammed in to mugs by their side. Unfinished canvases stood upright; a few good, others truly terrible. I caught sight of an unsigned sketch of nudes and wondered who had been given the talent. We walked hand in hand viewing the work as if we were in a West End gallery. The fresh smell of paint drenched the room and I felt high on it.

Then Lana led me out into the corridor and we started to explore the maze of rooms. I so wanted her that moment, her skin peach-like, ready to be kissed and ravaged. At the end of the hallway, there was a store room which was filled with canvases and sheets of paper of finished work. We started to kiss each other passionately and I spoke as I took off my shirt.

'I love you, I love you, you are my first love and I will love you forever.'

She was naked and as she touched my body I craved not just for sex but a deep intrinsic longing for someone to love. I pushed her towards the shelves and some of the paintings crashed to the ground. I kissed her deeply and in an instant I was inside her and felt as one with another soul for the first time. I kissed her large breasts and she gasped and her noise shuddered and made my whole body convulse. I reached an excitement that brought wonder to my world. I came inside her and rested my head on her chest as she clawed my back.

There was no detachment, just a sense of time standing still and never wanting it to move. For at that moment, I truly loved another soul. We walked back to the house and reached it just in time for roll call.

'I'll call you tomorrow, I promise.' I touched her neck. Nothing more was said and I walked into the hall at peace as I had never been before.

* * *

We sauntered into the room as if it were a funeral parlour. I sat in the third row and waited patiently for our examiner to appear. At ten to nine he ordered us to be quiet, chalked on the blackboard the exam we were taking, which I felt was strange as we had been given our exam timetable weeks before, and then he handed out our crisp papers face down. With the tension mounting we looked up at the loud ticking clock and at the stroke of nine o'clock with a deep breath Mr Rose said, 'And begin'.

Maths was not my favourite subject; perhaps the one that I dreaded most of all. It was a bit like being drawn away to the hard men of Leeds United in the third round of the FA Cup. But lo and behold, the exam was relatively straightforward and a win was on the cards.

About halfway through I noticed Butcher and Snedden passing notes furtively to each other. I couldn't believe my eyes and immediately felt the risk that they were taking. Mr Rose would take the occasional walk around the desks, slow and with assurance. It was posturing rather than anything else and after he took his short exercise, he would return to his desk humming quietly to himself, pen in mouth, resuming his *Times* crossword.

The exchange of notes continued and I started to be distracted and in a strange way protective of their daring ill-conceived exploit. Each time that Mr Rose looked up from his paper and scanned the room I coughed loudly as if I were warning the perpetrators of a crime.

At eleven o'clock we were ordered to stop writing and hand in our papers.

'I told you to stop writing, Dugdale,' shouted Mr Rose. Exam fever had clearly caught him as he was generally a softly spoken man. Poor Dugdale looked shot to pieces - clearly the last two hours had not gone well.

Between each examination, I would meet Burford and Troubles in Dunsmore Wood to chew over what had gone before and to have a puff on a cigarette. I felt sorry for Spit, who being a year younger still had another twelve months to wait until he took his exams. 'How fucking old are you?' asked Burford.

'I'm fifteen,' replied a less-than-confident Spit.

'Fuck, we have been hanging out with a child.'

Burford was playing the role of superior although he was only sixteen months older. But it is something that never leaves you. When you are more senior at school to some, you can still act that way towards them for many years.

And so the exams continued for three days, each following the other without any distraction and I had firmly secured the witnessing of the two cheats away in a locked box. That was at least until the headmaster called me to his office on the Friday of that week.

'Did you at any time see anything untoward happening during your Mathematics examination on Monday?' the headmaster asked. It is strange how pompous masters become when dealing with breaking of the school rules.

'No sir, I was too busy dealing with exponent and logarithm as functions of power,' I replied.

'Don't be clever with me, young man.'

I shrugged my shoulders, not believing that I was in trouble for just being in the same room as a couple of idiots.

'I don't want this to go further but it seems that two boys have been cheating and they were sitting directly in front of you.'

'What, Ash and Lonsdale, sir?' I purposely named two boys who'd been sitting behind.

He dismissed me and shook his head. 'Get out, boy, you are a waste of time.'

Not a particularly good few minutes with the man who could decide my future at the school. I could sense that he wanted me out of the school and my tight rope had just become a little more fragile. But I was no snitch, no squeal, no stool pigeon and however stupid I thought those two had been, they weren't going to have my finger pointing at them.

It was later that day, the housemaster made the executioner's walk to the Hall. Butcher, who boarded in Crescent House, had left earlier in the day. I could see no sign of Snedden; he had packed his possessions an hour before too and had last been spotted, bag in hand, climbing into a Land Rover that had driven away from the school grounds. His father, another old boy, took the news badly. He was a racehorse owner and although the Derby was upon us and he had a horse running, he decided to avoid Epsom after the news of his son's disgrace hit the newspapers. In the eyes of the public school hierarchy and society, 'cheating' rates near the top of scandalous reasons for being expelled; perhaps just behind murder, stealing or homosexuality.

'Today two boys have been expelled for cheating.' The housemaster spoke with clarity. 'It was with great discredit that they resorted to this behaviour. Even if they had achieved an A grade, their victory would have been hollow. You will not be seeing Snedden or Butcher again on these school grounds; shame on him. Enjoy your long weekend and I will see you on Monday morning. I remind you that the opening of the new Main Hall by a member of the Royal Family will be in three weeks. Please make sure that your parents have replied to the invitation.'

*　　*　　*

It was a weekend exeat and I took the usual train back to my home in Oxfordshire and was met at the station by my mother, looking a little tired but with a smile on her face. 'Aunt Flo is staying with us for the time being. Poor love, she is under the weather, so go easy on her, Samuel.'

'Of course I will, Mum; and don't forget Lana is coming down for lunch on Sunday,' I replied.

'How could I possibly forget that, my dear boy?'

I had made the momentous decision to invite my girlfriend to meet my parents and although I was longing to spend the day with her, I was full of dread of what my father's mood might be. This was going to be the first time that an introduction such as this had happened.

Poor Aunt Flo had been totally disabled by her broken foot and my mother ran around answering her every call.

'Bloody woman; she's working your poor mother off her feet,' railed my father, projecting his own behaviour. It was the first time that I had seen him since I had been given my final warning and he didn't once that weekend bring it up in conversation. He seemed distracted, probably with a business deal, but happy, as he had received earlier that day a letter from Tom full of optimism and probably full of lies.

'Your brother seems to be having the time of his life and he speaks highly of his girlfriend. Tell me, what's she like?'

I spoke of Suzy with the highest praise and he seemed to enjoy hearing about her. It was evident that every time Tom's name was in a conversation, he took on a totally different demeanour. His voice was light, his movement was gentle.

'You are going to meet my girlfriend on Sunday, father.'

'So I hear, I hope I'll like her.'

'You will. She's glorious.'

And with that I went to my room, closed the door and started to read my old football annuals.

* * *

It was Sunday and I waited at the station with the peculiarly intense British heat. The train was on time and as

213

Lana walked towards me along the platform, her beauty helped banish all the trepidation that had engulfed my weekend. Harold, of course, was welcoming and courteous and I sat in the back of the car hardly saying a word whilst Lana and he talked of the beauty of the countryside.

I felt my father always wanted to distance himself from his working-class background and the fact that Lana was a local girl had played with my mind for days. I prayed that he was not going to be either rude or embarrassing and on the journey to the house, although Lana would turn and look at my face to seek reassurance for her forthcoming meeting, I was so tense I could hardly raise a smile. And yet in truth I had little to worry about.

On stepping out on to the drive, my father was waiting by the front door and immediately gave a warm greeting. 'Welcome, welcome, you are indeed most welcome.' It was clear from the off that my father took a gleaming shine to Lana; the apple hadn't fallen far from the tree. He totally took over and taking her hand led her into the house and introduced my aunt and, to my surprise, my cousin Rupert who seemed to have appeared from nowhere. Rupert was Aunt Flo's only child conceived on her wedding night and was a photographer by trade, who took photographs not of models but of still lifes.

Lunch was full of conversation mainly dominated by Rupert himself. In his extremely posh tone he recalled an adventure.

'I was leaving by train from Oxford to London to have a meeting with Selfridges the other day. We were to discuss a project of taking photographs of umbrellas for their winter catalogue. So my mind was full of concepts and consumed with ideas. As we arrived into Paddington I unwittingly picked up the umbrella belonging to the man opposite.

' "Hey, what are you doing?", he asked.

'I apologised profusely and handed back his brolly. I then had the meeting with Selfridges and got the job, and as I left they handed me thirty umbrellas of different colours to take back to my studio to photograph. I got back on to the train, sat down, placed my thirty umbrellas at my side and then noticed sitting opposite was the exact same person whom I had sat opposite earlier that morning.

'He looked at me, glanced at my thirty umbrellas, and said, "Had a good day then?" '

The whole table fell into laughter with my father leading the plaudits. 'You're so witty, Rupert.'

'I think he's a pompous, boring old fart,' I thought to myself. I helped Harold carry the plates out to the kitchen where Mum was helping Violet with the apple crumble.

'I think she's lovely, Samuel,' Mum beamed.

'I do too and I think so does Dad?' I asked, still not sure.

'I told you he would be all right. I think you are very hard on your father.'

And she was not wrong; I enjoyed seeing my father be kind that afternoon, laughing and hosting Lana with charm and generosity; it gave enormous pleasure. I just didn't think my father liked me very much.

'And he got his ear pierced, would you believe it?' Aunt Flo was gossiping with Rupert.

'Oh God, how disgustingly vulgar,' my cousin responded.

I had walked in and overheard the two sharing the family news. As I sat on the sofa opposite, the conversation dried. We smiled at each other and there was silence until Rupert fractured it.

'Terribly D, that girlfriend of yours.'

' "Terribly D", Rupert? What does that mean?'

'Terribly "decent", silly,' he snorted, 'but of course not really one of us.'

'Of course,' I replied through gritted teeth. I was not going to enter into that class arena as it would have undoubtedly turned nasty.

Poor Rupert, henpecked by his mother, was pompous and lost but talented and good at his job. He admitted once at a particularly vulnerable moment that all he wanted to do was be a photo-journalist in war-torn areas but his mother wouldn't even consider it. When I suggested that he was over eighteen and could do what he liked, he hunched his shoulders and went quiet.

I walked Lana through our garden and spoke of childhood memories. How my father had collapsed on the tennis court and, thinking he was dying, I had run terrified to the neighbour for help. No one was in our house at the time as my mother was with my brother in the village; I was only six and petrified. In the end, after being 'flat out', he was up and serving by lunchtime. It was heat exhaustion and he was simply dehydrated. Lana listened and occasionally kissed my cheek as a sign of affection and reassurance.

The weather was glorious that day and before returning to school, we all had tea outside. Aunt Flo spoke about her foot and Rupert tittle-tattled about London society. Dad continued to entertain Lana, whilst my mother was working hard to make tea a success, although she had Violet helping.

I gave Lana a glance. It was the right moment to escape to my bedroom; I had wanted to grab her since she arrived. So I got up, and Lana followed.

'No sex in my house,' shouted my father as we were disappearing.

'Thanks, Dad,' I replied and we heard loud laughter drifting from the garden and following us up the stairs.

'They are lovely, your parents,' said Lana.

'Yes they are, aren't they?' I replied avoiding conversation, trying at the same time to hurriedly take off her shirt. We kissed quickly and fiercely and we fell on to the bed, hands clasped round each other. Here I was in the room where I grew up, the room where I had heard my mother read bedtime stories, where I'd played table football, listened to my records, and now I was making love to my beautiful girlfriend on the blue blanket that had warmed my body from my earliest memory. Strange, but much of that was dancing through my mind at the time. We were making the most frightful noise which was only broken by my father yelling from downstairs.

'Samuel. Time to go back to school.'

We finished seconds later and scrambled ourselves down the two flights. My father was waiting at the foot of the stairs.

'Your bag, young man?' One of his eyebrows was askew and I returned to my room to fetch my uniform and wash bag. It seemed different now, the innocence of youth seemed to have been rubbed away and I spoke out loud as I was closing my door: 'See you soon.'

My mother drove us back. Aunt Flo gave her usual 'Don't be a naughty boy' routine as I climbed into the car and I threw a wave goodbye to my father and cousin Rupert. As the car left the drive, I had this urge for the car to turn back, my stomach sank and I was consumed with a foreboding; I dismissed it as 'returning to boarding school blues' and spent the journey in the back of the car transfixed by the moving traffic whilst Lana, her essence still in my mouth, sat up front with Mum making spasmodic but polite conversation.

* * *

Burford was sitting in my chair looking out of the window taking a heavy draw on a Camel cigarette. He looked miserable and his heart was breaking.

'You look terrible,' I said.

'I feel like shit. Zara has had enough and has dumped me,' Burford replied.

'Out of where?'

'Out of her life.'

He then explained that since she lost the baby and since the story broke in the papers, things had not been the same. 'Heck, we *are* young and I suppose we were too young to cope,' he moaned.

I apologised for being distant and that I had been unable to hear his troubles.

'No, I've been the prick. I regret not being there after you returned from New York. You clearly needed a friend and I let you down. I promise it'll never happen again.' We hugged and then Troubles and Spit barged in and interrupted our moment of bonding. I spoke of Lana and how well the visit had been.

'It was amazing, my father was very civil and he was even pretty nice to me.'

'And did he break your balls about the final warning?' asked Troubles.

I shook my head. 'No, strangely he never brought it up. Mind you, he never asked how my exams went either.'

We all took our turns puffing up the chimney and blowing smoke out of the window and then made our way down to roll call.

There were two letters waiting on the sideboard, both with US Mail stamps. One was from Chiara and the other had my brother's address with the name Suzy Somerville on the back. I didn't read them immediately and instead placed them in my back pocket to pore over later in the evening.

The mood in the hall was light. First we had just returned from an exeat so most of us were high from the freedom, and secondly we were on the home straight for the summer holidays that were now a mere two and a half weeks away.

*   *   *

'You won't make the end of term – and get your hair cut,' was Summerfield's warm welcome message. I ignored his threat but there was no question that I was reaching the zenith of our battle. He was leaving at the end of term, and I had promised myself that one way or another he was to pay for all the suffering he had heaped on me since my arrival.

The housemaster spoke of the success of the term except for the few notable exceptions. I felt eyes piercing my back but I remained firmly upright. He explained that bringing the school together within this central building would transform the rhythm of the school. Never before had the houses been able to communicate in the way that would emerge in two weeks' time. Money had been raised by generous donations from the parents and the school planned to celebrate it with vigour and respect. It sounded as if he was running for the office of Prime Minister and whilst he was pontificating, Troubles gave me that look. I gave one to Burford and Spit caught my eye. We were all in agreement this was something we could have fun with.

*   *   *

The Film Society once a term gave a special screening to the whole school. We all gathered in the Speech Room and watched what tended to be a highly commercial movie that did not tax the brain or encourage debate afterwards. This term was different. They showed the public school film *If....* from 1968 directed by Lindsay Anderson an ex-public schoolboy himself, and starring Malcolm McDowell as the anti-hero of the piece, Mick Travis. And from the very

219

moment the new boys were ordered by a prefect to 'Run! Run in the corridor!' I was gripped.

I suppose seeing the gang of outsiders waging their own war against the system made me feel that I was not different. That it was all right to be angry and to be in search for another world. Ever since the 1st XV had laid into my body with their fists and boots, I had felt even more isolated. The film resembled my struggle and Travis's insolence and struggle with the gradation of order gave a clarity that the system depicted in the film had not changed. I felt both liberated and angry after seeing the film. What was odd was the film depicts a revolution and yet the school decided to show it as their special screening. How English! The way that the hierarchy, in order to diminish the impact of the piece, welcomes the sign of insurrection and pretends that it belongs to them. Back in my room with these thoughts and emotions still swirling, I opened the letters from New York.

First came Chiara's, who spoke of New York becoming her friend and how modelling was only good because it paid the bills. She said that she missed me and knew that my brother did too. 'Come back, darling, there is a big party awaiting you,' she wrote. I was consumed with Lana at the time and however ravishing, sexy, passionate or intoxicating this Italian beauty was, my head was firmly turned in a different direction.

And then I opened Suzy's letter:

Darling Samuel – We miss you and we talk about you every day. How you put magic back into our lives, with your wisdom and your love.

I questioned whether I should mention this but you should know. Tom had another setback the other day and we went through the same process over again. He

220

collapsed at work where he had scored some drugs from another waiter. It sounded as if it were dramatic as he fell behind the bar and glasses cascaded over his body. Anyway, Mr Miles the owner called 911 immediately and they saved him.

He is truly remorseful and he is of course very vulnerable and very weak. I love him so dearly and pray that he is going to get well. He has started to attend NA meetings again and I have gone with him a few times to that one we first went to on Fourth and Bleecker. He is determined and has promised never to return to the drug and I believe him. I have also promised that if he does I will leave him forever, as I can't go on like this any more. Believe me that was tough but if it helps him rid himself of this darkness, I am glad to make this threat.

I thought you should know all this. Give him a call if you can. We hope to visit your parents in August so we will meet each other again.

Love, Suzy x

I collapsed to my knees and sobbed like an abandoned child. The torment, the suffering I felt that moment and sense of helplessness just overwhelmed me.

I placed the letters together in a file resting on my desk and then placed it carefully in my trunk and went in search of my friends. I found Troubles lying on his bed throwing darts at a poster of the movie *Rollerball*, the scene we had just seen in *If....*

'Fed up?' I asked.

'Bored and fed up,' he replied.

'Get the others,' I ordered, 'I'll see you in my room in ten minutes.'

And there we gathered, Spit, Troubles, Burford, all

reaching the same crossroads in our short but full journey at the school.

'I need to brighten and change my life,' I declared and then with all the hurt and no doubt confusion submerging my head, I suggested we made plans to make the opening of the Central Dining Room, now known as the Main Hall, a 'tad' more interesting than was originally planned.

'Are sure you want to be involved?' I was looking at Spit Smith, younger and therefore giving me a sense of being an older brother.

'I wanted to be involved on day one.' And it was true – from that very first afternoon it was clear that Spit did not fit and that each day that followed developed into a tortuous marathon. I grabbed hold of his shoulders and gave him a warm shake. And as a band of brothers we all joined hands in a circle in the middle of the room, and I gave out a boisterous cheer, 'To the future and whatever it may hold'.

*　　*　　*

The sound of the fire bell crashed into my room disturbing me once again from having my way with matron. Tonight's dream featured us attending a fancy dress ball in a château somewhere deep in France. I know that because before the bell rudely disturbed my dream, I had been driving out of Paris, Eiffel Tower in the background with matron sitting beside me looking not unlike the portrait of Madame de Pompadour, mistress of the King. I was not Louis XV though, but Batman in full costume; all very complicated and perhaps a good thing the bell had rung to break it up.

*　　*　　*

There was no warning for the practice and as there had been a real fire a few weeks before, I thought this again was the real thing. I dressed quickly and ran downstairs.

We gathered outside exhausted, looking at each other suspiciously, half-expecting flames to be bursting out of the building in front and Andrew Grafton to come running out.

'The bell has gone off by mistake but we will continue the roll call as we have before,' announced Mr Webster. And then with the house in order and gathered to hear their names, without warning, the Websters' pet rabbit, the biggest rabbit that you could possibly imagine, came dashing out in front of us covered in a deep purple dye. He jumped around as if he were a performer in the circus. Mrs Webster, who had always kept a very low profile and was rarely seen in the house, let alone in the school grounds, came flying out stage left in pursuit of her bunny.

'Salvador,' she shouted but the rabbit was not listening and made a surge past the now cheering boys to the bottom of the garden. Mrs Webster dashed off in pursuit clad in floral nightie and an aquamarine dressing gown, her shocking red hair flying to the side. The sight of this purple coloured creature was bound to start a huge investigation in the house. Who did it? Who would be so cruel? And then I caught Burford's eye and he gave a slight smile and I knew that my aristocratic buddy was the culprit.

*   *   *

'What happened?' I asked him the following day.

We were gathered in my room talking about this and that, until I asked how a white bunny came to be purple. Burford chuckled and explained with a devious tone.

'I was mixing some test colour to drop into the fountain, and had started it down at the bottom of the garden after lights out. And then out of nowhere this huge fucker of a rabbit knocks over the dye I'd mixed, slips, rolls once and bounces away; tragic, unfortunate, but very funny. At least I now know I can concoct the whole colour thing.'

223

A huge fountain had been built outside the Main Hall as part of the elaborate design for this state-of-the-art building. This water was to be switched on as soon as the VIPs took their seats after the official opening had been sanctioned with a cord being drawn from a plaque. We planned to place pellets under the shafts and when the fountain ejaculated the water, it would be a delicious purple; not an aggressive action and perhaps childish but at the time the best idea of its age.

Those long days of reflection gave an expanse of freedom I rarely have had in my life. I had decided that I couldn't take on the dictatorship that defined my journey. Perhaps it was because I was now sixteen and in search of something new but it seemed I was left with no choice; never once did anyone in authority tap me on the shoulder and say to me, 'Hey son, it is OK to be different.'

*   *   *

The Main Hall building was now near completion and the inauguration was just a week away. The builders had reduced their countless tea breaks to just the one at eleven o'clock. They scrambled up and down scaffolding putting the finishing touches to their work. I got to know one called George, who, like me, supported Spurs but didn't have a good word to say about anything, especially our team ('not as good as they were in Blanchflower's day'). He moaned and moaned about his work and the hours he had to spend assembling a building for 'posh kids to eat and play in'.

We used to share cigarettes in the basement, with this sixty-year-old taking deep drags on his Woodbines. He looked worn and tired with a grey face and grey hair swept back with a generous dollop of Brylcreem. He had heard of my Uncle Louis as he used to attend the fights back in the good old days.

'I wouldn't go now, though. Big bunch of pansies.'

'But Joe Bugner may come out of retirement one day and become heavyweight champion?' I teased.

'More chance of me doing a full day's work,' he replied.

'Have a good evening, George.' And I left him mumbling about something or other and went straight to my room. I did not call Lana as I wanted and needed to read Suzy's letter again and to pore over each word.

My friends were all in my room smoking away and in good spirits. I went over to my trunk and immediately saw the padlock had been broken.

'Who the fuck has done this?' My friends gathered round as I opened the top, and sure enough a wad of money had been stolen, a Cartier watch given by my father for my thirteenth birthday, and my letters. I hadn't collected many over the years but the few that I had saved were precious. Mostly from Lana, some from my parents, but most importantly the one I had just received from Suzy. I was angry, so angry and cursed my bad luck.

'I bet it was Summerfield,' accused Spit.

My hands formed a fist and I punched the wall with such ferocity that the plaster cracked. I looked at my hand, now red and bruised.

'I have had enough of that cunt,' I spat, and stormed towards the door. My friends threw away their cigarettes and tried to hold me back, but I was having none of it and looked at them and said, 'My time has come'. They tried to follow, whether it was for support or just to watch I do not know, but I wanted to be alone because I knew that I was now only seconds away from being expelled; I was going to crush him with years of pent-up hate, vindication topped with pleasure.

I stormed down the stairs leaving my friends behind, muttering expletives and with not a care in the world except for revenge; that was until I reached Summerfield's room, and outside his red door I stopped in my tracks. It was strictly forbidden even to knock on the door of the head of house, let alone go in without being invited. It was almost the first rule that was instilled in me when I learnt my new boys' doctrine. It was so deeply wedged in my brain that it stalled the wrath and the dogmatic march.

I stood still, took a deep breath and without knocking, burst into the room. It was so dark inside I could easily have marched straight out but for the sound of whimpering coming from the far corner. I turned round, searched for a light and in one action, I found the switch and suddenly the light flashed on. And there, meshed together and naked, was my tormentor Summerfield in the act of sodomizing Warwick.

My eyes sprung from my head. 'What shall I do?' I instinctively asked.

'Try walking out of the door,' Summerfield dryly replied.

I turned away, embarrassed that I had walked in at such a moment, and the two scrambled in search of clothing to cover themselves.

There was silence; as silent a moment as I had ever encountered before. I looked at the two, hardly believing what I'd encountered; Warwick was staring at the floor, Summerfield looking, as if frozen, straight back at me.

'Well, well, well,' I said.

This was a gift that was going to be difficult to refuse. 'What are we to do?' I thought.

Summerfield had been wickedly and cruelly homophobic and had for many a term bullied a junior called Worthington simply because he was feminine and beautiful. Summerfield would jeer, 'Look what the cat has dragged in,' or 'You perverted bastard,' or yell 'Ooh, ducky,' as he walked by. Worthington was too weak to fight back and the public display of bullying went uncontested, which was shameful, especially as we had all shared the tragedy of Langley.

'There is nothing you can do, we will simply deny everything. Who do you think the housemaster, let alone the headmaster, would believe – a revolting arse like you or us?'

I had no answer except for my incredulous face. Summerfield bore little shame nor any humility. He had come out fighting like a wild animal trapped in a corner. Warwick's demeanour on the other hand had totally changed. He was now sitting down shaking his head. It was as if it were all right to be homosexual as long as no one knew about it. Now it seemed that the spell had been broken. He seemed tormented by his sexuality.

'Now get the fuck out of here and consider yourself lucky that I haven't put you into detention for walking in without permission,' Summerfield attacked.

I wasn't going to let this go lightly and suddenly without warning I realised I knew something that I wouldn't otherwise have guessed. Summerfield had been having an affair with Worthington. The head of house's constant berating of this poor junior added up to his lack of acceptance of what he was doing; he was consumed with guilt and that self-loathing pursued his every step.

'I am not leaving' I said, 'I'm staying and then I'll take the walk to the headmaster's office and report what I have just witnessed and also report your continual abuse of Worthington, a boy who has spoken privately to me about how you would go to his room late at night. I will make sure your time here ends in disgrace and any chance of attending Oxford will extinguish just like that,' and I snapped my fingers.

I was going for it, unsure at that time if what I was claiming had any truth. But I could tell as soon as there was a pause that there was veracity in everything I had said. For the first time since I had encountered this bullying vermin, I had the upper hand.

Summerfield's mood suddenly changed and he cordially asked me to sit down. Warwick was awkwardly getting dressed.

'Listen, there is no need for this,' he spoke calmly. 'I know we haven't generally got on but let's forget the past and look to the future.' The devil smiled, speaking without fear, and I shuddered.

'No, let's not forget the past. My distaste for you holds no bounds. You have, from my first day here, made my life hell and it's difficult to forgive and forget that. You are the most disgusting of creatures.'

I wanted to let my words hang and so I turned my back and went to the door. I looked back once more and Summerfield had remained static making no move with his body or expression. Warwick's demeanour had changed, he slouched and looked younger and uneasy. He was far different from the bully who had taunted me throughout my life at public school.

I left the door open and walked briskly through the long corridor, so often cold but for now warm and comforting. And as so often in life, who did I bump into but the very person I was in search for, young Worthington. I led him to my room which was still full of cigarettes and friends. They were impatient to hear what had transpired. In all the excitement I had completely forgotten why I had stormed to Summerfield's room in the first place and my trunk remained open and empty.

'I will have to tell you later, but for now, can you leave my room?'

My friends shuffled out somewhat bemused and left Worthington alone with me.

I spoke with maturity far beyond my adolescent years. It was clear though that this beautiful, timid boy had a strange attachment for the head of house.

'In private, he is very kind.' He spoke quietly.

'But he's cruel to you in front of all of us. Surely you want him to pay for how he has treated you?'

His eyes started to cloud and he looked to the ceiling, hands gently wiping away the tears that flowed freely down his face.

'No I don't, please, I don't want anyone to know.'

And here age did get the better of me, for I did not know what to do. I asked myself whether it was because he couldn't stand the sneers or names that would follow him throughout his life at the school and potentially after he left or because he truly cared for this boy. Making a decision I thought would be easy, there would be no question. I would go straight to the headmaster. But then even with my desire for revenge I held myself back. It may have been the world of the public school in which I was living or the fact that even with hate flowing through my veins, I did need or want retribution. Worthington left my room unsure of where he stood; my heart yearned and yielded and I was left confused.

I immediately went in search of my friends and found them very quickly. They were gathered by the fire escape. Although we lived in huge grounds, finding my mates was never daunting. I told them exactly what had happened. Their mouths dropped in unison and they devoured every syllable and consonant of what I reported.

'And why were you with Worthington?' asked Burford.

'Oh, that was about something different. I heard he knew who the thief was but he didn't.' I lied.

The consensus was clear, I should go straight to the housemaster and report them. 'Get the bastards,' Spit demanded.

'Not so fast,' I retorted. 'I want to hold on to this just a little longer and I ask you all, however difficult, to keep this to yourselves.'

It was not what they wanted to hear but they had faith in my judgement and grudgingly agreed, and we returned to our puffing and all looked a little shell-shocked.

I returned to my room later and immediately saw that the watch, money and letters had been returned, not back in my trunk but neatly piled on my desk. I sat alone looking out of my window. The sky had turned from blue to black and was flecked by uncountable stars. They gazed down and somehow I felt very insignificant. My mind was racing and I was in desperate search for solace. I read Suzy's letter again and again, wept and realised that my insignificance may be true in the universe but in my world, the world I walked and knew, it was very real and at times confusing and daunting. I had experienced true loneliness few times in my life: on the train to prep school aged nine; that first night at Montgomery; and again now. I was in search of answers. The trouble was I did not have the right questions.

*   *   *

The attention to detail held no boundaries. If they could have cleaned each individual stone leading to the Main Hall with a toothbrush they would have done so. The school had hired a team of manual workers to finish off the surroundings of this very impressive structure. The team wore red fluorescent coats with 'Montgomery' labelled on the back and were led with shouts by a Sergeant Major type in a particularly fetching yellow jacket. To their credit, they worked meticulously at creating a garden surrounding the fountain, painting the flag pole, finishing the shine on the brick work and assembling a temporary

VIP grandstand together with a spotless lush red carpet leading to the stairs. George, lazily painting the window frames, gave me a wide yawn as he watched this hive of workers doing their job.

*   *   *

Mr Baresi had been invited to the new kitchen to prepare the lunch for invited guests. 'It will be the most magnificent Italian feast, my greatest work,' he said and for a fleeting moment I felt guilty that our plan was to make this a day to remember but not for the food.

'Your food will bring great comfort to the stress of the day.' I chose my words carefully.

It was twenty-four hours before the event and I was having a coffee with my Italian friend. He remarked that I seemed different of late.

'There is anger in your eyes where before there was not.'

He was right and I looked into his face and saw a kind man with a concerned expression. He looked far older than his age, with lines deeply marked around his mouth and eyes. 'You have been kind to me, Mr Baresi, and I thank you.'

'You make it sound as if we won't be seeing other again.'

I shook my head and turned away from his gaze.

'Anyway, from now you call me Fabio and if it is all right with you, I will call you Sam.' And we gave each other a firm, enthusiastic handshake.

It was the Wednesday, twenty-four hours before the grand opening and forty-eight hours before the end of the summer term. The holidays loomed and the atmosphere on the campus along with the warm weather made everybody far more amiable, cheerful even. Mr Yates in passing waved a warm hello and Mr 'Noddy' Sumner, whom I had never even spoken to, gave me a friendly pat on my shoulder as he strode by. My mother had called earlier in the day to say that my father could not attend the opening as he was involved in a complex business deal and it had reached some sort of a crisis. She was feeling a 'bit poorly' and if I didn't mind she would miss the celebration too. It was a relief that neither would be there but I said that I was a little disappointed but understood.

That afternoon, I met Lana in town earlier than usual.

'Where shall we go?, she asked.

The choice was by no means wide: it was either the Wimpy bar, her house or the cinema.

'You know, I would love to walk past Mrs Wheeler's place. It was about now every Wednesday that I would be with her.'

She took my hand, didn't utter a word and together arm in arm we walked to Mrs Wheeler's street.

* * *

The street was as it was the day she died except for two boys playing a game of football using gates either side of the street as their goals. One of the boys was commentating on their make-believe game: 'O'Leary to Stapleton, on to Malcolm Macdonald and he scores,' and then he ran the length of the street to celebrate his goal.

The street rarely had cars driving through and today was no exception, but there was also a slight smell of burning rubber wafting through the air as if a car had just braked too hard nearby. I looked at Mrs Wheeler's door and a wave of mournfulness swept over and I thought of her warmth.

'You really are lovely,' whispered Lana in my ear.

'What do you mean by that?, I snapped, unable to accept the compliment.

'You just are.' Then we kissed, first tenderly and then

passionately and then I wanted to take her into Mrs Wheeler's garden and make love but thought I might be pushing the bounds of decency.

A fire engine then came screeching around the corner and right in front us five firemen dashed to Mrs Wheeler's neighbour's door and banged hard. There was no answer and the now impatient fire fighters started to break down the door. Flames started to flare out from the top windows and by the time the hose had been unrolled and water was jetting out towards the house, a street that had always seemed empty was now full of the curious, all gawping at the fire that was increasing by the second.

It was time to move on and we crept away from the street and its crowd for the last time. Another dream crushed: things are just never somehow the same when you go back.

As we passed the now familiar shops in town, I caught sight of an old costumiers tucked away on the corner of a side street. I had not noticed it before and yet I had passed that point many a time. In the window stood an over-used mannequin oddly dressed in a costume dating from the First World War. The shop was small and unassuming; it seemed to have a charm that belonged to a different era. We entered excitedly, not at that point knowing what we were going in there for. We disappeared into the shop and tried on a variety of costumes, our demeanour changing with each link to history.

Full of laughter, I walked Lana back to her house and we started to kiss again outside her front door; I had no concern that we would be caught by either parent, I simply could not stop kissing this sublime creature. Perhaps it was our youth, but it could have continued for hours with hardly a pause to take in breath.

'Do you want to pop inside to have a cup of tea?' Lana's

mother, Peggy, called out, looking down from the top window. I immediately pushed Lana away and became embarrassed and walked self-consciously into the kitchen. There I told both mother and daughter about my discovery in Summerfield's room earlier in the week. Lana looked stunned, her Mum acted as if she had heard it all before.

'So what are you going to do about it?' asked her Mum.

'I'm still not sure, as in a bizarre way I want to do nothing. I have already learnt that sometimes by doing nothing you can gain everything. But having said that, it's young Worthington that haunts me and so I'm still not sure what to do.'

'I'm sure you will make the right decision,' Peggy said, sipping her well-brewed tea.

The right decision unfortunately was beginning to weigh me down. I finished my drink and started to wash the cup under the hot water.

'Oh, leave that, dear,' said Peggy. 'Now, are you darlings planning to see each other during the summer holidays?'

'Forget the holidays,' I replied, 'we are planning to see each other tomorrow for the VIP day.' And the two of us gave each other a naughty smile as if we were hiding a secret; which of course we were.

*   *   *

An excited Spit Nimmo Smith grabbed me as I was walking back to the house. He literally took my hand and led me to the fountain in front of the Main Hall. The spurts of water were now non-existent and it was being drained of the strange-looking purple water. In fact it was the same purple that had drenched Mr Webster's pet rabbit only a few days before. I looked on as a number of harassed workers tried to look efficient.

'Troubles gave it a test run,' whispered Spit.

Well, it certainly worked. It was as if he had wanted to warn the authorities there might be a few who needed to disrupt the following day's progress. Within a short time the fountain had been drained, and the headmaster had gathered a group of masters and was a delivering a curt set of instructions to them. His orders were clear and precise; they would have to take it in turns to mount a guard on the fountain throughout the night.

'No one, and I repeat no one, is going to spoil this important day,' he ordered, his voice raised and slightly hysterical. Then he marched off into the distance. The remaining masters immediately started to sort out their roster, each one trying to grab the most comfortable time. We watched as these grown men, our guides in education, argued and fought for their preference. Poor Mr Oxlade was handed the short straw, a graveyard stretch between two and four o'clock in the morning. As he would have to conduct the choir later, an important element in the following day's proceedings, this did seem harsh. He walked away from the others, sulking, head lowered and wounded. Perhaps, I thought, there is bullying amongst adults too.

*   *   *

The Hall itself seemed monumental with tables lined one after another; it resembled a prison dining room, but with privilege. The Main Hall was grand and the beautiful carved tables were far worthier than boys going through their destructive teenage years deserved. The pristine white walls already had countless house photographs framed and hung. They covered the last seventy-five years of the school's history and to have a photograph of Field House next to the headmaster's House only a year before would have been unthinkable.

Spit hovered behind as we took the tour and it wasn't

long before I heard a loud crash. Spit had clumsily walked straight into a tray of wine glasses and they had shattered across the stone floor.

'Shit,' he cried and within an instant three masters came rushing in. We were scolded and told to leave 'sharpish' and so we did. As we left the hall we could see the fountain was being steadily refilled and Mr Rose was marching around it in a circle, like a Nazi guard at Stalag 57, alert for any trouble.

*   *   *

Although I saw Summerfield and Warwick at roll call we avoided each other's gaze. They meant nothing to me now and I was still at this point ready to walk away and abandon any justice to the years of taunting and downright bullying.

*   *   *

Back in my room, Burford was pointing out of my window at the masters and the fountain. Although it was still light, each master had a torch and each was taking their role extremely seriously.

Burford had three small bags of what looked like purplish-black crystals in his hand. The sky was turning and as darkness set, Burford expertly lobbed the three sachets in one shot from our strategically placed window straight into the fountain, marking the target with a gentle plop. It was a direct hit and within seconds you could hear Gripper Yates call out, 'What was that?' Panicking, he switched on his torch, but could see nothing. He continued his guard duty scratching his head, and the four of us fell over bursting with laughter and kicking our legs into the air. Naughty boys with glee on their faces.

*   *   *

Once again England was at its finest. Bright sunshine hurtled through my window and as early as six o'clock I was up and ready for the longest day. And then I heard this haunting noise, resembling the sound of a laughing hyena, a continuous resonance of a chuckle, prolonged and piercing. Out of my window I saw Burford hanging out of his room looking at the Main Hall. He was pointing and as I followed his finger to the wall above the main entrance. I saw written in large capital letters 'MUNRO'S SHIT CAFE'. The white paint was running at the edges but the work was clear, unhurried and dominant. The masters who had meant to protect the site overnight looked despairingly at the damage. Poor old Cripps had been summoned and the old man was reviewing the vandalism. Shaking his head, he knew that he had a near impossible job to clear the markings before the royals and other notables arrived that afternoon. The graffiti from a few weeks before was still highly visible. Jock, his dependable lad, arrived struggling with a long ladder. Between them they tried to reach the inscription but it was clear that the ladder was not tall enough and the two started to argue; the pressure of the day had started very early and well before anyone could possibly have imagined.

Boys from the headmaster's House were now hanging from the windows bemused by all the goings on. Burford had finished his laughing and was by now dressed and hanging around in my room. We were for the day to be dressed in our Sunday tails wearing a waistcoat of choice. Burford had chosen a fetching tigerskin number. I went for plain white silk as I had work to do and did not need to unnecessarily stand out.

*   *   *

A knock slammed on my door and before I answered, I knew that there was trouble. A junior spoke with his voice

237

still unbroken. 'I think you should know that your friend Winter has been expelled from the school.' I looked at my watch and saw it was not even eight o'clock. Burford and I looked at each other unbelieving but before our senses could take in the true impact of the news, Spit appeared, half-dressed, out of shape and out of breath.

'The fool was seen painting at about four o'clock by a not-so-dozy Mr Oxlade. His mufti was found under his bed and was covered with strips of fresh paint. Bottom line, he was caught in the act.'

Troubles was packing his trunk, dressed in jeans and a tight black T-shirt marked with white paint. He pointed at the evidence and gave a laugh not unlike the one I had heard from Burford's mouth a short time before. The expulsion was immediate and he was ordered from the grounds before breakfast.

'I thought the headmaster was going to hit me. His anger reached frightening proportions.'

He, or rather his parents, were going to be charged for the damage he had caused. He was accused of the vandalism carried out weeks before.

'That I did not do,' he said, defending his corner with the innocence of a choirboy. He had a resigned air about him as if he were glad it was finally over. By being a year older, and perhaps it was an illusion, Troubles seemed to have a more experienced outlook on life. He tended to live for the moment and the consequences that were dealt fell comfortably into his lap. His foolhardy act was a 'school suicide note' and it was no surprise that none of us knew what he was planning.

His trunk was to be sent on and his worn duffel bag was packed with a pair of jeans, sneakers and toothbrush, his favourite black T-shirts and tape recorder with his over-played Who cassette lodged permanently inside. His parents would be waiting, probably resigned to their son's behaviour, in their modern, rather garish house in Buckinghamshire's stockbroker belt.

'Fuck it,' he said and pulled the bag over his shoulder and said his goodbyes.

We in turn gave Troubles a warm heartfelt hug. I looked him straight in the eye and his face resonated relief and freedom. Perhaps this was the look shared by prisoners on their last day in the slammer. And out of the door he went, broad-shouldered, walking from the school grounds for the last time. And so another bottle fell crashing from the wall. It left just the three of us, standing dressed in tails – but all with shirts hanging out – waiting for the bell to sound for breakfast.

'Dear God, this is going to be a long day,' I said out loud. The tension broke and we once again burst into nervous laughter.

There was no announcement as to the demise of our late friend. As the roll call was checked, Winter's name was simply left off. Cripps, meanwhile, was working hard to remove his pre-dawn work from the stone and it looked as if he had finally found the right detergent to remove embedded paint. Poor man, age was certainly not on his side and it looked as if life had sped up over the previous few weeks.

*   *   *

The whole school, dressed in tails and top hats, lined the road and waited patiently in the intense heat for the royals to appear. Minutes crawled by and despite the expected arrival at eleven o'clock, by half-past they were still not in sight. Then rumours spread that their car had had a puncture and I overheard a flustered Mr Webster suggesting that they should send the boys back to their houses and recall them when they had word the visitors were round the corner. 'Round the fucking corner,' bellowed the headmaster, 'How do you expect to organise over five hundred boys to return in a matter of minutes?' Mr Webster made some remark about heat stroke but the head had no time for the discussion. He was losing it and I smirked at his discomfort. Huffing and puffing, he was marching up and down and sweating in a most un-attractive fashion; the welcome committee was at this point anything but welcoming. And then Munro came running towards us and shouted at top volume that the car was in sight. The school, as one, looked to the west in the direction, we were advised the entourage would be emerging from. However, it had taken the back lanes, and arrived from the opposite direction, missing the line of sweaty boys who were prepared to doff their hats as the cars crawled by. Instead, the huge Daimler arrived fifty yards up the road. The welcoming committee then made the short dash to meet the opening of the door.

The Princess emerged looking radiant, sexy and under-standably cool as her expensive air-conditioning must have been blasting at top volume to keep her looking that mystical vision for the school and the waiting press photographers. I caught sight of her long brown legs emerging from her car as a bowing headmaster waited to meet her eyes. She wore a tight sky blue dress, perfectly cut; her grace and poise would have made anyone in the land fall for her, let alone a prince. Her husband meanwhile followed in a grey suit, his regiment's tie and brightly polished brown shoes. Perfectly turned out, the ever-charming husband allowed his wife take the centre stage.

The presentation line consisted of the headmaster, the head of school, the five most senior masters, one of whom was Mr Webster, and three prefects drawn by lot. Summerfield was one of the so-called lucky trio. There were strong rumours that he had rigged the draw but it was never challenged and his place stood uncontested. He bowed so deeply on his introduction that I thought his head would finish in the Princess's groin. He wore a polka-dotted waistcoat and for the first time I noticed how camp he was. With each handshake or bow the click of the camera captured the moment for posterity. It was time to drift away as the chosen ones were led to the dining room to meet the parents who had donated large chunks of their inherited or hard-earned cash for the construction of the building. After cakes and coffee were served the ceremony would begin in earnest and the school would gather again for the unveiling of the plaque with the customary words on it.

*   *   *

The stables clearly had not changed for years. A courtyard was surrounded by a dozen battered horse-boxes, with slates in danger of falling from its roof. Stable girls in tight jodhpurs were dashing around to do anything to make the horses more comfortable in the potent heat. The courtyard stone was being hosed down, drowning out an old radio playing 'My Coo Ca Choo' by Alvin Stardust. Mr Oliver, the owner, a short man in his mid-forties, was shouting out orders to his nubile stable girls with a gruff voice, a hand-rolled cigarette mysteriously hanging from his bottom lip. The hive of activity resembled a stable on the Epsom Downs before the Derby, instead of just a local riding school.

Lana was waiting and standing next to a large proud chestnut mare. She stroked its neck and seemed at ease with the animal. Mr Oliver shook my hand and offered to give me a guided tour of his business. I said that I hoped to have time later but first I had an appointment to meet.

Spit had already placed milk bottles under each of the Daimler's tyres. How the royal driver and the security people missed this misdemeanour, I have no explanation. But Spit had been in an edgy mood all day and the expulsion of Troubles had sparked aggression rather than joyful oppression. His fight against the school's authority was concluding; he had fought the system from his very first hour on the school grounds and it seemed only right for him that with all his close friends leaving one by one, his journey in this very English institution would end at the same time.

Unbeknownst to Spit, it was my Italian friend Mr Baresi who would knife the final blow into his rebellious heart. He had witnessed Spit on his knees placing the glass under the tyres. He was in the middle of a mad flustered rush as he had failed to deliver the biscotti in time for the meet and greet hour with the royals. He simply took note of the act and was ready to report it after he had completed his job.

By the time Mr Baresi had run desperately into the reception, the hour was nearly up and the food that needed to accompany the coffee had been already been devoured in the shape of chocolate digestives. Mr Baresi was so concerned about missing out on this rather bland item that he started to stalk the royals with tray in hand, urging them to try his home-made biscotti. As the Princess was leaving the hall to make her way to her seat for the unveiling, Mr Baresi accosted her with a plateful. 'You must try one of these, Your Majesty, please,' he insisted.

'Oh no, thank you, I have had enough,' she politely declined, but he was not taking no for an answer so he literally picked one up and tried to force-feed the beautiful Princess. He had completely lost his senses and a break-down that had hovered over him ever since his wife had left with his children came crashing down. The last sighting of my Italian friend and advisor was the poor soul being marched away by two security men.

*   *   *

An intensive search of specific rooms in the house had been ordered to commence as we had gone to line up in the streets waiting for the royal couple. The whole operation was led by Warwick and I suppose it was of little surprise that my room was duly ransacked. Warwick was going on the attack and was in search of some demonstrative evidence to decisively hammer the final nail in my coffin. There would be nothing to find, with perhaps the exception of an old copy of *Mayfair* magazine – but even that would not have been enough to guarantee dismissal.

It was under David Burford's bed that Warwick claimed his ultimate prize. A small box full of plastic bags filled with potassium permanganate. Warwick was unsure of what it was but knew that he had found something which would eventually lead to yet another expulsion. Before lunch was even served, he was to be proved right.

*   *   *

The headmaster was seated next to Her Royal Highness on plastic chairs that looked harsh and uncomfortable. The Prince was sharing a polite one-sided conversation with the headmaster's wife. A brass ensemble, in the guise of the school band, started to play Martin Luther's hymn 'A Mighty Fortress is our God' followed bizarrely by Rod Stewart's 'Maggie May'. The prime suspect for this contrasting abomination was a serious Mr Oxlade who was fervently conducting the band.

I was only seconds away and could hear the grating music blast out across the fields. I had changed from school

243

tails into my Indian chief costume hired from the local shop and Lana donned a beyond-sexy Indian squaw outfit. As she was changing I grabbed her around the waist.

'Behave,' she said, 'we don't have time for that; and put those feathers on your head.'

My costume was most appropriate: no top, as I had worked desperately on my weights left in memoriam by Grafton, suede shorts, and a pair of cowboy boots. Fully pumped, I dispensed with the bow and arrow but did have on the most magnificent Indian chief's headdress made of thirty eagle, hawk and crow feathers trimmed with horse hair and strips of leather. It was heavy but devastatingly attractive. My sensual and desirable squaw wore a suede fringe top and a buckskin mini-skirt with slits on the sides. I would have duly gone into battle and died for her; that is how I felt as I climbed on to Blaze, our strong-willed mare, and pulled Lana up to the saddle. She held tight as we rode towards the sound of the tuneless brass band. As the music grew and I was merely moments way from starting the chain of events that would lead to probable expulsion, I felt contented and calm and had no fear. I was prepared to leave this institution and wanted to go with a sense of humour rather than with anger.

'Those feathers represent you going into war,' remarked the costumier as I first fitted the monumental creation on to my head.

'But I go in peace,' I had replied.

And it was true. As I rode my horse that summer's day with girlfriend by my side, I did not possess an ounce of malice.

The band was drawing to the close of 'Maggie May' when I trotted in front of the Prince and Princess who were now preparing to unveil the plaque. The music dying down was not the only reason there was a sudden hush. The headmaster, seeing my right hand raised and saying 'How' in a deep voice, with Lana's legs strapped around my thighs left his mouth and the mouths others wide open in an absolute shock as if they had just witnessed a brutal car crash. It was if time had stood still for the moment and the hundreds gathered were unable to move; that is, except the Princess, who started to applaud and shriek 'How charming, how charming.'

The cord was pulled and the inscription was revealed. We, meaning Lana, myself and the horse, stood to attention as the celebration continued and I realised at that moment I hadn't made a plan of what to do after my dramatic entrance. Mr Webster walked calmly over and signalled me to move towards him.

'Get rid of the fucking horse and the tart and report to my office.' He spoke quietly with gritted teeth and a fake smile plastered over his face. It was at this point that the fountain was switched on and the slow ejaculation of clear water burst open. Within seconds, it had changed to the colour purple and was spurting out of control over anyone who was in close proximity. The packets that Burford had thrown in the night before had not been detected and the colour flew in countless directions, soaking few but enjoyed by many, including Her Royal Highness who once again thought it was part of the ceremony.

I dismounted from the horse and as if arresting me, two prefects held my arms sharply. 'Bring him over here,' demanded the Prince and for a second I had regressed to Tudor times and I was about to meet my executioner.

I shook myself from my captors and made my way with Lana to present ourselves to our honoured guests. In fact it became clear that the Princess was more interested in the horse than anything else and the Prince had a penchant for my Red Indian girl.

'That is quite a figure, I mean costume you have,' laughed the Prince. His eyes looked her up and down and up again.

'Thank you, sir,' Lana replied and gave a low naughty curtsy.

I thought he was going to ask for her number at one point whilst the Princess was being distracted stroking the horse incessantly. 'Beautiful animal, beautiful animal,' she kept repeating.

Their royal security decided enough was enough and moved their charges on into the dining room. One heavily built guard was splattered in dye and his face personified indignation. He did not look best pleased and if he had found the culprit, Burford would no longer be with us. The Princess turned and gave a warm farewell. I smiled back and then in a movement as she turned her back, I was locked by the arm and escorted away. I turned and glanced at Lana as she stood alone with the horse by her side.

'Goodbye, my love,' whispered Lana, 'be brave.'

I stole a kiss and told her to go home. Then I was taken away. It was as if I were being led to a firing squad and there was nothing left, only glory.

*　　*　　*

'They found the potassium permanganate in my room.'

It was Burford who was sitting, waiting patiently for the headmaster to read out the last rites of his public school education. I asked who did and the reply was Warwick. I bit my lip and sat beside him. The wait was long and protracted; the minutes moved leisurely and a heavy ticking resonated each passing second of our last hours at Montgomery. The headmaster was having lunch with his guests before the execution, minus the chef, Mr Baresi, who was now in the custody of the royal protection officers. My mind started to play anomalous games and at one point I was convinced, as the grandfather clock standing tall in the corner struck two, that I would be allowed to remain at the school as my stunt had obviously been appreciated by our royal guests. Burford was upbeat, humming and tapping annoyingly on the arm of his chair. He was in a jovial mood, casual in behaviour and acting as if he were about to go and see his favourite movie. The headmaster's sour-faced secretary tutted constantly under her breath until it reached the point where I said, 'Could you please stop it, this is difficult enough.'

She huffed once more and returned to her other irritant, the typing of end-of-term reports.

Finally the door opened and in walked the headmaster, uttering no word. He walked straight into his office and closed the door firmly behind; I took a deep breath and prepared for my summons. Even the secretary now seemed a little nervous, sharpening her pencil pensively with a knife rather than the simple pencil sharpener; and for a second, and I mean a second, I found her attractive in a rather bizarre way. It made me question my judgement and I was at this point quite unsure if what I had done that morning was after all the right decision.

I was drifting into the realm of secretaries and matrons when my silence was fragmented by the third musketeer, Spit Nimmo Smith, being escorted by the head of school into the room where Burford and I were waiting. Munro knocked on the headmaster's door and without answer walked straight in. Spit glanced back and threw me a wink. Spit then returned to the waiting area, being told most firmly to sit and wait until he was called. And so once again we were together in what seemed to be the inevitable conclusion to our journey at this chapter of our rite of passage.

Spit sat next to me with hands lodged in pockets, and legs stretched out in a laid-back manner. He recounted that the royal front tyres had burst viciously and that Mr Baresi after witnessing the deed had turned him in. He accused Baresi of trying to save his neck, and that may have been true, but it was clear that my Italian friend was far from being himself. The tyres went flat rather quickly and their Royal Highnesses had to hitch a lift from one of the following security cars. The Prince reportedly had the face of wrath and rumour has it that he swore he would never return to the school again. A splodge of purple dye resting on his favourite brown shoes could have been the reason.

The phone shook and then rang on the secretary's desk and Burford was the first to be called in to meet his school's maker. I looked at my watch and looked at Spit and then I looked at the office door and wished I had penetrating hearing. Behind that door yet another friend of mine was being asked to leave the institution early. The room had suddenly changed from being light to feeling claustrophobic. Eventually Burford emerged with a benign smile on his face.

'You got away with it?' I asked, encouraged by his whole demeanour.

'No, I have to be gone within the hour. Painless, really.' And with a squint of the eyes and an eyebrow raised, he shook back his curly brown hair and walked out of the office to prepare his return to Warwickshire.

Spit was the next in line and as he marched in to the study to meet the head I saw someone younger, someone struggling, as I suppose we all were, in search of an identity. His shirt was hanging out from his grey waistcoat and his stomach hung over his belt. His top button was undone and his tie pulled halfway down. He did not care and knew his time was up. He was never well turned out and becoming tidy for the first time in his years at Montgomery was not going to change the result of their blunt conversation. I once again sat alone with the secretary and she continued to type, hitting each letter as if swiping a fly with a rolled-up newspaper. I tried to grab her attention, as my dark fantasy was beginning to emerge once again and helping to distract from my oncoming encounter. But she was having none of it and steadfastly kept her eyes glued to her large and sturdy typewriter.

Spit seemed to have taken more time in the company of our headmaster than Burford. It nearly got to the point where I wanted to tell the secretary that I knew what was going to happen and to thank the headmaster but say I could not wait any longer as I had another appointment.

But finally Spit emerged, looking as if he had just witnessed an accident and was in a state of shock. Poor boy, the reality had finally pierced his core.

He kept repeating, 'Why, why, why?'

'So what did you tell him?' I asked.

'That I just did not like it here and could not think of a better way to go.' Unconvinced as he spoke these words, I had the sense that he had made a mistake and should have made more of his life at the school, but I was the last to justify the observation. On balance though, all his friends would have left, so the following terms would have been chillingly lonely. He made a hand sign that he would call me and before he disappeared from my view I asked, 'Any regrets?'

'Not for a second, not for an instant, just relief.' So perhaps I was wrong, but his green eyes told a different tale.

Again the phone rang and the decidedly distant and again unattractive secretary pointed to my executioner's door.

His office seemed to have grown since my last visit. The window behind his desk was more expansive and the afternoon sun shone through and caught me like a spotlight as I walked towards his paper-scattered desk. I half-expected him to ask me to sit down and offer me a drink, but of course the meeting was not to be so cosy. His voice was clipped and sharp and he looked tired. Four expulsions in one day before teatime must have set some sort of record.

I wanted the final chance to have my say, but it was clear that it would be a lecture rather than a two-way conversation.

He talked of his disappointment as if he had grown to know me well over the years, and of how an exciting school career had twisted to be nothing better than a calamity. He spoke of how the failure would stain my life and it would take a concerted climb to distance myself from the stench of the sewer in which I now stood.

'Where do you go from here?' he asked as if I would have an immediate answer. Throughout my audience, he continually punched one hand with a tight fist that grew sharper as we touched a subject that drifted out of his realm or vision on how the public school system worked.

'Do you know, one day, you will look back at these years as your most liberating?' he continued. 'What you do not know is that life grows increasingly more difficult and that freedom condenses. For now, you do not have bills to pay, nor children to care for, nor any responsibility for staff you may in the future employ. You are free, my boy, and yet you have snapped that liberty with both of your hands. I feel sorry for you that given this extraordinary privilege, you have rejected it. Remember these words, because they will return to haunt you.'

My parents had been telephoned and my mother was driving up the A40 to take her son home. I have often thought of what went through my mother's mind as she drove through the deep gap in the road where the county of

Oxfordshire begins and ends. What a disappointment I have must been on that summer's day to both my mother and my father, but that is not how I thought on that Friday.

I was dreaming of the future; of what excitement this enforced freedom was going to bring. I had no space for empathy for my parents and certainly no room for remorse. I was exhilarated in a giddy way and in my teenage head I was high with anticipation.

* * *

'Yes, I do have something to say,' I answered when the headmaster finally gave me a chance to say my last words; they fell easily from my mouth. 'When I passed my examination, I thought at the time it was the most rewarding day of my life. I was going to the school that my brother and father had attended. I was full of joy and I remember when I heard the news I yelled out to the universe that I had never been so happy. I had been accepted and that was an incredible boost. But virtually from my very first step, I knew that just because my family had been here did not mean that it would suit my soul. I tried to find the rhythm and pulse of the school but the harder I tried, the lonelier I became and my salvation was a small group of friends and eventually a girl from town that I met when I left the school on a Saturday night without permission. Never did a master or any Senior take me to one side and ask if everything were all right. Never did anyone notice that I was troubled and in search of guidance. I never received any words of wisdom from you or your masters during my time here and I felt and feel bereft of guidance.'

The headmaster listened intently and for the first time that afternoon his anger subsided. But then he resumed his bearing and rose from his deep chair and we were eye to eye.

'Now leave, and do not set foot on these grounds again.

251

I've heard what you've said but you are to blame and it is about time that you took responsibility for your life. Now get out.'

He pointed to the door. I turned my back and walked away from the severity of his voice and when I reached the exit from my school's stage, I turned and without any pre-meditation said, 'Before I leave, and you should believe this, the other day I walked into Summerfield's study and found him having sex with Warwick. You may find that acceptable and simply part of public school life but what is not acceptable is Summerfield's continual abuse of Worth-ington, a junior boy. And I believe the only reason Worth-ington has sex with the bully is because he is terrified.'

I did not wait for a response. I simply stood tall and walked away.

I strode to my study and packed my trunk with haste. Burford and Spit had both left notes saying that they would call in a few days when the heat had calmed. I looked out of my window for the last time and saw Cripps hard at work sweeping away the rubbish from the day's celebration; the sound of 'Fool to Cry' by the Rolling Stones drifted over the windless day. The graffiti on the building remained and the fountain had been drained but purple residue had stained the bottom. I then saw my mother's car drive towards the house and although she was a distant figure, I believe I saw her pained expression. I reached for my trunk and tried in vain to lift it; it was too heavy and so I walked into the corridor in search of help.

A boy new to the school that term was walking towards me. I asked him for his help and he smiled and was eager to assist in carrying my trunk. And so down that stairwell we descended, passing no one. My mother's slight figure was waiting, standing by the side of the car, the engine still running. She lifted up the boot and with the help of this junior, we struggled to squeeze in the trunk, the evening was suitably setting.

'What's your name?' I asked the young man who had shared my final walk out of the house. It was true that although I had shared the last twelve weeks with this boy, I had no idea what he was called.

'William Mason, sir,' he replied. 'And may I say that was the coolest thing I have ever seen when you arrived on your horse with that beautiful girl.' I could see instant admiration resonating from his eyes and also a hint of the rebel about him.

'First, there is no need to call me "sir", and second, be careful with your time here. Try to enjoy most days and do not just throw it away without serious thought. It is far easier to get yourself into trouble here than it is to walk that straight and narrow line.' We shook hands and for an instant I believed I was growing up.

My mother then put the car into gear and without a word we passed the old buildings that had shadowed my privileged life. As she drove away from the school grounds, I turned to my old house and for just a fleeting second, had a spike of regret at the passing of my youth.

*　　*　　*

Two hours or so later we turned into the drive at home. As soon as my mother stopped, I sprang out of the car.

I saw my father. He was waiting by the front door. I first recognised his anger, then saw scorn etched on his face. I walked cautiously towards him, desperate to avoid a moment that was, of course, impossible to avoid.

'Who the hell do you think you are?' he yelled

'I don't know, father, who am I?' I replied and brushed past him into the house in search of an answer.